MORE PRAISE FOR *DEADLY POLITICS*

"Welcome to Molly Malone's Washington ... where parties and power go hand in hand with mystery and murder."

—Brian Freeman, author of *Spilled Blood*

"Sefton entertains while providing an unnerving behind-the-scenes view of D.C. politics, where power and politics can make a lethal combination."

—*The Free Lance-Star* (Virginia)

BLOODY POLITICS

New York Times Bestselling Author

MAGGIE SEFTON

BLOODY
POLITICS

MIDNIGHT INK
WOODBURY, MINNESOTA

First Edition
First Printing, 2014

Book design and format by Donna Burch-Brown
Cover design by Kevin R. Brown
Cover images:iStockphoto.com/2294733/©Kativ,
    iStockphoto.com/7856918/©bkindler,
    iStockphoto.com/28787972/©rotofrank,
    iStockphoto.com/21882515/©Jelena Aloskina,
    Shutterstock/59621926/©fstockFoto
Editing by Patti Frazee

Midnight Ink, an imprint of Llewellyn Worldwide Ltd.

This is a work of fiction. Names, characters, places, and incidents are either the product of the author's imagination or are used fictitiously, and any resemblance to actual persons, living or dead, business establishments, events, or locales is entirely coincidental.

Library of Congress Cataloging-in-Publication Data
Sefton, Maggie.
  Bloody politics / Maggie Sefton. — First edition.
    pages ; cm. — (A Molly Malone mystery ; 3)
  ISBN 978-0-7387-3130-8 (softcover)
  1. Murder—Investigation—Fiction. 2. Washington (D.C.)—Fiction. 3. Political fiction. I. Title.
  PS3619.E37B58 2014
  813'.6—dc23
                        2014026219

Midnight Ink
Llewellyn Worldwide Ltd.
2143 Wooddale Drive
Woodbury, MN 55125-2989
www.midnightinkbooks.com

Printed in the United States of America

ONE

Washington, D.C., October 2007

RAIN WAS COMING. THE scent of it was on the breeze that blew in from the coast. Whipping up small whitecaps on the Potomac as it flowed past. Fast river. Currents shifting, rising, as it surged toward the sea. The Atlantic, birthplace and Mother of Storms.

"Watch the river," I remembered an old fisherman once saying. "It will always tell you when a storm's coming."

I watched the Potomac as I ran along the parkway trail that bordered the river all the way to Mount Vernon. The fast-flowing current seemed to swell as it rushed toward Chesapeake Bay and the sea. Any storms Mother Atlantic spawned would surge up the Potomac on its strong tides, flooding lowlands filled with beautiful homes as easily as it flooded colonial farmlands hundreds of years ago.

The grayish-white clouds above had darkened in the last few minutes, and I decided I'd better cut my Sunday afternoon river run short. My lightweight running jacket had a flimsy hood that would thwart a light spring shower. But this was mid-October. Still hurricane season, officially. There were few light showers this time of year. Now was when the rainclouds thickened and brought forth drenching downpours. Some of the Atlantic's most capricious and brutal hurricanes had come in October, bringing vicious storm surges up the Potomac, the Rappahannock, and the James rivers, flooding Virginia throughout the Tidewater areas, the capital city of Richmond, and all along Virginia's river lands and coastline.

I checked over my shoulder and made a quick U-turn on the trail, heading back toward the parking area where I'd left my car. It had been sunny and warm when I began my run, but no more. A gust of wind blew my hair toward my face from the back. I watched a seagull swoop overhead, then hang suspended for several seconds as it rode the air currents above the river. A storm was definitely coming.

I glanced over my shoulder again and saw the clouds had blackened and thickened, angry now. I picked up my pace, faster, then faster, hoping I could make it back to my car before the rain began. No such luck. Raindrops appeared on the trail before me. Only a few now, but there would be more. The wind whipped up and I sprinted, hoping to outrun the rain, but my gut told me there was no way I was going to escape the approaching storm no matter how fast I ran. This storm was no longer coming. It was already here.

Monday morning

I watched the black stream pour into my oversized ceramic mug. I inhaled the aroma of the dark, strong coffee as it wafted upward to my nostrils. *Ahhhhhh.* Brain cells were snapping awake. Coming online, I took a drink of the hot brew made by Luisa, Senator Russell's housekeeper—shocking my taste buds and nervous system at the same time. *Now*, I was awake.

"Morning, Molly," Casey said as he headed for the coffee urn on the counter beside me. "Don't you just love these gray fall Mondays."

"I'll tell you when I wake up," I said to the senator's African-American security guard. "Another sip should do it."

"Did you and Danny get out to the Blue Ridge Parkway this weekend?" Casey asked as he filled his coffee mug. "I remember you saying you wanted to."

"No, we didn't. Danny's plans changed. One of his consulting clients needed his attention," I said, catching the former Marine's eye. "So we had to take a rain check on the parkway leaf tour."

"Ah, yes, consulting," Casey gave a knowing smile, then sipped his coffee. "I'm sure you two will get to reschedule it."

I leaned against the counter as I drew the mug close to my chest. "I never know how much to worry when he goes off on those trips, or even if I should. Sometimes he swears he's in meetings most of the time. Part of me believes him, but there's another part of me that wonders if he's out in the field, or wherever, getting shot at."

Casey and Danny had served together years ago in the early 1980s when Danny was a young Marine lieutenant. Casey had helped carry out the dead bodies of Danny's men from the bombed-out barracks in Beirut. Older now, gray darting through his cropped hair, Casey smiled at me. "Don't worry. Danny knows enough to get out of the way of trouble. You develop a sixth sense in special forces. He'll see it coming."

I thought about that while I took another deep drink of coffee and felt the caffeine rush hit my veins. "Yeah, but what if it sneaks up on him when he's not looking?"

Casey chuckled as he turned toward the doorway leading out into the Russell mansion's hallway. "Danny can take care of himself. Trust me, Molly."

I followed after him. No doubt my computer screen was filled with tons of new messages, waiting for me to answer, blinking, demanding. There was no escaping. Why was it that Mondays made everything loom larger? Especially dismal Mondays. That's when the Dreaded Monday Lethargy struck. Both Casey and I must have been affected, because I noticed we walked more slowly down the polished walnut hallway of the Russell mansion. Normally, we were each fast walkers but not today. Not on gray Mondays. Especially an Autumn Gray Monday.

"I assume the senator and Peter returned on the usual nine-thirty nonstop from Denver last night," I said. "When I got in this morning, I heard Peter in the library working the phone."

"Actually, I picked them up from the airport early Sunday afternoon. Peter said they both had to catch up on committee research before today."

"Wow, that Senate Banking Committee appointment has really added to the senator's workload. He and Peter have been putting in pretty long hours since late July."

"At least he cut back on his entertaining," Casey said as his cell phone buzzed. "I'm sure that's made it easier for you to balance the senator's budgets."

"Amen, to that." I turned toward my office at the end of the hall as Casey headed toward the front door. There was no escaping Monday morning routines for either of us.

Monday afternoon

Trask's cell phone buzzed on the glass table beside him. He reached for the phone as he relaxed in the Adirondack chair. Shaded from the morning sun by a dark-blue canopy above, Trask took a sip of coffee as he saw Raymond's number flash on his screen. "Hello, there. Haven't heard from you in a couple of weeks. Everything still quiet?"

"Yep. Just the way I like it," Raymond's scratchy voice came over the phone. "Where are you now? Still cruising the Bay?"

"No, I'm at one of those resorts along the Eastern Shore. Got in right before the storm hit Sunday. It's sunny now, so it should be a great day on the water."

Raymond's raspy chuckle sounded. "Are those other sailors drooling over your new boat?"

"Ohhhhhh, yeah," Trask said with a smile as he looked out on the broad expanse of still-green lawn that sloped down to the water. White wisps of sails dotted the waters of the Chesapeake Bay that surrounded the grounds. "You should have seen their expressions when I told them I bought it in the south of France."

Raymond laughed out loud at that. "I'll bet. Whatever you do, don't tell them the price tag. They'll choke on their Scotch."

"I'll remember that. Well, if everything's all quiet, I may plan a sail down to the Caribbean next month. Winter in warmer climes."

"Between you and me, I hope you get the chance. It was starting to get a little messy there with Quentin Wilson and that staffer

Levitz. Those two jobs, following so close to each other, really set the committee off. Spencer said they were panicking like a bunch of schoolgirls. Especially after the Malone woman almost walked in on you while you were searching her computer files. That really upset some of the original members. The ones who've been here the longest."

Trask took another sip of his Bloody Mary. "She really spooks those guys. Some day you'll have to tell me exactly why. It's gotta be more than her congressman brother-in-law's death years ago. No one's ever questioned that car crash. Not even in his hometown Denver press. So the Malone problem must go back farther."

"Well, you're right about that. But, it's complicated."

Trask laughed softly. "That's what you always say."

"That's because it's all dead and buried, like the congressman. And let's hope it stays that way."

Trask changed the subject. "Is that voice transcription software I set up on Natasha Jorgensen's phone still working? I haven't heard any complaints since I left two months ago."

"No problems. I've checked it every day, but all her phone calls are either work related or personal. She's had a couple of calls to Malone to meet for lunch, but nothing that aroused attention. I think we damped that situation down for good."

"You may be right, Raymond. But my gut still has this feeling about Jorgensen and that Malone woman. You know the feeling."

"Yeah, I know that feeling. But let's hope your gut is dead wrong. Those guys would not handle it well. Personally, my gut and I are both hoping you get the chance to winter in the Caribbean. Nothing would make those guys happier."

Trask laughed out loud as he signaled a server who was walking across the green.

Monday evening

I slid across the dark wood bench in the high-backed booth. That way I could sip my Guinness and watch the front door of Billy Martin's tavern at the same time. The nights were getting chillier, and the normal Georgetown crowd was trickling into the landmark pub. Hopefully, my old friend Samantha Calhoun wouldn't be late, or I'd have to bribe the waiter to let me keep the booth. Just then, Samantha appeared in the doorway, and I gave her a wave.

"Hey, there," I welcomed as she approached. "Has the rain started up again? You look a little wind-tossed."

"That's the residue of aggravation from having to direct the taxi driver through Georgetown rush hour traffic." Samantha hung her raincoat on the booth hook before she sat down. "I swear, he will not survive long in D.C. unless he learns these streets. Don't they have to take an exam or somesuch?"

"I have no idea. I simply try to dodge them in traffic. Thanks for coming on short notice. I wanted company for dinner on this dreary Monday. I didn't want to eat alone in Fortress Malone."

Samantha gave me a warm smile. "I know exactly how you feel, sugar. Once you've gotten used to having a companion for dinner, it feels lonely when you don't. Where's Danny Dangerous off to this time? Out of state?"

"Yeah, he headed for Dulles Saturday morning, which totally cancelled our plans for a Blue Ridge Parkway getaway." I sipped from the last of the froth atop my Guinness.

"The leaves will be around for a couple more weeks, barring any big storms. You know October." She glanced up at the approaching waiter. "I'll have your best Kentucky Bourbon. Neat."

"Now that my friend's here, could you bring us two bowls of your oyster stew, please? I'll bet you've been selling a lot of that today."

"Yes, ma'am, we have. Shall I bring it now or wait?"

"Bourbon first, please, then the stew," Samantha ordered with her best Southern belle smile.

"You got it, ma'am," he said with a grin, then scurried away.

I leaned back against the booth. "So, tell me what you've been up to this last week. What's been on Eleanor's social agenda? Last I heard you both attended the symphony season opening night. Dvorak, as I recall. Now that the Kennedy Center's fall season has started, you won't have an evening to spare, I bet."

"You bet right, sugar," she said, settling into the booth. "Eleanor's in her element now that fall has come. Every night is filled with performances of some sort. Concerts, theatre, recitals. If it's on a stage, we're there." She smiled and thanked the waiter for the amber-filled glass. "And of course, daytimes are filled with charity lunches, tedious lectures, and poetry readings. Some good, but mostly bad."

I laughed as she sipped her bourbon. "Ah, yes... culture and charitable works. The nuns would be proud, Samantha."

She rolled her eyes. "To tell the truth, I've actually enjoyed the charity lunches. Thanks to Eleanor, I've discovered some new groups that I've started supporting. Got to keep spreading it around, as Beau always said."

Samantha's husband, elderly Alabama Senator Beauregard Calhoun, was one of the most powerful men in the Senate until his death several years ago. He'd left Samantha as one of the wealthiest widows in Washington—and the merriest until last summer's scandal. I recalled the events that had sent her to the Grande Dame of Washington society, Eleanor McKenzie. Samantha had been serving a very public and dramatic penance under Eleanor's protective wing since August. Her days and evenings were filled with activities overseen and supervised by the Queen Mother herself.

"I daresay all that generosity on your part has silenced any wagging tongues for good. Charity is truly good for the soul, right?" I raised my glass.

"And the reputation," Samantha raised her glass, then sipped. "Nary an eyebrow is raised when I walk into a room now. I swear, it's gotten so calm it's almost boring. I'm tempted to misbehave just to rile them up a bit."

"Please tell me you're kidding." I gave her a pained look.

"Of course, I am, sugar. You know I've reformed." She grinned at me over her glass. "I'm done with the scandalous liaisons. Of course, now there are no liaisons at all. So I'm doomed to boring celibacy, I suppose."

Somehow I doubted my dear friend would remain in that state forever. "I'm proud of you, Samantha, and I know Eleanor is. You've totally silenced all the critics and vicious gossips. And even the Widow Wilson has stopped making snide comments to the sleazy *D.C. Dirt.*"

Samantha stared off into the tavern's main room, more crowded now than when she arrived. People were escaping the chilly weather.

"Sylvia Wilson has her hands full trying to transform herself into an effective congresswoman, from what I hear."

"Good luck with following in Quentin Wilson's footsteps. I've heard nothing but high praise about him since his death last summer. Even from politicians on the other side of the aisle. Everyone I've spoken to said he was one of the hardest-working congressmen on the Hill."

Samantha slowly turned her glass on the tabletop. "Quent was a workaholic. So Sylvia Wilson has big shoes to fill if she aims to live up to her husband's work ethic. From what I've heard from my sources, she's got all she can handle just trying to get up to speed on her committee work. She should have kept more of Quentin's staffers. Now she's having to deal with her Cleveland group's learning curve."

"Common rookie mistake," I added with a wry smile. "They have no idea how important the former staffers' institutional knowledge is. I'm just glad Natasha Jorgensen jumped ship to Sally Chertoff's office after Wilson's death."

"So am I. Sally is a congresswoman on the rise. She's impressing several of the higher-ups in the party, from what I hear."

Samantha's army of friends, staffers, spouses, and higher-ups spread across Washington—her mice, as she called them—kept my friend on top of the latest gossip as well as any changes blowing in the wind. In Washington, the winds were always blowing. "What are your mice saying about my boss? Anything I should know about?"

"Nothing but good," Samantha said after sipping her bourbon. "He's continuing to impress the movers-and-shakers with his work ethic, especially now that he's been appointed to the Senate

Banking, Housing, and Urban Affairs Committee. Apparently he's stepped forward on the International Trade and Finance Subcommittee. He's been asking penetrating questions, which indicates he's doing his homework."

"Well, I can vouch for that. He and Peter burrowed into that international banking and finance research in July and are still at it. He even cut his Colorado trip short this past weekend." I spotted the waiter approach with a tray. "Ahhh, here comes the house specialty."

"Oh, Lord. That stew is as deadly as it is delicious," Samantha said when the waiter deposited two bowls of creamy-white oyster stew before us. Steam wafted up from both.

"They make it with real cream, you know," I teased as I scooped up a spoonful and watched the steam rise.

Samantha paused, creamy spoonful raised. "Don't remind me. I'm trying to ignore the calories."

"Forgive me, but I needed something to drive away the dismal fall Monday before I returned to Fortress Malone." I tasted the rich seafood mixture and sighed inwardly. Calories be damned. This was exactly what I needed after a gloomy day. "Delicious, simply delicious."

"Sinfully so," Samantha added after closing her eyes in obvious enjoyment. "Now that you've mentioned Fortress Malone, I wanted to catch up on how things have been. You haven't had anything else occur that's alarmed you, have you? Be honest, Molly."

I savored another mouthful before answering. "No, not a thing. The entire house is locked down tighter than a drum. Special codes and alarms. Both house and yard are totally being watched by the cameras outside. Lights come on even if a neighbor's cat comes prowling. Even Bruce has set them off."

Samantha closed her eyes. "Oh, thank God. I'm so relieved to hear that. It really concerned me that a prowler had gotten in last summer. Lucky you happened to return and startled him away. Some people come home and find their places vandalized."

"Well, thank Danny for bringing in that specialty security team. They're responsible. They are way above the norm for security, and they've done a super job." I took another sip of Guinness. "And, yes. I am relieved that I came home before that prowler could find any bank or credit card statements where he could steal account numbers. I don't need those kinds of problems. So, I guess I was lucky."

Funny, I didn't feel lucky. I still felt violated by that intrusion in August. And no amount of high-end, top-of-the-line security systems could take away the memory of the fear I felt as I stood over my old desktop computer and discovered it running with My Documents file on the screen. Desk drawers halfway open, my murdered niece Karen's daytimer pulled out. Even though my common sense told me the burglar was simply looking for financial information he could steal, there was still something that bothered me. A niggling little thought in the back of my mind.

"Lord, Molly, you need to sign up for one of those credit-watchdog agencies that oversees your accounts. That's what I did. Too many prying eyes are on the web." She drained her glass, then added, "I'll send you an email with their website and link. Promise me you'll check them out."

I scooped up another spoonful of heavenly calories and smiled over at my friend. "I promise, if you promise me you'll join me again for a Monday night dinner. It looks like that's the only evening free on Eleanor's Washington schedule. No need for you to dine alone, either. And I can stay in touch with the Washington whirl. The senator isn't entertaining as much as before. Most evenings he's still absorbed in research."

"You've got a deal," Samantha said with a smile as she signaled the waiter with her empty glass.

TWO

Late Tuesday morning

LUISA APPEARED IN THE doorway of my office. "Can I bring you some coffee, Molly? I just made a fresh pot."

"Thanks for asking, but I filled up a few minutes ago. Mid-morning break." Senator Russell's housekeeper of thirty years straightened a stack of books on the corner of my desk. Then she turned to the bookshelves, giving the books a pat to even the spines. "It looks like you're searching for things to do now that we don't have caterers rattling around in the kitchen three times a week."

Luisa smiled. "Maybe I am missing all the activity. It certainly feels so much quieter these last few weeks. We've only had a few dinners. I guess I got used to that busy, busy pace."

"Addicted to the action, huh? Or maybe it's the politicians you miss?"

"Lord, no!" she said with a hearty laugh before turning away. "I think I'll go to my sorting list and put this extra time to good use."

"A sorting list?" I made a face. "I shudder at the idea. Going through clutter by choice rather than necessity is a scary thought." I heard Luisa's laughter echo down the hallway.

My personal cell phone burst into life, sending the sounds of Aretha Franklin's voice belting out "R-E-S-P-E-C-T." I saw Danny's name and number flash on the Blackberry screen and picked up as Lady Soul took a breath.

"Hey, there. How's the consulting going?"

"It's starting to wrap up. With luck, we'll finish tomorrow and I can catch a flight home. Maybe be back by six or so."

"That would be great. Shall I thaw out some of those gourmet leftovers we have stashed in the freezer?"

"Naw. Let's go out. I've been chowing down on seafood this entire weekend, so a steak sounds good."

That comment immediately caught my interest. "Seafood, huh? You must be near the water. Some place with a lot of really big ships, I'll bet."

Danny's low chuckle sounded over the phone. "Good guess."

My office Blackberry came to life this time, and a saxophone wail sounded throughout the office. Wicked Wilson Pickett with "Mustang Sally." This was classics month on my playlist.

"Okay, Squad Leader. Keep me posted."

"Roger that. You and Sally behave until I get back."

"No promises."

I heard Danny's laughter until he clicked off.

———

Raymond grabbed both sides of the bathroom sink, holding on until the coughing fit ceased. His fingers bled white with the effort, body shaking. Finally, the spasms eased, the shaking calmed.

Jesus God ... that was the worst one yet.

He spat out phlegm into the white sink. That's when he saw it. Tiny red droplets in the sink below. He'd figured it was only a matter of time before it started. Inevitable. He stared into his office bathroom mirror. The bluish-gray shadows beneath his eyes were even more noticeable now against his sallow skin.

Raymond splashed cold water on his face and rinsed the incriminating droplets down the drain. Then he rubbed the hand towel across his face, hard. Tried to get the blood moving, get some color into his face so he didn't look like a goddamn corpse.

He walked back to his office and sank into the desk chair. The fatigue was getting worse too. Another sign. Raymond knew all the signs. He'd read up on it a couple of years ago. The warning signs. Opening a lower desk drawer, he brought out the bottle of thirty-year-old Scotch Spencer had given him last spring. It was the last bottle in the case. He picked up a crystal glass sitting beside the old-fashioned electric clock on his desk and poured himself two generous fingers of the molten gold. He took a drink and let the liquid heat coat his cough-ravaged throat. Better. A little better.

Raymond slowly rose from his chair, taking the glass of Scotch and the bottle as he walked down the hallway to one of the inner offices. No windows in this room. Shelves of equipment lined the walls, along with cameras and various other pieces of equipment. On a long table against the wall was a monitor screen, showing the front yard and driveway of a two-story brick townhouse. Beside the monitor screen sat more equipment, one with a smaller, gray monitor screen.

Raymond checked his watch and sat in the upholstered chair beside the table. He stared at the blinking white cursor on the smaller screen. He entered a few lines of type and symbols on the keyboard below.

Let's see who the Jorgensen girl talked to last night, he thought as the screen suddenly showed lines of white type scrolling backwards. Raymond watched the time clock at the top of the screen that revealed the hours and minutes as they also sped backwards.

Raymond checked the log sheet on the clipboard beside his elbow. He logged off at 6:35 yesterday evening. As he hit the play button, the monitor screen showed lines of white text separated by lots of space—pauses in the recorded conversations that rolled by on the screen. Raymond scanned the lines of text. It was a personal call. Then a hang up, and another personal call. Jorgensen must be answering voice mails.

By 10:15 that evening, he noticed a large amount of empty space roll past on the screen. *Bedtime,* he thought and scrolled forward faster as he sipped the Scotch slowly. He watched the clock register 7:00 in the morning. Two more personal calls scrolled by. Raymond leaned back in the chair and watched the screen clock. Only a couple more hours, and he would be synchronized with his watch.

Just then, another conversation started. Raymond abruptly sat up after the caller identified herself. Congresswoman Sylvia Wilson was on the line, talking with Natasha Jorgensen. Raymond leaned forward, reading the lines of a phone conversation that took place only a half hour ago.

He watched several key words pass by in the text of the phone call. Words he'd hoped he wouldn't see again. Congressman Quentin Wilson. House Financial Services Committee. Quentin's notebook. *Quentin Wilson had a notebook? What the hell!*

Raymond leaned even closer to the screen, not wanting to miss a single word. Research on banking and international monetary policy. Chairman of the House committee, Edward Ryker. At the mention of that name, Raymond's gut twisted. Why was Sylvia Wilson sticking her nose where it didn't belong? Asking if her husband ever mentioned Congressman Ryker. *What the hell?*

He watched the white text roll by on the screen. *Jorgensen doesn't know anything. Quentin Wilson never mentioned Ryker. She's acting surprised. Or, is she lying to the congresswoman?* He'd heard that Sylvia Wilson had run roughshod over her husband's congressional staffers, so there was definitely no love lost between the staffers who jumped ship and the widow. Certainly there would be no desire to help the nosy new congresswoman.

A pause on the screen. Then the congresswoman asked Jorgensen to drop by her office and take a look at the notebook. See if she recognized anything. *Holy crap.* That was all they needed. Jorgensen making connections, finding out what her former boss had learned from his research.

More text filled the screen. Jorgensen was busy tonight with a visiting Iowa delegation and Congresswoman Chertoff. She'd be free Wednesday night. Sylvia Wilson suggested 6:30 at her office in the Rayburn Building. The lines of white type stopped.

Raymond stared at the blank monitor screen. *Dammit!* Everything had quieted down. Quentin Wilson's death had disappeared from the media spotlight. He was dead and buried. All questions had been answered. He overdosed deliberately because his bitch of a wife was going to divorce him and expose his affair with Samantha Calhoun to the world. His political career was ruined. And now this. *Dammit to hell!* What was Sylvia Wilson up to? And what did Quentin Wilson have in his notebook?

Raymond pushed away from the table and returned to the front of his office to retrieve his cell phone. The morning sun threw a bright swath across his worn oriental rug. He pressed Trask's number, then searched through his pockets for more throat lozenges. When he didn't find any, he opened his center desk drawer while the line connected. Finding a half-filled bag of the honey-coated throat lozenges, he dumped the contents on his desk. Trask's voice answered as Raymond popped a lozenge into his mouth.

"What's up? We talked yesterday."

Raymond sucked on the honey-coated drop. "You need to come back to town. The phone bug picked up a conversation between Sylvia Wilson and Jorgensen. It seems Wilson found a notebook from departed hubby Quentin. Lots of stuff about international banks and money transfers. She called Jorgensen to ask what she knew about it. Jorgensen acted surprised. Claims she never knew about any notebook."

"So, what's the big deal? It sounds like the same stuff he was researching."

"It also had Ryker's name in it."

"*Aw, crap.*"

Raymond could hear the disgust in Trask's tone. "Yeah, that's what I said. We're gonna have to take a look at that notebook. Or find out what's in it," he said, walking back into the office with the monitors. "Jorgensen will be busy with visiting Iowans till tomorrow. She told the congresswoman she'd come to her office Wednesday night to take a look. We need to find out who she sees and talks to when she's not on her phone. You're gonna have to be right on her."

"Roger that. Let me get the boat prepared and boarded. Then I can drive back tomorrow."

Movement on the smaller monitor screen caught Raymond's attention and he leaned over to read the lines of white type. The words "text message" appeared first on the screen. Raymond read the following two lines of type, and his gut took another twist.

"*Dammit to hell*," he muttered into the phone. "Jorgensen just sent a text message to Malone. 'You'll never guess who called me a few minutes ago. Sylvia Wilson.'"

"I'll take the boat over now. Keep me posted. I want to hear what Malone says."

"You and me both."

"We warned them about Jorgensen. Never leave loose ends." Trask's line clicked off.

Yeah, we did, Raymond thought as he went to retrieve another lozenge.

Tuesday afternoon

"Sorry to dump all this on you, Molly," Peter Brewster said, handing me another folder. "But those subcommittee sessions will consider these issues of international banks and financial institutions in a couple of days and the senator needs those summaries."

"That's okay, Peter. I didn't have anything planned for tonight anyway." I checked the headings on the folders. "So you simply want me to go through these reports and copy only the headings and summary paragraphs, right?"

Peter nodded. "Exactly. And I promise this won't happen again. I'll be interviewing tomorrow for the two new research staffer positions. They can take over after that. Meanwhile, the senator told me you can have a few extra-long weekends as his thank you." He grinned. "I imagine you and Danny might want to escape to some warmer winter climes when the snow starts to fall."

"Tell the senator thank you, and I'll take him up on that offer in February when the ice starts coating the streets," I said, following Peter from his office and into the mansion hallway. "I don't mind snow. It's the ice that causes problems. D.C. traffic is bad enough without everybody sliding into each other on the roadways." I grimaced.

"Oh, I told Luisa you'd be staying here for dinner tonight. The senator and I are off to Senator Dunston's reception." Peter paused in the hallway. "You and Luisa and Albert can order out if you want. Put it on my credit card."

"Now you know Luisa would take that as an insult," I teased. "Besides, I'm looking forward to listening to Albert and Luisa brag about the grandchildren. I'm sure they've got new pictures."

"Oh, yeah. Albert showed me this morning," Peter said, heading toward the front door. I could hear his cell phone's music ringing from his jacket pocket.

Back to work for both of us. I paused on the way to my office at the end of the hallway and pulled my cell phone from my pocket. A text message came in from Natasha Jorgensen. I clicked on it and read. "You'll never guess who just called me. Sylvia Wilson."

I had to smile. From what Samantha told me the other night, Widow Wilson was still trying to find her footing on Capitol Hill and was still stumbling. She was probably calling Natasha to ask her to come over and explain the filing system. That was what happened when you let all your experienced Hill staffers leave and brought in Cleveland rookies. Unlike professional baseball, Capitol Hill had no minor leagues where you could work your way up. Congress was Major League ball. You'd better know how to play, or you'd be played.

I shut my phone off completely and stashed it in my jacket pocket. No time for Widow Wilson stories right now. I would be working late for Senator Russell. And he was definitely a Major League player.

THREE

Wednesday morning
TRASK DEPOSITED THE TALL carryout cup with the familiar green and white logo on the table beside Raymond. "I brought an extra coffee, double cream." He dug into his navy-blue jacket pocket and pulled out a package of honey throat lozenges, then dropped them beside the coffee. "I figured you could also use some of these."

"Hey, thanks," Raymond gave him a tired smile. "You were right on both counts."

"Did you stay here all night? You look like hell."

"Naw, I went home at seven or so. That way you escape the worst of rush hour on the beltway." He took a big drink of the creamed coffee and felt the heat slide down his throat. He glanced back at Trask and saw that expression he'd spotted once or twice before. When something else appeared briefly in Trask's ice-blue eyes. A flicker of compassion? Sympathy? Raymond wasn't sure. It never lasted long enough for him to decipher.

Trask sat in a nearby swivel chair, took a drink from his coffee, then pointed toward the smaller monitor screen. "Has Malone called Jorgensen yet?"

"Not yet."

"Have you talked to Spencer?"

Raymond shook his head, then took another drink of coffee. A deeper one this time. "No, I want to have more information first. We need to find out what's in that notebook. According to Spencer, Wilson only overheard bits and pieces of conversation."

"But you said Ryker's name was there."

"Yeah … there's that. But Spencer said Ryker swore he and Ambassador Holmberg only talked about the bill and when it was coming up in committee. So, there may be nothing more than Wilson's speculations in that notebook. You know, his overactive imagination." He shrugged. "After all, he was an ambitious junior congressman itching to advance."

"With a prescription drug habit," Trask said, mouth twisting with a crooked smile. "Or, so I've heard."

The gray screen flickered into life then, the white cursor flashing. Another call coming in on Jorgensen's phone. Both men turned their chairs and stared at the screen.

———

I leaned back in my desk chair and listened to Natasha's phone ring while I sipped my first mug of Luisa's coffee. "Hey, Natasha. Sorry I didn't call yesterday, but I was working late. I had to help Peter with some extra reports for the senator."

"No problem, Molly. I figured I'd hear from you today."

"The senator's new committee assignment has really piled on the research. He and Peter have been buried since late July."

"I know what you mean. I've been taking home congressional reports for weeks now. Ever since I came over here. Nightly reading."

"Antidote to insomnia, right?" I joked. "So tell me, what's up with Widow Wilson? She can't decipher the filing system?"

Natasha gave a short laugh. "Actually, it was kind of a strange phone call. It seems she found a notebook in Quentin's desk at the office, and she asked if I knew anything about it."

I took a sip of coffee and let my imagination run free. "Oh, brother. Don't tell me he had a secret porn collection."

"No, no, nothing like that. She said it was filled with notes about reports and articles he'd read. I thought it sounded like he was doing research for his subcommittees and told her so. But she said that the research was on international banking and monetary policy. And financial legislation. So, she was confused because none of that was related to his committee assignments. Which are now *her* committee assignments."

My little buzzer went off inside. "Sounds like the same stuff you told me he was researching last summer."

"That's exactly what I thought. Remember those files I gave you? They were filled with research reports and articles on those same subjects. So I'm thinking that notebook is where Quentin kept his research notes."

"Did you tell her that?"

"Yeah, I did. I told her he'd gotten interested in that subject last summer and started researching it. That's all I knew."

I knew there was a whole lot more to it than that, but I didn't want to share it with Natasha. That information had been given to me in confidence by Samantha. So I worked around the edges. "That makes sense to me. What did she say?"

"Well, that's when she asked me to come over and take a look at the notebook. It seems Quentin jotted down some other things that made her curious."

"Like what?"

"Well, he'd written in Congressman Edward Ryker's name and his committee. He's the chairman, you know."

That name burned its way through my brain. No longer the same heat, but singeing all the same. It had not lost its power over the years. "Yes, I know," I said, unable to keep the chill from my voice. I also knew the reason Quentin Wilson had Ryker's name in his notebook. Wilson had overheard Congressman Ryker and former EU Ambassador Holmberg talking with each other about upcoming legislation in Ryker's committee. "Did he write down any other names?"

"You know, she rattled off a few, but I don't remember them now. One of the staffers was signaling me, so I was only paying half attention."

"So you plan to go over and take a look at the notebook? Maybe you'll remember something else. Help out the struggling new congresswoman." I deliberately let the sarcasm creep into my tone.

Natasha snickered. "Part of me doesn't want to, but in the spirit of congressional cooperation, I guess I'd better."

Now it was my turn to snicker. "Congressional cooperation. We certainly need more of that. Harder to find nowadays." An idea wiggled from the back of my brain. "Say, would you do me a favor, Natasha? If you take notes when you're going through that notebook, could you give me a copy, please? I'd appreciate it."

"Sure, Molly. She kind of suggested that I take some notes. She wants me to go through my old daytimer from the office and see if there's any correlation. Of course I told her I would, even though it's really presumptuous of her to ask. After all, I'm up to my neck in work here in Chertoff's office."

I laughed softly. "Ahhhhhh, yes. The spirit of congressional co-operation seems to be a one-way street for the Widow Wilson."

"You got that right. Listen, I've got a call on another line. Why don't I call you tonight and tell you what I found? I'm going over to her office right after I leave here tonight."

"Uhhhhhhh, tonight won't work for me. I'm already booked," I demurred. This evening Danny and I would be enjoying fine food, fine wine, and each other. "Why don't we meet tomorrow morning at the Canal for a run? I can get there by six-thirty … I think."

"Sure. I'll be finishing up by then, but we can do the last stretch together. Why don't we meet at that bridge on Thirty-first Street over the Canal? I'll be on the way back from the Key Bridge turn, so we can run together toward the Parkway. I'll make a copy of what-ever notes I take. How's that?"

"Sounds like a plan. I'll see you tomorrow morning."

"See ya."

I was about to add my customary "take care," but her phone had already clicked off.

———

Raymond leaned back in the upholstered chair, still staring at the gray screen. The blinking white cursor didn't move. No more phone calls. Glancing over at Trask, he saw him smiling. That insolent, I-told-you-so smile he'd seen before. Raymond let it slide. He didn't have the energy to spare for petty aggravation. He had to stay focused.

"Well, that was informative."

Trask snickered as he laced his fingers behind his head and leaned back in the swivel chair. "Yeah, I'd say so. I knew Jorgensen was going to be a problem. I just didn't know when. Now there's Congresswoman Wilson sniffing around. That's the last thing those guys want."

"Yeah, you're right." Raymond turned the takeout coffee cup on the chair arm.

"I say we eliminate Jorgensen before she can pass along any more information. That way, Sylvia Wilson will hit a dead end in her snooping, and so will Malone. Once Jorgensen is gone, there's no one else who can answer questions about that notebook."

That made sense, Raymond thought. Leave it to Trask to always cut to the brutal truth. Simple. Surgically simple. Excise Jorgensen, and then maybe they could seal up the wound. Maybe.

"You know, I got the feeling Malone knew more than she was letting on to Jorgensen," Trask said, leaning forward in the chair, coffee cup dangling between his knees.

"Yeah, I got that too. Makes me wonder how much she knows about Quentin Wilson. Or, rather . . . how much her friend told her."

"You mean Samantha Calhoun."

"Yeah. The 'paramour' as the *D.C. Dirt* called her." Raymond gave a snort.

"Do you think Wilson told Samantha Calhoun about seeing Ryker talking with Holmberg that day?"

"I don't know. But it makes me wonder. I got the same feeling you did. Malone knew more than she was saying to Jorgensen. And the only one who could have told her was the Calhoun woman." Raymond stared off into the office.

"First, we take care of Jorgensen. If we're lucky, that could stop all the snooping. And Jorgensen should be stopped before she meets Malone tomorrow morning and can hand off any more info."

"Agreed. I'll run it by Spencer. I think he'll authorize it."

Trask smiled a cold smile. "There's no time for him to go through a committee on this one."

"Nope. *He'll* have to authorize it." Raymond upended his coffee cup.

"I was gonna get more coffee. You want another cup?" Trask asked, rising from the chair.

"Yeah, matter of fact. And wouldja bring me one of those breakfast sandwiches too?"

"Sure thing." Trask headed toward the hallway.

"Are you gonna take care of her tonight?"

Trask glanced back over his shoulder as he put on his shades. "Nope. Tomorrow morning before daybreak. Under Key Bridge." His cold smile returned. "Surgical."

Later Wednesday afternoon

Raymond poured two fingers of Scotch into the crystal glass. He held the glass up to the sunlight shining through the corner window at the back of his office. The sun beam caught the crystal edges in the glass. It was the only thing he took from the house when he left. And that was only because she threw it at him. Nothing else. She wouldn't even let him say goodbye to the kid. But she saw him. He'd spotted her little face at the bedroom window, staring solemnly, brown eyes huge. He'd blown her a kiss before he got in the car and driven off. She'd seen that. He knew she did.

He swirled the Scotch in his glass. Funny thing, memories. Different ones popped out of the quicksand of your mind. Out of nowhere, you're back in time. He took a large drink, then pressed Spencer's name on his phone directory.

"Raymond, how're you doing?" Spencer's deep voice came over the line. "How's that case of Scotch holding out?"

"Funny you should ask. I'm halfway through the last bottle."

"Well, then, I'll have another case sent out today. How's that cough doing?"

"It's okay," Raymond lied. "The Scotch helps. So does hot coffee. Listen, we've got a problem. I've been monitoring that girl Jorgensen's phone since August. Nothing unusual showed up until yesterday. Sylvia Wilson called Jorgensen and asked questions about a notebook she found in Quentin Wilson's office desk drawer."

"What kind of notebook? What was in it?" Spencer's voice had lost all trace of warmth.

"Sounds like Wilson took notes on all that international bank research he was doing. But he also had some names written down. Ryker's for one."

"*Shit!*"

"I know. Jorgensen said she didn't know anything about a notebook and acted like she'd never heard Wilson mention Ryker before."

"*Dammit!*"

"Yeah, then the congresswoman asks Jorgensen to come over to her office tonight and take a look at the notebook, take notes, even. Then compare them to any old office records Jorgensen may have."

"*What the hell!* What is Sylvia Wilson up to? She's not on any banking subcommittees. Why is she poking around?"

"Beats me. It may be because Ryker's name is mentioned. And apparently there are other names, too, but the Jorgensen girl couldn't remember."

"Wait a minute! Who else was that Jorgensen girl talking to?"

"That's another problem. After Sylvia Wilson's call, Jorgensen texted Molly Malone. Malone called her back this morning and asked questions."

"*Goddammit!*"

"And it gets worse. Malone asked Jorgensen to make her a copy of any notes she takes. They're planning to meet early tomorrow morning along the canal where they both run." Raymond held the phone while Spencer cursed again, a longer stream this time.

"*Crap!* We'd gotten everything quieted down, and now this," Spencer complained.

"Yeah, my thoughts exactly. Well, you know what I'm going to say next. Trask and I agree Jorgensen needs to be taken out before she can hand off any more information to either Malone or Sylvia Wilson. She's the bridge. Eliminate her, and the other two hit a dead end."

"*Damn...*" Spencer whispered the word this time.

"I know. You're worried about the rest of the committee."

"Damn right. There's no time to even run this past them."

Raymond detected a worried tone that he hadn't heard in Spencer's voice before. "You said they took on some new members. Any word about them?"

"Montclair said a couple are from Southeast Asia. Another one is Russian."

"Well, if you think we'd better not make a move, okay. It's your call. We can only hope there're not many names in that notebook. But every time we think there's nothing more that can come out, something else appears."

"Yeah, I know."

There was a resigned sound in Spencer's voice that Raymond had heard before, so he pushed a little more. "Now, we've got Congresswoman Wilson snooping around in addition to Malone. There's no way we could touch the congresswoman, and you guys decided hands-off Malone. For now, at least."

"Yeah, yeah … ancient history. I know where you're going Raymond, and I agree with you. If we can shut it down now with Jorgensen, then we should. It's just …"

Raymond let the pause grow, feeling Spencer's reluctance over the phone. "Trask has already picked out the perfect spot. Under Key Bridge along the Canal. The Jorgensen girl runs before six, so it'll still be mostly dark then."

"I thought you said she was meeting Malone then."

"They're set to meet later on Thirty-first Street where it crosses over the Canal. Jorgensen would be on her return run. Trask has followed her several times along the Canal. Malone too. He knows that stretch and knows their habits." He waited for Spencer's response.

"Yeah … go ahead. Do it."

"Okay …" Raymond said, hearing the hard edge in Spencer's tone. "I'll tell Trask." Maybe this time, things would quiet down and stay quiet. Maybe.

FOUR

Early Thursday morning

I ZIPPED MY LIGHTWEIGHT running jacket closer to my chin. A slight breeze had picked up, rustling the leaves of trees bordering the Chesapeake and Ohio Canal. I hadn't been chilly when I first started running from my house on P Street down through the darkened predawn Georgetown streets toward the Canal. But now that I was no longer running, I felt the fall temperature change more keenly.

Walking up and over the arched roadway where Thirty-first Street spanned the Canal, I stood at midpoint of the bridge and stared down the towpath once again. Natasha must be running late. Early dawn had brought a little more light, which made it easier to make out the faces of the runners getting in their morning workout. No sign of Natasha yet.

I pulled my cell phone from the pocket of my running pants and searched for any missed text messages. Maybe I hadn't heard the little beep with the sounds of morning traffic. More cars on the streets now. I'd heard a siren's wail a few minutes ago. It sounded only a few blocks away. Probably an early morning fender bender.

I also checked for any unanswered phone messages and only saw Loretta Wade's message last night. She was the senior researcher at the Congressional Research Service of the Library of Congress and had a question. I hadn't been able to get back to her because Danny was picking me up from the office and the rest of the evening we planned to be incommunicado. Only talking to each other.

I glanced down the towpath again and decided to start running in the direction Natasha would be coming. And I might as well return Loretta's call at the same time. Heading down the paved incline that led from the bridge to the Canal below, I punched in Loretta's number as I jogged slower along the towpath. No sunshine this morning. It was gray and gloomy. On the verge of rain.

Loretta's phone rang a couple of times, then her no-nonsense voice sounded. "Hey, Molly! We're both up and at 'em early."

"Well, I'm not getting at anything right now except the Canal towpath. I'm not even at the office yet. I'm waiting for a friend to show up. She promised to meet me."

"I just got in here to my office. It's quieter now and I can work on the long to-do list hanging over my head."

"I know what you mean. Hey, your text message said you had a question about my deceased brother-in-law Eric Grayson's research. Did you find something?"

"I found a whole bunch of topics that he'd researched. European Union banking regulations, financial institutions. Kind of strange since it was Europe. He had searched international banking regulation in general. But he had also searched U.S. legislation, which involved transferring money to European banks. I thought that was strange because he was never on any banking or financial subcommittees or committees. I know it was years ago, I wondered if he left any notes explaining what he was searching for."

Eric Grayson's notebook. I remembered my niece Karen talking about her father's notebook, how she'd kept it and gone over his notes sometimes.

"Matter of fact, he did. Karen kept her father's research notebook, and I remember she said he made notes of things he was investigating. I put it in her safety deposit box along with insurance policies and other legal documents after her death. I tried to put her things away. They were a reminder she was gone."

"I'm sorry, Molly. I didn't mean to bring back painful memories."

"No, no, it's okay. I could take a look at that notebook and see what's there." A woman runner passed around me as I ran, and I picked up my pace. I thought I spotted a cluster of people farther ahead, near the Key Bridge overpass. Probably a college track team doing an early morning run before class.

"If you get a chance to go through it, let me know. Especially if you find any notes that might explain why he did all those searches. He showed up at the Library of Congress three times a week for several weeks. I remember because I worked there during that time period. This puzzle was too easy to solve. I need a challenge. A new puzzle."

"I'll take a look at the notebook, Loretta. If I find anything, I'll let you know. Maybe we can share over another Irish pub dinner."

"Sounds good. Talk to you later."

She clicked off, and I slid the small phone back into my running pants pocket. Meanwhile, it looked like the cluster of people farther ahead weren't running. And the same-color shirts weren't team jerseys. They looked like uniforms—Washington, D.C. police uniforms.

A chill passed through me then, and it wasn't because of the breeze. Another runner approached me, coming from that direction. I waved at him as he neared and yelled, "What's happening by the bridge?"

"D.C. cops and medics. They blocked off the towpath," he said as he passed, slowing his stride to glance back at me. "Saw a girl on a stretcher. Lots of blood." Then he took off running again.

His words stopped me in my tracks. A cold fist twisted my stomach. *Natasha. God, no.* I took off, running faster, drawing closer to the uniformed personnel clustered beneath the huge span that was Key Bridge. I spotted an ambulance parked on the roadway directly above the Canal. Two white-uniformed men hurried down the steps that edged the stone wall bordering the Canal and towpath.

"Ma'am, stop! You can't run here. You gotta turn around now," a heavyset D.C. policeman commanded as he approached, waving at me.

I stopped immediately. "What happened?" I asked him, my voice higher pitched than normal. "I'm … I'm going to meet my friend. She's up ahead." I pointed toward the bridge.

"You'll have to meet her somewhere else, ma'am. Now, turn around and head back the way you came, okay?" He directed me in a no-nonsense tone, pointing down the towpath behind me.

I obeyed without a word, retreating a few paces. The policeman made a shooing gesture with his hand, and I turned around and started slowly walking back down the towpath, looking over my shoulder as I did. The white-uniformed medical personnel were hovering together at the far end beneath the bridge span. Several other runners and onlookers stood on the side of the towpath along the Canal, watching the proceedings. I left the towpath and joined them. We were far enough away so we did not attract police attention.

The cluster of police separated as two medical personnel carried a stretcher out from under the bridge. Two other medics accompanied them. The person on the stretcher was covered totally by a white sheet or blanket, including the face. The person had to be dead. The medics angled the stretcher as they slowly started up the steps bordering the stone wall.

Suddenly a slender leg slipped from beneath the white cover and dangled over the side of the stretcher. One of the medics walking beside stopped the stretcher carriers for a moment while he tucked the gray-clad leg beneath the white shroud once again. The men resumed their careful climb.

It was only a moment, but it was long enough for me to spot the bright-yellow running shoe on the foot that dangled over the side. The cold fist in my gut squeezed tighter. Natasha wore neon, bright-yellow running shoes. She joked they were her nighttime and early morning alert system. Drivers and cyclists couldn't miss the bright-yellow shoes.

I stared, unwilling to move until the medics had the girl on the stretcher safely loaded onto the ambulance. That's when I took off, running as fast as I could down the towpath. Back to Thirty-first Street and back toward my house. It was too early to call Natasha's office. No one would be answering the phones. But my gut told me what I didn't want to know. Natasha was the girl on the stretcher. I *knew* it.

Digging my phone from my pants pocket again, I scanned the directory and slowed down long enough to press Casey's number.

He was the only one I knew who could find out the girl's identity and what happened to her. Maybe. I listened to his phone ring three times before his gruff voice answered.

"Molly? Has something happened? Why are you calling so early?"

I slowed enough so I could make sense. "Casey ... I'm here on the towpath. I was supposed to meet Natasha Jorgensen ..."

"Who?"

I let loose a torrent. "She used to work for Quentin Wilson, but I was gonna meet her because she had notes from Quentin Wilson. But she never showed up at six thirty, so I went down the path toward Key Bridge where she was running, and ... and I saw cops, Casey. D.C. cops and medics and a body on a stretcher. It was all covered up, so I knew the person was dead. I knew it. And I saw Natasha's running shoes! I recognized them."

"Whoa ... slow down, Molly! Where are you now?"

"I'm running down the Canal, heading home. But I wanted to ask if you could check with your D.C. cop friends to find out what happened here. I *know* it was Natasha, Casey! I just know it!"

"Okay, hold on. You get home, Molly, and I'll see what I can find out while I'm heading to the senator's house. Hell, I haven't even gotten in the shower yet. The cops probably don't know much, to be honest. Whoever it was probably didn't have an ID on them. Most people don't carry an ID when they run. So it may take a while to identify her."

I hadn't even thought of that. "You're right. Okay, find out what you can. I'll see you at the office. Thanks, Casey. I—I appreciate it."

"Talk to you later, Molly. And for God's sake, be careful while you're running. Pay attention. It's rush hour. Where's Danny?"

"He's probably sitting in rush hour on the way to a meeting at Quantico."

"Well, better him than us. See you at the office."

"Thanks, Casey."

I shoved the phone into my pants pocket and picked up my pace, running as if the Devil himself were behind me. For all I knew, he might be. That had to be his handiwork beneath Key Bridge this morning. Too close. Much too close.

———

I stood in the hallway of the Russell mansion and watched Casey pace at the other end of the hall, next to the living room and the French doors leading to the garden outside. He was still on the phone with one of his D.C. cop friends trying to find out details about the dead girl found beneath Key Bridge this morning. Clasping my coffee mug with both hands, I held it close to my chest, absorbing its warmth.

Peter stepped out of his library office down the hall, glanced to Casey, then walked over to where I stood by the door to my office. The emails accumulating in my inbox would have to wait.

"Have you called Chertoff's office yet? Any word on Natasha?" he peered at me in concern.

"I called as soon as I got back to my house. I asked them to let me know the moment Natasha came into the office. I said I was worried something had happened to her, because she didn't show up to meet me this morning. I didn't say anything about seeing a body on a stretcher." I closed my eyes. "Just in case I'm wrong. God, I hope I'm wrong. I hope Natasha spent the night with some fantastic guy and totally blew me off this morning. God, I hope so." But my gut didn't believe it.

Peter made an attempt to smile, but his smile couldn't make it past the worry already on his face. "I hope so, too, Molly. I don't want to think about the other."

I wished I couldn't think about it, but that image of a dead girl's body shrouded on the stretcher, slender pant-covered leg dangling over the side. Neon-yellow running shoes. How many people wore shoes that color? I had only spotted one pair like that since I'd been running in Washington, and they were on Natasha Jorgensen's feet.

"I checked with some friends in the Rayburn building," he continued. "Their office is next to Congresswoman Chertoff's. So if anything happens there, like police show up or something, they'll give me a call."

"Thanks, Peter. Let's hope they don't see anything." Just then, my attention was drawn to Casey. He was pocketing his cell phone and walking down the hall toward us.

"That was Lieutenant Schroeder. He said they're checking into the dead girl's identity now. Her throat was cut. They think it may have been an attempted sexual assault and she fought back. No witnesses, of course," Casey added. "Any drunks sleeping under the bridge would take off the minute they heard a scuffle."

I felt a shudder run over me at that image. "A guy on the towpath told me he saw a girl on a stretcher and there was lots of blood."

Peter flinched. "Good God. With all those people running in the morning. You'd think you'd be safe."

"It's fall now and still Daylight Saving Time. So it's actually dark before six a.m. Schroeder said the girl had her cell phone and keys but no other ID. I told him about your planned meeting with Natasha Jorgensen, Molly. And your concerns, especially after you witnessed the medics taking the body away." He looked at me sadly. "Schroeder said to thank you for the information. They're going to contact Congresswoman Chertoff's office."

Lieutenant Schroeder was the D.C. police detective in charge of investigating my niece Karen's murder last spring. He was very good and worked very hard trying to find the killer. "Well, that's something. Detective Schroeder is certainly thorough."

Peter put his hand on my arm and looked at me solicitously. "We don't know it was Natasha, Molly. Try not to worry." The sound of his cell phone buzzed from his jacket pocket. "That's probably Jackie from the Hill reminding me of a meeting."

"Go back to work, Peter. You've got to stay on task. I'm okay. I'll keep you posted if I hear from Natasha's office."

Casey gave my arm a squeeze before he started toward the front entry. "I promise I'll call as soon as I hear from Schroeder, Molly."

Peter gave me a half smile as he backed away. "I'm still hoping it's that hot-date scenario you described."

"See you later, guys," I half waved to them as I headed toward the kitchen. I needed another mug of coffee to keep away the chill that had penetrated through my clothes.

FIVE

Thursday, Mid-morning

RAYMOND JUMPED AT THE sound of his cell phone on the table beside him. He'd been staring at the smaller monitor screen, watching to see if any phone calls or texts appeared. There was nothing. Which meant Jorgensen wasn't using her phone like she did every morning. Trask was successful. There was a little blip on the monitor for a second, then nothing more.

Noticing Trask's name flash on his cell phone, Raymond snatched up the phone before it rang again. "It's about time. I was starting to worry. Any problems? How'd it go?"

"Messy, but effective. She screamed like hell when I grabbed her. Woke up a drunk under the bridge, so I had to move faster, that's all. It took me longer to get rid of my clothes behind the university, though. I had to wait till the old maintenance guy wasn't watching the incinerator."

"Anyone else around that might have spotted you running away?"

"Nope. No one else was on the towpath. I ran up the steps and changed clothes halfway to the street. Put all the bloody stuff in the backpack, then I watched it burn."

Raymond relaxed a little. "Good. Good. So you got the list. Better bring that over. And her phone."

"I got the list but wasn't able to get her phone. I searched her jacket pockets, but she was flailing around on the ground so much, I couldn't search her pants. Meanwhile, the drunk was starting to make noise, waking up. I had to take off. Didn't want to risk anybody else coming close."

Raymond grimaced to himself. "Damn," he said softly. "That means the cops have her phone. They'll find the bug."

"Maybe. Maybe not. Depends on who checks the phone. Besides, there's no way to trace anything to us."

"Yeah, I know. It's just another one of those loose ends that keep appearing."

"Look, let me jump in the shower, then I'll come over there with the list. I think you're going to be surprised what's on it. And those guys will be glad we took care of Jorgensen before she could pass it on. Put a lid on this."

"Okay, sounds good. And bring more of that good coffee, wouldja?"

"Sure thing."

Put a lid on this, Trask said. *If only*, Raymond thought as he turned off the smaller monitor screen.

———

I saved an email to one of my computer file folders as I reached for my office phone. Casey's name flashed. "Hey, there. Have you heard anything yet?"

"Yeah. I just got off the phone with Schroeder."

I could tell what Casey was about to say from the sound of his voice. "It was Natasha, wasn't it?"

"Yes, it was. They checked the cell phone card for her name and identification, then contacted Congresswoman Chertoff's office. The staff confirmed Natasha hadn't come into work yet today. They also described her car and where Natasha usually parked every morning while she ran. Officers found the car with Natasha's purse and photo ID. One of Chertoff's staffers is coming down to identify the body."

I felt an old chill ripple over me. Last spring, I'd been the one to find my niece Karen shot dead in her car, blood everywhere. I didn't wish that experience on anyone. Gruesome didn't even cover it. "Good Lord. I feel sorry for that young staffer. You said Natasha's throat was cut. That's going to be hard to forget."

"It's not a pretty sight, I can vouch for that. Listen, Molly, I'm on the way back to the mansion. Senator Russell is holed up on the Hill all day. Peter too. Is there anyone else you'd like me to call?"

"No, thanks, Casey. I'll leave Danny a message. He's tied up all day. Then, I'll call Samantha. She needs to hear it from me rather than the newspapers."

"Okay. See you later." He clicked off.

I placed my office phone beside the computer, then pulled my personal phone from my purse. Taking a deep drink of the barely warm coffee, I pressed Samantha's number in my directory. Mid-morning. She should still be home. Probably preparing for another charity luncheon with Eleanor. After three rings I heard Samantha's warm Mississippi drawl sound in my ear. Honey-smooth. I found that somehow reassuring.

"Hey, there, Miss Thing. How's the charity circuit going?"

"It's heating up, believe it or not. Everyone is gearing up for the holidays. There will be fundraisers and galas and concerts galore, so keep your checkbook out. We're coming after your charitable dollars."

I heard the humor in her voice and it felt good. Familiar. And it chased away a little of the chill. Unfortunately, I was about to spread that cold feeling to my dear friend. "Thanks for the heads-up. The nuns would be proud of you, Samantha. They're probably smiling down beatifically at you from heaven right now."

She snickered. "Well, that's a pretty picture, but I'm not so sure. I was not one of their favorites. But, I did see one of the sisters a few weeks ago, believe it or not. She's in her eighties and still working with the charities. In fact, she introduced me to the person in charge of arranging support groups for the veterans returning from Iraq and Afghanistan."

"Well, that's certainly a worthwhile effort."

"Absolutely, so I will gladly add them to my donation list. How's it going over at the Russell ranch? It's been pretty quiet these last couple of months."

"It's still quiet. Listen, Samantha, I wanted to call you and share some pretty awful news before you read it in the papers."

"Oh, Lord, Molly ... what's happened? The senator hasn't had a heart attack, has he?"

"No, no, he's healthy as a horse. This bad news concerns someone we both know. Natasha Jorgensen. She … she was killed this morning on the Canal towpath while she was running. She runs really early, and some bastard must have been hiding in the dark near the Key Bridge underpass. Waiting for some young girl to run past so he could jump her."

Samantha gasped. "*No! God, no!* Not Natasha! How horrible! How did you hear about it? I've seen nothing on the news."

"It probably won't be on the news until tomorrow. I know because she was supposed to meet me at the bridge on Thirty-first Street and we were going to run together. But she never showed up this morning. So I walked down toward Key Bridge, because that's where she always turns around. When I got there, D.C. cops and medics were swarming all over. I saw them carry off someone on a stretcher, and I glimpsed Natasha's yellow running shoes." I released a tired sigh.

"Oh, Molly … you were there?"

"Yes, so I ran home and phoned Casey to find out what the cops knew. They called him a few minutes ago after they'd identified the victim. It was Natasha. Someone from Chertoff's office is going to identify the body. Casey said that bastard slit her throat."

"Good Lord … I can't believe this," she said, shock evident in her voice. "I simply cannot. I don't *want* to believe it. It's too awful. We're losing these wonderful people. I don't understand. *What is happening?*"

Samantha's question gave me pause. She was right. In the past six months four bright lights on the Hill had been taken from us. Some prominent, others laboring behind the scenes. Karen. Celeste. Congressman Quentin Wilson. And now, Natasha Jorgensen.

"I can't understand it, either. All four of them. Dead from vicious attacks in the streets or by random accidents. All gone."

It was true, Karen was shot in her car, Celeste Allard—a co-worker and friend of Karen's—died in a horrible explosion, Congressman Wilson died of an overdose, and now Natasha, killed on the C & O towpath.

"Thank you for telling me, Molly," Samantha said sadly. "I'm going to send some flowers to Chertoff's office. I imagine they'll arrange a service for her here like they did for Karen. If I remember correctly Natasha's parents live in Minnesota."

"Yes. Flowers are a great idea. I'll do the same. I'll arrange for some to be sent from me and from the senator and Peter."

"I'm going to have to meet Eleanor in a little while for lunch. Smithsonian lecture this time. But let's get together later this week if we can."

"Sounds good. Danny leaves on Friday again. I'll give you a call. Take care. Give my regards to Eleanor."

Samantha promised to give her regards, then she clicked off, and I returned to my computer. Only immersion in work would drive away the memories of violent deaths that lurked at the edges of my mind.

Thursday evening

I took another sip of the delicate and luscious Pinot Noir Danny had opened and settled back into the sofa cushions, my head resting in the crook of Danny's arm.

"I guess it's crazy to hope there was someone who witnessed the attack. Like some guys who were sleeping under the bridge.

I remember you saying drunks slept under that Key Bridge overpass."

Danny took a sip of wine, then shook his head. "Those guys would have taken off fast. Waking up to see some guy killing a girl that close. They've gone to ground by now. No way would they talk to the cops. They could wind up being accused."

"That makes sense, I guess. If you can make sense of anything this awful."

"Washington is as dangerous as any other big city. People get mesmerized by all the beautiful buildings and parks and places like the Canal. They forget predators can be lurking in those beautiful places. They let their guard down. That's when they're vulnerable. Sounds like Natasha had been running along the towpath for a long time. She probably assumed that running early in the dark of the morning was as safe as in the daylight."

Danny was right. Washington was seductive in its beauty. Far too easy to become entranced. "It's just so tragic. Natasha was smart and talented. She had such a bright future. Just like Karen." Painful memories of my late niece's violent death crept from the back of my mind.

"And that's another reason this is so painful for you. It reminds you too much of Karen. Thank God you weren't the one to actually find her, Molly. Once was enough." Danny leaned over and kissed my temple, his lips warm from the wine.

I took another sip of the rich wine, pondering what Danny had said. More old memories crept from the dark. "Actually, it would have been the third time I walked in on death."

Danny grimaced. "Damn, I forgot about Dave. Sorry I said anything."

The painful memory from long ago returned—my walking into our home to find my young husband Dave facedown on his desk in a pool of his own blood, gun in his hand. "It's okay. We've lost lots of bright talented people over the years. Too many."

I stared out into the fireplace; the three logs Danny had placed on top of each other still blazed with the flames, sending a wonderful warmth toward us on the sofa. A remembered thought slipped in, dancing over the flames in the fireplace. "I keep remembering something Samantha said when I called her this morning. She was fond of Natasha, so I wanted her to hear about Natasha's death from me and not the newspapers. Samantha said 'What is happening? We're losing these wonderful people.'"

Remnants of the consumed top log collapsed onto the others in a shower of sparks. Danny got up and took the fireside poker to prod the remaining logs. "She's right. Quentin Wilson died nearly three months ago."

"Yeah. And after she said that, I couldn't stop thinking of them. Karen, Celeste, Quentin Wilson, and now Natasha. All of them have died within the last six or seven months."

"Didn't that Hill staffer die too? You know, the one who was providing Wilson with the drugs. I thought you told me he committed suicide out of town. The cops were closing in on him, I guess." He sat down on the sofa again and pulled me closer.

"Yeah, you're right. I don't know anything about him other than what Natasha told me. They were old friends from Minnesota. She said he was smart and funny and really a good guy. So he probably had a bright future, too, until he started delivering drugs on the side." I took a deeper sip of wine. "Too many deaths, too close together."

"Thinking about it won't make more sense of it, Molly. Take it from someone who's had way too many encounters with death. Bad things happen to good people as well as bad people. We can't help that. Or them. Believe me, I've tried."

I nestled in closer, seeking his warmth. "I know what you're saying. Good people die in terrible accidents every day. Bad things happen. It's just…"

I couldn't find the words to explain what was bothering me, because I wasn't really sure what it was. But there was something about those recent deaths that I was missing. Some connection I hadn't spotted yet. Why I felt that way, I didn't have a clue. It was simply a feeling, and I couldn't shake it. Ever since Samantha asked "What's happening?" I'd been asking myself that same question and finding no answer.

"It's just that Natasha's death reminds you too much of Karen's. Hers was a deliberate murder, but Natasha's was a brutal, senseless killing. Poor Natasha was in the wrong place at the wrong time."

"You're right," I said, nestling into his warm embrace.

"We're going to change our running routine starting tomorrow morning. No more towpath. We'll come back next spring, and we're going to switch locations. I don't want you running alone outside when I'm out of town. Promise me. You can run at my gym instead."

I felt his warm lips on my neck. That was a promise I could easily make as I let Danny take the wine glass from my hand.

SIX

Friday morning

I TILTED THE OVERSIZED coffeepot and watched a hot, black ribbon of Luisa's primo-blend coffee pour into my mug. She ordered it from some specialty shop in Colorado. I inhaled the rich aroma before I drank, then returned to the tabloid newspaper spread out on the Russell kitchen counter. Leave it to the sleaze rag, the *D.C. Dirt*, to reel in more readers with lurid headlines in bold type.

CONGRESSIONAL STAFFER'S THROAT SLASHED IN BLOODY ATTACK! IS THERE A KILLER LOOSE IN GEORGETOWN?

Natasha Jorgensen, former chief staffer for the late Congressman Quentin Wilson, had found a welcoming place in Congresswoman Sally Chertoff's office. Super smart and quick, according to her friends, Natasha had a bright future ahead of her until she ran beneath the arching span of Francis Scott Key Bridge early Thursday morning. Friends say Natasha had been running along the C & O Canal towpath for years, but usually later in the morning when there were more runners about. Thursday morn, Natasha chose to run earlier than usual, when it was still dark, no doubt unaware of the predators that lurked in the shadows. Jorgensen was attacked, her throat slashed, and left to bleed to death along the scenic Canal towpath. Police think the attack may have started as a sexual assault, then turned fatal when Jorgensen tried to fight off her attacker. With no witnesses, the police have no leads yet as to the killer's identity.

I stared at the dramatic prose and remembered Danny's comment last night about predators hiding in the dark.

Luisa bustled into the kitchen then, two plastic grocery store bags in hand. "Goodness, Molly. Is that your second mug of coffee already? I swear I saw you filling up when you first came in before eight."

"Guilty," I confessed, holding up one hand. "I came in early to catch up. Yesterday I was only able to finish half of what I needed to." I took a deep drink, savoring.

Luisa pointed at the tabloid newssheet, and she visibly recoiled. "That was a horrific attack! Simply awful. To think someone was under the bridge lying in wait for your young friend." She shuddered visibly. "What monster would do that?"

"A sick one, Luisa," I replied as Casey entered the kitchen, coffee mug in hand. Both of our caffeine habits were considerable.

"How're you doing, Molly?" Casey asked as he refilled his mug. "I trust you changed your running route this morning."

"*Madre de Dios*," Luisa waved her hand as she returned to emptying grocery bags. "You need to get a treadmill, Molly, and run inside your house. Stay off the streets. It's dangerous out there."

Casey and I exchanged smiles. "Don't worry, Luisa. Danny and I went running on the track at his sports club this morning. And I promised him I would not run along the towpath again without him. In fact, we're staying away until spring. Winter will be coming soon anyway."

"Thank the Lord," Luisa decreed, giving me a maternal nod as she opened cabinets. "You'll be much safer with the Colonel."

I had to smile at Luisa's continued use of Danny's former military designation. Ever since Danny had expedited some paperwork for Luisa and Albert's oldest son in the Marines, they had been Danny's biggest admirers.

Casey caught my eye and beckoned me into the hallway. "See you later, Luisa," I said, following after him.

"What's up?" I asked once we were in the hallway and away from the kitchen. No one else was about. Albert was evidently still running errands, and Peter was with the senator on the Hill.

"I had another call from Schroeder last night. He told me they found a bug on Natasha Jorgensen's phone."

That caught me up short, and I stared at him. I'm sure my mouth was open in surprise. "*What?*"

Casey's dark eyes mirrored my surprise. "Do you have any idea who would be listening in on her calls?"

"No! She was a congressional staffer, that's all. The Hill's packed with them." I stared down the hallway. "Who in the hell would listen to a little staffer's calls? It doesn't make sense."

"No, it doesn't. Do you think she was involved in that friend's drug business? You know, that guy, Levitz, who had a side business on the Hill delivering prescription drugs. Is there a chance she was more involved in that than she admitted?"

I shook my head. That picture didn't come into focus. "I don't know, but it seems unlikely. I talked to her right after Gary Levitz was found dead in Texas, and she was genuinely broken up about what had happened to him and to Congressman Wilson. And she blamed it all on those prescription meds." I looked him in the eye. "If she was lying, she was one helluva good actress."

Casey frowned. "It doesn't make sense that someone would bug her phone without a reason. Of course, there's always the possibility she was issued a phone that had previously belonged to someone else. That's kind of unlikely, though."

We started walking down the hallway together. There were tons of emails awaiting me in my email program's inbox, and for once I was glad. There would be lots of work to distract me from the ideas bouncing around in my head right now.

Who in the hell would bug Natasha's phone? She didn't have any enemies. Did she?

Other memories from the not-so-distant past came forward.

I paused at the doorway to my office. Work was waiting. I'd have plenty of time to ponder and think this through tonight at home. Danny had already left for a short trip to Chicago.

"Don't let this bother you, Molly. None of us can ever know what is going on in someone else's life. Natasha Jorgensen may have been involved in things we don't even want to know about."

"That's true," I said. "I think I'll ask Samantha to put out feelers to see what deep background gossip she can find. Let's see what comes up."

"Sounds good." Casey turned down the hallway.

"And for the record. The security team that did Peter's rental house I'm living in, Prestige Systems, they swept the house before they started installing the system and found a tiny listening device in my living room wall. Right above my desk. You know, my desk with the computer and the file drawers the thief was so interested in." I gave Casey a crooked smile.

His eyes widened in obvious surprise. "You're kidding."

"Nope. I was shocked, of course. Danny and the security team said that maybe the bug was placed there to listen in on a former occupant. Peter said the previous renter was a Swedish business-man. So, who knows?"

Casey shook his head. "Jeeez. I shouldn't be surprised. This is Washington. Everybody's spying on someone. See you later." He headed toward the front entry once again.

This is Washington, I repeated to myself as I entered my office. The sound of my personal phone buzzed with a message. I clicked on as I settled in my desk chair. A text message from Samantha. There was a memorial service for Natasha Jorgensen scheduled for tomorrow afternoon, Saturday. Samantha offered to take me, then we could return to her home for dinner.

Perfect, I thought to myself as I clicked into message mode on my phone screen. I needed some time tonight to sort through all the thoughts bouncing around inside my head right now. Once I had made sense of them, I could talk to Samantha. I'd need a sounding board. Someone to bounce ideas off of. Samantha had a personal history with Quentin Wilson and Natasha. She could help me make sense of them. Or not. Maybe she'd simply laugh and tell me I was "crazy as a bedbug." Maybe so. We'd have to see. I was hoping for crazy.

Friday afternoon

Raymond lifted the glass of Spencer's premium-aged Scotch and let the golden heat numb his throat. He sank into the buttery-soft beige leather sofa in the corner of Spencer's window-wrapped office. Sunshine streamed through the large expanse of glass.

"I ordered another case. You should receive shipment by tomorrow," Spencer said as he sat on the loveseat directly across from Raymond, then he reached out his hand. "Okay, let's have it. See what precipitated this bloody mess."

Raymond removed two folded papers from inside his jacket pocket and handed one over. "Here's the original. I made a copy for you to give to higher-ups. You don't want to offend their sensibilities."

Spencer gave him a sardonic look as he unfolded the paper. "Offend their sensibil—*Aw, Christ!*" He screwed up his face in obvious distaste. "Is that what I think it is?"

"You mean blood? Yes, it is. You can't slit someone's throat without blood getting everywhere," Raymond said, deliberately smiling. Spencer never was one for hearing about the details of a death. He simply ordered it done. And kept himself antiseptically removed from the operational details.

"Jeeeeeez!" Spencer dropped the paper on the glass table between them and bent over it. "It's hard to read her writing."

"The top note mentions both the House and the Senate committees where the legislation was introduced. But scan down and you'll see Ryker's name. And others." Raymond deliberately didn't say more. Let Spencer discover it.

Spencer did as he was directed, scanning the paper for a minute. "*Dammit!* There's Ryker. And ... *Holmberg? Aw, crap!*"

"Keep going," Raymond said, secretly enjoying Spencer's consternation.

"Wait a minute ... she's got 'Stuttgart bank' with a question mark. *Son of a bitch!* Ryker said he never mentioned the bank's name!"

"He may not have. But you said he and Ambassador Holmberg were talking about international transfers. So it would be easy for those two words to slip out."

Spencer let loose a stream of curses as he sprang from the sofa and marched over to the liquor cabinet. Raymond sipped his Scotch, watching. A strange feeling of detachment was creeping around the edges of his mind. Spencer returned with the bottle of Scotch and poured more than half a glass for himself. "Here," he offered, extending the bottle toward Raymond's waiting glass.

"That paper ought to placate the committee's objection to the termination. Both Trask and I had a feeling about Jorgensen from the start. She was going to be trouble, and we were right."

Spencer drank deeply, then shot Raymond a harsh look. "The others are furious at how this was handled. What a bloody mess! That sleaze rag will run with it for days. Killer stalking girls in Georgetown! *Jesus!*" He tossed down more Scotch.

Maybe it was the Scotch, but Raymond allowed himself to relax into the sofa cushions. "Not every termination can be neat and tidy like Quentin Wilson's overdose or that Celeste Allard on the Eastern Shore. Those take planning. We didn't have time for this one. Jorgensen was meeting Malone that morning. And she was going to pass along that information." He pointed to the paper on the coffee table. A particularly bright-red swath of bloodstain covered the top left corner of the page.

Spencer scowled at the paper for another minute. "Yeah, you're right. We didn't want Malone to start snooping around again."

"That's what I figured. Better to remove Jorgensen. That should stop Sylvia Wilson and Malone. We hope."

Spencer looked at him sharply. "What do you mean?"

Raymond sipped and savored the liquid gold on his throat. "Well, there's the off chance Malone would contact Sylvia Wilson herself, but that's unlikely."

"Why?"

"Because Malone and Samantha Calhoun, Quentin Wilson's girlfriend, have been best friends since high school. They're tight. So, it's doubtful Malone thinks too highly of Sylvia Wilson."

"Yeah, women do hold grudges," Spencer said with a smirk, then tossed down the rest of his Scotch. "And the Malone woman is a champ. I heard she spotted that chief staffer Jed Molinoff at that talk Holmberg gave last spring at Dumbarton Oaks. Apparently she was staring daggers at Molinoff because she blamed him for keeping her niece outside so a mugger could find her. Molinoff turned tail and ran." Spencer snickered as he poured more Scotch into his glass, then sank back into the loveseat. "You guys are gonna have to lie low. The top committee heads are furious. They'd just taken on three new members, and the word was they were not too pleased by the notoriety. So, go to ground. Send Trask on a Caribbean trip. Whatever. Quiet is the word."

Raymond raised his glass. "I'll drink to quiet." And he took another deep sip. He could use some quiet time. But he had an uneasy feeling he wasn't going to get it.

Saturday late afternoon

"Your mice are reporting in already? Impressive." I took a sip of the crisp sauvignon blanc Samantha had pulled from her fridge. We'd returned from the sad and somber memorial service and sought out Samantha's cozy library. A fire blazed pleasantly in the nearby fireplace.

"My mice are nothing if not efficient," Samantha's fingers flew across the cell phone's tiny keyboard, then she placed it on the end table beside the loveseat where she sat with her legs drawn up. "That was one of the staffers who's known Natasha for years, and she swears Natasha was not involved with Levitz in his drug delivery business." She took a sip of her favorite bourbon. "Natasha was squeaky clean, says this girl."

"Well, that resonates," I said, kicking off my heels and stretching my legs as I relaxed in an upholstered armchair across from her.

"We'll be hearing from more of them as the evening progresses. Now, why don't you tell me what's been eating at you? You said earlier that you'd been going over some things. So, what's up? Are you thinking about making some investments? If so, I'll be glad to give you my financial guru's number."

I recognized Samantha's teasing tone. "Don't I wish. No, I spent last night and this morning going over those files Natasha gave me of Quentin Wilson's research. Then I dug out Karen's research files on some of those same topics. I even went over those email files Celeste Allard sent me."

Samantha peered at me. "What were you looking for?"

"I'm not sure exactly. I guess I wanted to see if anything jumped out at me."

"Did it?"

I shook my head. "No, not really. But all the while I was looking at that stuff I had this feeling there was something else. Something I was missing." I scooped up several almonds Samantha had placed on the end table beside me.

"Why dredge up all that stuff those poor souls were working on before they died? Let the dead rest in peace." She gave a little shiver, then sipped her bourbon.

"I'm not digging *them* up, just their research."

"I thought you'd finally let all of that stuff go. Why go back into the past again?"

"Because I learned something yesterday that caused me to take another look. It made me think there was something else going on that I had missed."

"What was it?"

"Schroeder, the police detective handling Natasha's murder investigation, called Casey and told him they'd found a bug, a listening device on Natasha's cell phone." I watched Samantha's eyes widen in surprise.

"*What!* Who on earth would be tracing her calls?"

"Precisely what Casey and I said. Casey wondered about the possibility that she was more involved in Gary Levitz's drug business than she'd let on. We now know that's not true. And the only other possibility would be if Natasha was issued a cell phone that belonged to someone else. But that's not likely either."

Samantha looked puzzled. "Where are you going with this?"

"I started seeing some connections. Karen was researching the same international banking topics Quentin Wilson was. They're both dead. Celeste Allard was researching Karen's office emails on those topics and some others I'd asked her to check. She's dead. And Natasha had all of Quentin Wilson's research files and had started asking questions. Now, she's dead. Karen and Natasha, Wilson and Celeste were all asking questions on those same topics."

Samantha looked at me, clearly incredulous at what I'd just said. "Surely, you're not trying to make some connections with all those deaths, are you? I've gotta tell you, that's way more than stretching it."

Having listened to myself say it out loud, it did sound farfetched. "I know, it doesn't make sense, so how could it be possible? All I know is, I have a strong feeling those deaths were connected."

"I still think you're looking for something that's not there. What connections are there other than the research?"

"For one thing, the reason Celeste Allard left for the Eastern Shore was because an intruder got into her D.C. apartment while she was out running one evening. She's certain of that because things were moved around on her desk. And the guy even opened drawers and cabinets in her bedroom and her closet and bathroom."

Samantha screwed up her face. "That's creepy."

"That's what I said. But Danny was with me that night, and he said it looked like someone was trying to send Celeste a message. A message that he could get to her. Anyway, she headed for the Bay that night, and she was dead within a week. Gas explosion in the house where she was staying alone."

"Danny believed someone had gotten into her apartment?" Samantha's expression had now changed from skepticism to intense interest.

I nodded. "And there's another reason that makes me suspicious something else is going on. Natasha was going to bring me a copy of the notes she took from Quentin Wilson's notebook. That's what started all of this, remember? The Widow Wilson was curious when she found it in his desk drawer. So she called Natasha and asked her to come to her office to take a look. Natasha was convinced it was simply more of his research notes, but she told me she'd make a copy of anything interesting she found."

I took a sip from the delightful white wine before continuing. Samantha stared at me in rapt attention, not saying a word.

"Natasha also said Sylvia Wilson indicated there were several politicians' names in that notebook. So Natasha and I made plans to meet Thursday morning. She was going to bring me a copy of her notes, but she never got to because she was murdered right before we could meet." I stared off into Samantha's fireplace. "And now we know someone was listening in on Natasha's calls, so they would know exactly where to find her and when. We even set the time we would meet." I met Samantha's rapt gaze. "I've never liked coincidences, Samantha, especially when bad things happen. I called Casey this morning and asked him if the police found any papers in Natasha's pockets or clothing. He called back right before the memorial service and said nothing was found. No papers, just car keys and a cell phone."

I held Samantha's gaze and watched her expression change to worry.

"That's why I want to find out if there's a connection. I've decided to contact Sylvia Wilson and ask to speak with her privately. I want to find out what Quentin Wilson had in his notebook that may have cost Natasha Jorgensen her life."

Samantha stared at me for a long minute before speaking. "Be careful, Molly. That woman can be treacherous."

I gave her a crooked smile. "Don't worry. I've seen her in action. I'll be on guard. And don't worry. Your name will never come up."

Samantha simply rolled her eyes. "Well, I really hope there's nothing in that notebook that's important. So you can let that poor girl rest in peace along with the rest of them."

I had the distinct feeling no one was going to be resting in peace anytime soon. "Apparently there's one important name there. Congressman Ryker."

Samantha's eyes went even wider. "Good God, Molly. Promise me you won't do anything rash. Talk to Danny first. When's he coming back?"

"Tomorrow. And I promise I won't get in anyone's face." I gave her a sardonic smile.

Samantha drained her glass. "If there's anyone you should leave in peace, it's that man. Whatever Quentin or Natasha or Karen or any of them were investigating, it has nothing to do with you. You're not involved. So step away from all of this, Molly."

I savored the last of the wine before adding to my friend's worry. "I would, except there is one more thing that makes me suspicious."

"Oh, Lord. I'm afraid to ask." Samantha left the loveseat and walked to the liquor cabinet to refresh her drink.

I waited until she was relaxed on the loveseat once again, bourbon in hand. "The security team that installed the system in my house and yard found a small listening device in my living room wall. A bug. Right above the desk where my computer is. The same computer where the intruder had opened my documents files. And rifled the desk drawers and pulled out Karen's daytimer." I deliberately watched apprehension fill Samantha's gaze this time.

"You never told me that."

"I know. I didn't want to worry you. Plus Danny and the team said it was probably put there for the previous resident. Some businessman. That made sense at the time. But now, I'm not so sure."

Samantha stared at me, clearly worried this time. "Please be careful. You don't want to make any more enemies in this town. Trust me. I know."

"I promise," I said, even though I knew that was going to be impossible.

SEVEN

Sunday

"So, do you think I'm making connections that aren't really there? Samantha's hoping it's all my imagination."

Danny held my hand as we walked around the edges of the Tidal Basin. The leaves had all turned now with the chillier nights. Yellow and orange, reds dotted here and there, accenting.

"No, I don't think you're imagining things. I'm not sure if those deaths are connected or not, but they do raise questions. I don't like coincidences either."

Hearing that my suspicions had passed Danny's initial skepticism made me feel better. "I figure I'll know once I take a look at Quentin Wilson's notebook. If all I find is more research notes, then I'll chalk it up to imagination. But, I have a feeling there's something else there."

"You're talking about Congressman Ryker, aren't you?"

"Yes, I admit it. Once I heard Ryker's name, I knew there was something else going on. With Ryker, there always is."

"Okay, what's your next move, Corporal?"

I heard the tease in Danny's voice. "I'll call Congresswoman Sylvia Wilson's office first thing tomorrow morning and ask for a return call. I'll say it has to do with Natasha Jorgensen. That ought to pique her interest."

"It should. Meanwhile, I think you should start a document file to keep track of what you've learned so far. Put it in order. It'll be easier to see what you've got. I assume you've been keeping notes."

"Oh, yeah. I started writing notes in an old spiral notebook in my desk."

Danny looked at me with a sardonic expression. "Don't tell me you've got a notebook too? Get it on the computer, Molly. There are too many notebooks floating around as it is. Wilson's notebook. Your niece Karen's notebook. And that young staffer Natasha was taking notes. Take my advice and put everything you've learned into one document file. It's easier to make sense of it all."

I laughed. "You've got a good point."

"Now, why don't we forget about politicians and enjoy what's left of this warm October Sunday? Why don't we drive over to the waterfront and see what fresh seafood is available. We can feast tonight."

"Great idea, Squad Leader."

Monday

I tabbed through the spreadsheet of Peter Brewster's rental properties. A string quartet was playing Bach softly from my computer's speakers. Bach's ordered brilliance in the background even made entering rental expenses and revenues easier. Amazing how that worked.

Marvin Gaye's "Grapevine" interrupted my concentration, and I grabbed my personal cell phone. Caller Unknown flashed on the screen as I answered. A woman's contralto voice greeted me. None other than the Widow Wilson.

"Ms. Malone? Congresswoman Sylvia Wilson here. You're with Senator Russell's office, I believe. My staff tells me you wished to speak to me. Something concerning Natasha Jorgensen. It's tragic what happened to that poor girl. Were you a friend of hers?"

"Yes, I was. Natasha was smart and savvy, and she's gone much too soon," I said, wondering if I should try to ease into the conversation or simply jump in. As always, my natural forthright inclinations won out, so I jumped in. "The reason I called, Congresswoman, is because Natasha had been helping me with some research my niece Karen Grayson was doing before her death. Karen was on Congressman Jackson's staff. Her research involved recent legislation before the House concerning international banking. Natasha told me your late husband had done similar research before his death." I paused. "She also told me you had questions about that research and she went to your office to check your husband's notes in hopes of finding answers." I waited to see what Sylvia Wilson would say. I'd served the ball into her court. She could play it or simply let it drop at the net.

She played it. "Yes, that's correct, Ms. Malone. My husband had made some notes I couldn't understand. I was hoping Natasha could answer my questions. But unfortunately, she didn't know what the notes meant either. She was going to check her previous research for Quentin in hopes it would shed some light, but alas, she never got the chance. She was attacked that next morning under the bridge."

I debated how to follow up on this without seeming too presumptuous. A fine balance. I didn't want to arouse suspicion on the Widow Wilson's part either.

"I spoke with Natasha before she went to see you, Congresswoman, and she and I planned to meet after she'd seen your late husband's notes. She had great respect for Congressman Wilson's judgment. She told me if he was interested in that subject, there must be something there. And it might make sense of my niece Karen's similar research on the subject." That was a deliberate exaggeration, but I figured a compliment could help. It surely couldn't hurt. Both Quentin Wilson and Karen were dead and buried.

Sylvia Wilson paused. "That was good of her to say. But, I'm curious why you're so interested, Ms. Malone."

"I'm simply trying to complete Karen's research and find what conclusions she was trying to make. As a tribute to her, I suppose. She was another talented staffer on the Hill whose life was cut short far too early. Like Natasha, Karen died violently. Shot in the head while she sat in her car in Georgetown one evening last spring."

"Oh, I'm so sorry to hear that. That's … that's awful. Was it a mugger?"

"No, it was deliberate murder by her boss, Jed Molinoff, who was Congressman Jackson's chief staffer. Karen was ending their affair, and Molinoff panicked that it would come to light. He left a suicide note before he took his life last spring." I let the melodramatic moment hang in the air, hoping my blatant emotional pitch would register.

"I understand your desire to do something in your niece's memory, Ms. Malone. So, yes, I'll agree to let you see Quentin's notebook. Do you want to come to my office or meet elsewhere?"

"Why don't we meet elsewhere," I suggested, my old reluctance to walk through those Congressional office hallways reasserting itself. Too many memories from the past.

"All right. How about the Willard Hotel this evening? I've been to a couple of meetings there, and it's become a favorite."

Her choice made me smile. The Willard was one of my senator father's favorite places in Washington. He was a savvy, respected senator and a historian-at-heart.

"You must have studied history, Congresswoman. The Willard played a large role in our Capitol's history. Many politicians preferred discussing important political issues in the Willard bar than in the hallowed halls of Congress."

"Yes, I know. History was my late father's passion as well. There are some quiet corners in the main lobby where we can meet. I have a meeting that may run late, but I could be there by eight o'clock."

"Eight o'clock would be fine, Congresswoman."

Monday afternoon

Peter Brewster rounded the corner of his library office as I walked past. He had a preoccupied look of intense concentration. I'd seen that look a lot lately.

"How's it going, Peter? You've been so busy on the Hill these past two months, I rarely have a chance to talk with you when I arrive in the mornings."

His boyish grin suddenly appeared. I thought the increased Senate demands had wiped it away permanently.

"Hey, Molly. It's getting better, now that the senator and I have caught up with all that research we had to do for Senator Dunston's committee."

"You two have been buried in international finance documents and papers for weeks now," I said as we approached the kitchen. Luisa was cheerfully reorganizing cabinets, I could tell. No doubt another item on her formidable to-do list.

"I finally divided up all the financial topics and assigned staffers to each group. Way more efficient. Oh, and thanks for doing some of those summaries for us. We were heading into the home stretch. Now we're beginning to see daylight."

"Wow, I'm impressed," I leaned against the doorjamb. "Did any of those research files I gave you from Karen help at all? They sounded like versions of the same topics. Really dry, if you ask me."

"Well, you're right about that. I think the senator and I reached new levels on the caffeine-intake scale. We may even have rivaled you."

"Not possible. I'm world-class. Tell the senator that when you see him. He'll laugh. I haven't seen him in ages, it seems. He's always gone when I get here before eight. And you're both still at the Hill when I leave at night."

Peter laughed. "Sounds like you miss us. I'll tell him."

"I'm not the only one." I pointed to Luisa who'd moved on to another cabinet now. "Luisa is bored out of her skull with no caterers and guests to supervise these last two months. She's been reduced to working on her to-do list and reorganizing everything in sight. No cabinet or closet is safe. I'm forced to lock my office door when I leave in the evening." I deliberately spoke louder than usual.

"I *heard* that," Luisa sang out from the kitchen.

"She's got Albert upstairs turning mattresses. When she's not sending him all over town on errands."

Peter simply laughed. "Well, all of you will be pleased to hear the senator has decided to invite his entire Senate subcommittee for dinner in a couple of weeks. So, we'll be back, getting in your way again, Luisa."

"I'll look forward to it," Luisa said. "And tell the senator I reorganized his tie rack this morning. The colors were all mismatched." She gave us both a wicked smile.

This time I laughed out loud. Matching up ties was definitely beyond my patience level. "See, I told you. That dinner has come not a moment too soon. Luisa would be organizing your office next. I've seen that desk."

"Don't even come close, Luisa. I have live creatures hiding beneath the paperwork. And they bite." He laughed as he headed down the hallway.

I accompanied him toward the front entry, remembering something I'd wanted to ask. "Are you still keeping track of where all the Congressional members are living? You remember we were talking about the clusters of Congressmen shivering together, sharing townhouses, bunking in with each other."

"Kind of. I've got an intern keeping directories now. Were you looking for someone in particular?"

"I was curious where Congresswoman Sylvia Wilson was living. Did she rent a condo somewhere posh?"

Peter opened the front door and paused. "I think I recall someone telling me she was living in the same townhouse where Quentin Wilson lived. I think she bought it for him when he first entered Congress five years ago."

"Boy, was that a good investment. Real estate prices keep rising here." I smiled. "By the way, your properties are showing a profit as well."

"Always a good thing. I'll see you tomorrow, Molly," he said as he headed out the door.

Hopefully, Albert had finished turning those mattresses and was already waiting in the car. I headed down the hallway toward the kitchen and more coffee. Meanwhile, something about Sylvia Wilson living in her recently departed husband's townhouse buzzed in the back of my brain.

Monday evening

I walked through the Willard Hotel's opulent lobby. Strolled, rather. I was in no hurry since I enjoyed the opportunity to step back in time. Richly upholstered armchairs were clustered together with antique end tables all around the expansive lobby, inviting private conversations or exhausted tourists who simply wanted to rest. Tall ceilings and art-filled walls spoke of another era. Another century, actually.

I spotted Sylvia Wilson seated in a corner, conveniently away from the other groups of people who sat, lounged, talked, and chatted in groups.

"Congresswoman Wilson?" I said, hand extended. "I'm Molly Malone. Thank you so much for meeting me."

Sylvia Wilson's sharp eyes did a quick appraisal of me. Hair, wardrobe, makeup, shoes, jewelry. I doubt she missed anything. I wondered what grade I'd been given.

"So nice to meet you, Ms. Malone," she said, giving me what looked to be her official smile. She indicated the empty armchair next to the table beside her.

I noticed a half-filled martini glass on the lamp-lit table as I sat. "Please call me Molly," I said, placing on my lap the slender portfolio I'd brought. I noticed the congresswoman's briefcase beside her chair. "You're very kind to take time from your busy schedule, Congresswoman. I promise I won't waste any of it with too many questions."

"Actually, Molly, I'm hoping you can answer some of *my* questions." She reached inside the briefcase and withdrew a plain spiral-bound notebook, the kind bought in a drugstore. She paged through it. "Most of Quentin's notes have to do with rules and regulations on international banking, particularly transfers of funds. But after every section, he jotted down other things. Names, for example." She paused on one page. "Here's one. Epsilon Group. Have you ever heard of it? One of my staffers did a cursory check and learned it was an organization of international financiers, distinguished professors, and European finance ministers whose purpose was to educate the public about global financial issues. Writing papers and giving speeches."

I was about to reply when the waiter approached. I ordered a coffee, not about to dull my wits around the Widow Wilson. I sensed I'd need them all.

"I know Karen was researching the same group," I said. "She'd also learned the Epsilon Group had actually succeeded in getting some minor recommendations added to Congressional legislation in the last couple of years. I believe Congressman Jackson supported a bill with one of their recommendations. Karen worked on a lot of special projects for the congressman."

Sylvia Wilson listened carefully. "I see. Congressman Jackson was on the International Monetary Policy and Trade Subcommittee, so that would be right in his area. I'm still curious why Quentin was interested." She turned another page. "He's written down Congressman Edward Ryker's name. As well as Senator Dunston. Now Ryker is Chair of the House Financial Services Committee, and Dunston was recently appointed chair of the Senate Banking, Housing, and Urban Affairs Committee. So that makes sense. However, Quentin also wrote 'Stuttgart Bank' beneath Dunston's name, then drew several dollar signs." She looked up at me with a quizzical expression. "Does that ring a bell with Karen's research?"

It might not ring a bell with Karen's notes, but those names definitely rang loud bells for me. I opened the portfolio in my lap. "Karen's notes made no mention of Dunston, so that's interesting. Also, no mention of a Stuttgart Bank. But the dollar signs obviously mean money. Probably money transfers." I watched Sylvia Wilson nod, then I added. "But I do know that Congressman Ryker must have a connection with the Epsilon Group, because I attended one of their speeches last spring. I saw him there, acting really chummy with the speaker, Ambassador Holmberg, former EU Finance Minister."

Sylvia Wilson sat back in her chair, clearly digesting what I'd just said. "Interesting. Quentin had also written the name Holmberg in his notes. In fact, he'd put arrows between Ryker's and Holmberg's names." She turned the notebook around and held it out so I could see. Sure enough, Quentin Wilson had drawn an arrow linking the two men's names. I quickly scanned the rest of the page, hoping to see more, but she returned the notebook to her lap. However, I thought I glimpsed something at the bottom of the page.

"Had Karen come to any conclusions? What connection do these people have with each other? Are they all members of this Epsilon Group?"

"I don't know." I glanced at the pages in my portfolio. I'd taken Danny's advice and transferred all my notes to a document file. "According to Karen's research, the Epsilon Group members are all from the financial community. I searched them myself and found the same information your staff discovered. It described the group as a consortium of learned and prestigious experts who'd served various roles in international finance and governance. Stuff like that. The only names I found were those who were listed as speakers, like Ambassador Holmberg." I glanced up. "Could I take a look at the notebook? I think I spotted something written at the bottom of the page."

"Surely." Sylvia Wilson extended the open notebook.

I tried not to grab it greedily and glanced at the bottom of the page. Quentin Wilson had scrawled what looked like "son," then "Stuttgart." I made mental notes of the second repetition of Stuttgart.

"It looks like he repeated the word Stuttgart. Is that 'son' in front of it?"

"Maybe. Sometimes Quentin's handwriting got squished together when he was in a hurry."

Eager to see what else was written, I deliberately put on the most innocent expression possible—innocent for me. "Do you mind if I page through?"

"Go ahead. There are only a few more names mentioned. Perhaps you'll recognize them."

I pulled out a ballpoint pen and wrote down the little I'd learned so far. Stuttgart Bank, Senator Dunston, Holmberg, Ryker, and the word sun or son. Someone's son? I turned the pages slowly, scanning and making notes of what Quentin Wilson had written. *Geneva. Milan.* They were definitely places. At the bottom was another name. *Spencer* followed by a question mark. Was that a first or a last name? Considering how many people I had met passing through Senator Russell's dinners and receptions, it was impossible to remember all the names. I searched through my memory anyway to see if there was a connection, but nothing came to mind.

"I wish the name Spencer rang a bell, but it doesn't. We meet so many new people in Washington. Plus Senator Russell entertains frequently, so there's a constant stream of strangers visiting the residence."

A small smile tweaked the edges of Sylvia Wilson's mouth. "Yes, I've heard of Senator Russell's parties, and I confess I look forward to being able to attend sometime in the future. Right now, I'm hard-pressed to remember all the new faces and names I've met since I was appointed."

I returned the notebook to her, and the thought occurred that in a different time and different circumstances, Sylvia Wilson and I might have become friends. She had a no-nonsense attitude about her that I liked. "I've made notes of those names and comments that were new to me. I'll take a look at Karen's daytimer and other notes to see if they're mentioned. I promise to keep you posted as to anything I learn."

Sylvia Wilson closed the notebook and returned it to her briefcase. "I'd appreciate that. I certainly don't have time to delve into this area at all, and frankly neither does my staff. In fact, I'm still perplexed as to why Quentin would have wasted his valuable time on researching an innocuous group of financiers." She shook her head with a faintly disapproving expression. Then she focused her intense gaze on me. "And I'm still curious why your niece and now you have spent time researching the same thing. I can understand your wanting to do something in your niece's memory. But I sense there's something else behind your search, Molly." She looked at me with that half smile once more.

I toyed with my reply, then decided I owed the Widow Wilson an honest answer, considering how she'd been so cooperative. "Actually, there is another reason that has spurred my curiosity, Congresswoman. I returned to Washington last spring, and since then four bright, talented staffers who worked on the Hill have died. Two died violently in the streets—my niece Karen and Natasha Jorgensen—and two by accident—your husband and a young congressional staffer in Congressman Jackson's office, Celeste Allard. The only thing all four of them had in common was they each were asking questions about the Epsilon Group, international banking, and financial legislation. Such innocuous-sounding subjects, we both agree. But I have a suspicious nature, and it tells me something else is involved. Particularly since I learned the police found a bug on Natasha's phone."

I paused and watched Sylvia Wilson's eyes widen in surprise. She stared at me with rapt attention. "Really? That means..."

"That means that whoever was listening to her calls heard your phone conversation with Natasha asking her questions about your husband's notebook. And, they overheard my phone conversation with her saying we would see each other the morning following her meeting with you. Natasha was going to tell me what she saw in the notebook." I met Sylvia's shocked gaze. "Of course, we never got to meet that morning. I arrived at the towpath shortly after the vicious attack. I remember hearing sirens wailing in Georgetown. I thought she'd overslept so I walked toward the bridge, hoping to see her, but I saw the police instead." I stopped and let Sylvia Wilson conjure the rest.

"Oh, my God ... you were there?"

"Right afterwards. I watched police carry a shroud-wrapped body away on a stretcher. I had a sinking feeling even then."

Sylvia turned her face away. "And you think her death was connected to your niece Karen's?"

"I don't know if it was or not. But they were both researching the same thing." I paused before adding, "And I have Karen's research notes at home in my desk. This past summer, I uncharacteristically returned to my home one weekday morning, and I frightened away an intruder. Whoever it was had come in my locked back door. He stole nothing, but he had rifled my desk drawers and opened my computer files." Sylvia Wilson's face paled slightly. "I had an expert security firm totally redo my home and surroundings. And in the midst of that, they found a listening device in my wall. Directly above my desk." I sat back, letting my words sink in.

Sylvia Wilson stared at me for over a minute, white-faced. "It will take some time for me to digest all of this, Molly. You've certainly given me much to think about."

"I'm sure I don't need to tell you to please keep this entirely to yourself. No one else should know."

"I agree."

"Oh, and if I may give you some advice, Congresswoman. I've heard you're living in your husband's home, which you had purchased. My advice is to hire a special firm such as the one recommended to me. Have that house totally protected from intruders of any kind. Secure it completely. I'll be glad to give you the name of that company, if you'd like."

"I'd like that very much, Molly. And please call me Sylvia."

"I think you're being very wise ... Sylvia," I said with a small smile of my own.

EIGHT

Tuesday morning

LARRY FILLMORE TOOK THE Capitol South Metro escalator stairs two at a time, hurrying away from the throngs of commuters pouring out of the Metro station. Running his finger through his phone's directory, he pressed Spencer's name as he angled away from the mass of congressional staffers heading toward Capitol Hill. He listened to the phone ring three times before being answered.

"Good morning, Larry," Spencer's deep voice sounded. "How's it going over there on the Hill? Are you keeping Congressman Jackson's staffers in line?"

Larry could hear the amusement in Spencer's voice. "No problems. They're all under control. By the way, I made sure Congressman Jackson had a copy of that European Union report you sent over. That should answer most of his questions."

"Always happy to oblige, Larry. We want to keep the good congressman well-informed and allay any doubts he might have about the transfer of funds. Apparently Jackson had asked some pointed questions in that last subcommittee meeting."

"Yeah, he and Chertoff started asking about the limits on funds, and how the recipient banks are chosen. That report should help answer any questions."

"Good, good. We want to keep them content and quiet." Spencer's chuckle came louder.

Larry stepped off the sidewalk and onto the grassy area bordering the walkway. He stopped beneath a tall oak, its leaves already turning a rusty red. "Listen, there's another reason I wanted to call you this morning before I get into the office. I accompanied Jackson to a dinner with some of his Omaha donors last night at the Willard. You'll never guess who I saw when I was leaving the hotel. A really odd couple talking together in a corner of the lobby."

"I'm not good at guessing games. Who was it?"

"Congresswoman Sylvia Wilson and none other than Molly Malone." Larry waited for Spencer's reaction. It came quickly.

"*What the hell!* The two of them *together*?"

"Yeah. I figured you'd want to know."

"*Jesus!* What in hell would those two be talking about? Malone's best friends with the Calhoun woman."

"Quentin Wilson's paramour, as the *D.C. Dirt* liked to call her," Larry said, thin lips curving into a smirk.

"Sylvia Wilson hated Samantha Calhoun's guts from what I heard."

"That's why I thought it was odd."

"*Damn,*" Spencer mumbled.

Larry waited, expecting Spencer to say something else, but he didn't. Surprised, Larry volunteered, "I can start asking around if you want me to. See what Sylvia Wilson is up to."

"Yeah, do that. Quietly, of course. Don't draw any attention."

Spencer's voice sounded worried for some reason, so Larry ventured, "Don't worry. I've got my spies out there. I'll let you know what I learn."

"Okay. I'll talk to you later," Spencer said abruptly, then clicked off.

Larry checked his watch, then headed toward the Rayburn Office Building. Meanwhile, he paged through his phone directory for one of his many sources. Clearly, Spencer didn't like the idea of Sylvia Wilson having a tête-à-tête with Molly Malone. Larry had a feeling it didn't have anything to do with the late Quentin Wilson.

———

I clicked out of the email program and shoved the computer mouse aside. Finished for now. Emails were never completely finished. I could only catch up. They multiplied when I wasn't looking. I leaned back in the desk chair and indulged in a long stretch. Spreadsheets were waiting, but I didn't feel like staring at the screen again quite yet.

I took a sip of my recently refilled coffee and reached for my personal cell phone. There was a call I needed to make. I was about to press Samantha's number, when I noticed a text message waiting. It must have come in when I took a coffee break. I saw it was from Loretta Wade.

"Have you had a chance to check Congressman Grayson's notes yet? I have a slight break in my normal deluge, so I could start delving into those old records."

Natasha Jorgensen's death had wiped away the memory of my conversation with Loretta that morning by the Canal. I'd completely forgotten I'd promised her I would check Eric Grayson's research notebooks. Feeling guilty, I mentally revised my plans for tonight. While Danny was out with the veteran's group, I would retrieve Eric's notebook from the bank deposit box and go over it. Hopefully there would be some clues as to what my congressman brother-in-law was searching for years ago. I quickly keyed in a text message reply to Loretta, suggesting we meet for lunch in that small park near the Rayburn Building this week. I'd bring the notebook and let her have a look.

I checked my watch, then pressed Samantha's number. Mid-morning. She should still be home.

"Perfect timing, Molly," she said when she answered. "Another ten minutes and I would have left to join good sister Bernice at Walter Reed. She's going to introduce me to some of the people who're coordinating wounded veteran care."

"Wow, that's definitely more noble a venture than what I've spent all morning doing. Answering emails, placating overzealous congressional and senatorial staffers who have tons of questions."

"Well, remember what the nuns told us. We each serve in our own way," Samantha said, more than a hint of amusement in her voice.

"Oh, Lord. Hanging out with good Sister Bernice is rubbing off on you. You'll be quoting scripture next."

"By the way, would you remember to ask Danny the name of the veteran organization he's working with? You told me he volunteers with a group that assists returning wounded vets."

"As a matter of fact, he's going there tonight. I'll text him and find out the name. Meanwhile, I wanted to ask you a favor, Miss Thing."

"Name it."

"Could you ask your mice to check the gossip hounds to see what connections turn up on Congressman Ryker, Senator Dunston, and Ambassador Holmberg? I met with Sylvia Wilson at the Willard last night. She even showed me Quentin's notebook."

"You're kidding."

"No, she was clearly interested in finding out what those notations meant. Quentin had also written Stuttgart Bank and another name in there—Spencer, which I assume is a last name. I didn't recognize it."

"Hmmmm. Spencer. I know a lot of Spencers, but let's see what comes up in connection with Ryker and Dunston and Holmberg. I'll start spreading the word."

"Thanks, Samantha. I knew I could count on you." I reached for my mug and took a deep drink of coffee. "Oh, and ask your mice to concentrate on financial information if they can. Apparently, Quentin Wilson discovered a connection between Ryker, Dunston, and Holmberg. Unfortunately, Wilson's notes were kind of cryptic. But he did draw arrows between Ryker's name and Holmberg's. And he drew dollar signs lots of places. Particularly under Dunston's name. So, I'm curious."

"Now you've made me curious. Quentin was spot-on when it came to focusing on a subject, so if he found a connection, there's got to be something there."

"That's what I'm thinking."

"Frankly, I'm amazed Sylvia Wilson was so forthcoming with that notebook. You must have charmed the bejeezus out of her."

I laughed softly. "I don't know about that. I think it was more a case of each one of us helping the other. I had information and so did she. So we shared, I guess you'd say. She was curious about why Quentin was spending so much time researching something that wasn't part of his congressional committee work."

"That's understandable."

I could feel the unspoken concern coming from my friend. "Don't worry, Samantha. Your name will never come out of my mouth in her presence."

Samantha chuckled. "Thank gawd. Oh, did you get my email with the web link to the company that protects your financial information? I sent it this morning."

"I haven't had time to check my personal emails yet, but thank you. I'll give them a call." Another thought buzzed from the back of my brain and hovered right in front of me, claiming my attention. "And speaking of security, I want to make a suggestion for you. I'm going to email you the name and phone number of the contact person for the specialty security firm that took care of my home. And I want you to seriously consider having them totally redo your house and property."

"I already have security, Molly. A very good firm too. Remember all those surveillance videos we watched last summer after Quentin died?"

"I remember. And I'm sure they are a very good firm for average people. But you're a special case, Samantha. And I want you to have the very best protection out there."

"Thank you, Sugar. I think you're special too."

I could hear the laughter behind Samantha's voice, so I decided I had to get her attention. "Listen, Samantha. Most of Washington knew you and Quentin Wilson were seeing each other. That's why I'm worried about you. You also knew about Quentin's research, and I think you should protect yourself. Just in case."

"My God, Molly... now you're scaring me."

I could hear the worry in Samantha's voice. "I'm sorry to scare you, but I don't think you should take chances with your safety. It won't hurt for you to have a total security makeover. Lock your place down tight. And have them sweep for bugs in the process."

"Good Lord, I don't even want to think about that."

"I know. But we have to protect ourselves. And if you're wondering if I'm overreacting, I can tell you I gave Sylvia Wilson the same advice."

"You're kidding!"

"Nope. She wanted to know exactly why I was so interested in following up on Karen's research into this subject. So I told her exactly what I just told you. Three promising congressional staffers and a congressman are gone from Capitol Hill. And the only thing they had in common was that they were researching this same subject. I even told her about the bug found on Natasha's phone and the one found in my wall."

"What'd she say to that?"

"Not much, actually. She blanched and stared at me wide-eyed. So I guess I got her attention."

"Well, that takes some doing, from what I hear."

"Oh, and I told her I'd heard she was living in the same town-house where Quentin lived. And I recommended the exact same security firm and offered to send her their name. And *she* accepted my offer."

Samantha laughed softly. "Damn, Molly. You're relentless, you know that?"

I could hear surrender in my friend's voice and exulted inside. "It's one of my few virtues, Miss Thing. You of all people know that."

Tuesday afternoon

Raymond stood beside Spencer's wide office window, gazing down at Pennsylvania Avenue. Late afternoon and the October sun was arcing downward, inching toward a sunset. Another week and a half and Daylight Saving Time would be over. The autumn hours would abruptly shift and sunset would rush upon them. Night hastening right behind.

He sipped from the ample glass filled with Spencer's aged Scotch. Molten gold slid down Raymond's ragged throat. Another case had arrived on his doorstep this very morning. Thank the angels. Or Spencer, rather. Relief in a glass.

"*Dammit to hell*," Spencer cursed again from the corner of his office. "What is it with women? Why can't they leave well enough alone? Why do they always have to go poking into things? Things that are none of their business."

Raymond had to smile at the petulant sound in Spencer's voice. "The best laid plans oft go astray," he offered as he walked back to the corner sitting area. The leather sofa received him with a sigh as he sat down.

Spencer looked over his glass with a scowl. "Don't get philosophical on me. I don't need that right now." He tossed back a deep drink. "You gonna put Trask on Malone, or what?"

"Yeah. I'll have him watch her comings and going for a while. See who she meets, aside from that boyfriend of hers. He's there most of the time."

"Yeah, you ought to run a check on him too. We don't know anything about him, except he was the one who brought in the security company, right?"

"That's what I figure. Judging from watching him talk to those guys when they arrived and when they were outside later, I could tell he obviously knew them. So, I'm betting he's former military, but we need to find out more. We can't follow the congresswoman around, so I guess your boy Fillmore will have to keep an eye on her." He took another sip and let it slide down slowly, numbing his throat.

"I've already got him on it. Larry and his contacts can find out if the congresswoman stays on task with her own committee work. If she starts poking into other things, he'll find that out too."

"Okay. That's about all we can do for now. Keep an eye on them both. If they start getting too close to something, we'll hear about it. Hopefully, neither of them will push this any further. Hell, they don't have anywhere to push. Jorgensen is gone. Wilson is gone. Anyone who had access to information has been neutralized." He gave a crooked smile.

Spencer lifted his glass. "Let's hope you're right. I don't want to have a conversation with Montclair about any more leaks. It would not go over well."

Raymond noticed the slightly anxious tone that crept into Spencer's voice. He rarely heard it. So he sought to reassure. "Let's hope this was a case of an excess of female curiosity. And that will be the end of it."

"I'll drink to that," Spencer said, lifting his glass. "Damn aggravating women," he added, then tossed down the remainder of his Scotch.

NINE

Wednesday

"HERE, HELP ME EAT these fries, so I won't feel so guilty." I held out the paper cup to Loretta, who was seated beside me on a bench. We'd succeeded in finding a shady spot in a park between Louisiana and Constitution avenues near the Capitol.

"Oh, no. I'm not going there with you, Molly." Loretta waved her hand at me as she shrank away from the crispy temptations. "They are SO not on my doctor's list. His good list, that is." She forked through the last of her salad and stuffed the plastic container in her bag.

Now I wished I'd chosen yogurt instead of the greasy New York–style hot dog from the vendor cart on the corner of Pennsylvania Avenue. Too late now. "I shudder to think what's on your doctor's bad list. All my favorites, I'm sure." I tossed down the last bite. Fattening but delicious.

"And all of mine," Loretta said with a smile.

I drained half my water bottle, then withdrew an old hardcover notebook from my oversized purse. "I'm glad you texted me the other day, Loretta. Natasha Jorgensen's murder completely wiped away my promise to check this out."

"I'm so sorry to hear about your friend." She looked at me with concern. "It's always terrible to see younger people die way earlier than they should."

"We've had a lot of that these last few months, haven't we?" I caught her sympathetic gaze and watched it turn wary.

"Indeed, we have. Too many. Now, show me what you found. I need another distraction."

I opened the notebook and began to page through it. My brother-in-law's neat handwriting showed on every page. "It looks like he was taking notes on his research. A lot on European Union financial policy and regulations. I skimmed through, and most of it is pretty dry stuff. But he does have notes toward the end where he mentions some European banks. Also, Eric wrote down Montclair and Kasikov." I turned toward the back pages and pointed to the words. "I don't know if those are names of places or people. There's no clue."

Loretta leaned closer, focusing on the notebook in my lap. "What's that in red ink? I can't tell."

"That's Karen's writing. Her notations are mostly question marks throughout the notebook, so clearly she was puzzled too. But Eric didn't indicate what he was looking for. I was really hoping I'd find out something more. But most of his notes concern early EU financial policy, so that's old news today."

Loretta peered at the notebook. "Well, let me go over it and see if any of his entries jog my memory. I remember talking with him, but Congressman Grayson wasn't particularly chatty."

I grinned. "You're right about that. Kind-hearted but a bit taciturn, especially when he was working on something."

"Wait a minute," Loretta said, pointing at a page. "He's circled that word. Right there. What is it?"

"I saw that on several pages. It looks like *geo*, but there's no indication of what he's talking about." I paged back and spotted another place where the word *geo* was circled. "See, there it is again. And here too. Does he mean 'geography'?" I paged backwards over several pages, pointing out several instances.

"Hmmmmm. Now I'm intrigued. You know how I love puzzles. Let's see what I can find out. I promise I'll get this back to you in a few days. I'll expressmail it to you to be safe."

"Thanks, Loretta. I appreciate it." I handed her the notebook, then reached inside my bag and withdrew a folded sheet of paper. "And here's something else I think you'll find interesting. But you need to keep this information strictly to yourself. I obtained it confidentially, and it concerns Quentin Wilson's research this past summer." I unfolded the paper and handed it to Loretta. "He also mentions a European bank and a possible connection between some rather prominent politicians. And he clearly indicates that money is involved because he drew several dollar signs beneath their names in his notes."

Loretta looked at me, her dark gaze intense. "Those are pretty prominent names. Does anyone else know about Wilson's research?"

"Only a few people. One of them was Natasha." I watched Loretta's gaze widen, then turn wary.

"Good Lord. Did Congressman Wilson suggest to anyone that he found evidence of wrongdoing?"

"It looks like he was getting close, but he died before he could put all the pieces together. At least, that's my guess. I could be dead wrong too. Maybe Wilson was on a wild goose chase, but I figured you'd be able to find out if he was. I made this copy for you."

Loretta scanned the page, then gave me a small smile. "Now I see why you want me to keep this private. I promise, I will. The notebook and these notes will be delivered back to you by special delivery, I promise."

"Well, no need to go to that expense. Expressmail will do."

Loretta glanced toward the others relaxing and enjoying lunch in the park this late October afternoon. "I think it's time we both returned to our offices, Molly. We must look like we're plotting world domination or something. This is the second time I've caught that dark-haired guy with the mustache looking at us. He's on the opposite bench with a newspaper."

I glanced over and spotted a dark-haired guy reading a newspaper, remnants of lunch spread on the bench beside him. Cola can in hand. "Yeah, if we're attracting the attention of worker bees, it's best to head back to our own hives."

"Amen to that. I'll be in touch, Molly," Loretta said as we both rose from the bench.

"Thanks so much, Loretta. And next time, let's meet at that new Irish pub in your neighborhood. We'll attract less attention there."

"I'll drink to that," Loretta said with a smile as she turned and walked down the concrete path toward Capitol Hill and the Library of Congress.

I tossed my lunch trash into a trash can as I headed toward Pennsylvania Avenue and what I hoped would be a quick cab ride back to Georgetown.

Late Wednesday afternoon

"Where are you now?" Raymond asked as he leaned back into the chaise lounge, phone to his ear.

"I'm sitting in a café on New York Avenue. I finally threw in the towel after she changed trains in the Metro station. She got on the orange line and the doors closed before I could get inside. The middle of rush hour, and every car was packed. People were getting caught in the door. You know how it is."

"Not really. I avoid the Metro like the plague. Too many people to suit me. Give me rush hour on I-66 any day." Raymond picked up the glass of Scotch on the patio table beside him. The sun was just starting to set, casting a reddish glow through the oak trees bordering his Virginia backyard.

Trask's laughter sounded. "My bet is she was heading somewhere in the District, maybe Maryland. We'll know more once we find out who she is."

"All you've got is she's a middle-aged African-American woman. Tall, slender, you said. Cropped hair. Good-looking, right?"

"Yeah. Taller than Malone. Basketball tall. She walked that way too. Athletic. I followed her all the way into the Library of Congress but lost her when I had to go through the security checkpoint. So I couldn't see which office she went to. I left the building and sat on a bench not too far away where I could see the entrance. That way I'd spot her when she came out. I figured she might walk to the Metro station."

Raymond took a deep drink of the molten gold. "You said you got a photo of her with Malone?"

"Yeah. Damn near got caught too. She looked up just as I was putting the phone to my ear. I saw her looking at me again, just before they got up to leave. Next time I'll bring out the priest's collar."

Raymond snickered. "You'll have to show me that one. I can't picture it."

"With the glasses, it looks pretty convincing. One time, I actually had a cop ask me if I was looking for the Catholic church nearby. It was all I could do to keep a straight face."

Raymond laughed out loud at that, despite risking the cough's return. He took another big sip to stave it off. "Did you recognize the notebook Malone handed over?"

"Nope. It had a different cover than the ones I found in Malone's desk drawer at her house. But it must have had a lot of things in it, because both of them were fixated. Pointing out stuff to each other. Man, I'd like to get my hands on that."

"Fat chance. Not until we find out who she is."

"Oh, yeah. Malone gave her a separate sheet of paper. There was stuff written there, too, because they were pointing at different things."

Raymond let out an exasperated sigh. "Well, let's not get excited about this. That woman could be someone she's working with for Russell's office. Who knows? Let's wait and see what that Fillmore guy in Jackson's office can find out. If this gal works on the Hill, they'll have ID photos. Let's see what turns up. Maybe we'll get lucky." Somehow Raymond didn't feel luck was coming their way. Once Trask mentioned the Library of Congress, he'd gotten a bad feeling in his gut. Stirring up some old memories.

"If this gal works in the Library of Congress, then it sounds like Malone is following in Quentin Wilson's research footsteps. That's where he spent so much time. Once he overheard Ryker's conversation, that is."

"Yeah, that's exactly what I was thinking." Raymond scowled into his glass, then took another deep drink. "*Dammit.* I was hoping she'd reach a dead end and let it drop. It looked like she did for a while."

"Then enter Congresswoman Wilson," Trask said, in a sarcastic tone. "It looks like Malone's trying to follow up on whatever Sylvia Wilson told her when they met at the Willard. Who knows? Maybe Wilson gave Malone her husband's notebook. I never found anything that looked like that in his house when I checked last July. And it wasn't in his briefcase either when I got the chance to check. He must have always left the notebook at his office."

"You're probably right. *Damn!*" The cough was starting to tickle, so he took a drink. "That's another loose end. Like the phone bug."

"Don't worry. We've covered our tracks. Nothing comes back to us. These women have nothing. Just notes in a book. Nothing definite. Nothing that implicates the higher-ups. And I don't think they will. Let 'em research their asses off if they want to. We'll keep an eye on them. And if anyone gets too curious, well … they'll meet with an accident."

Raymond flinched at Trask's brutal assessment. Funny. He'd never flinched before. Not in all the times he was carrying out the orders. "Too many accidents add up, Trask. That's what bothers me."

"Don't worry about it. They're little people, with the exception of Sylvia Wilson. No one pays attention."

Raymond released a sigh and leaned over to pour more Scotch into his glass. "I hope you're right, Trask. I hope you're right." But his gut had other thoughts and he could feel it.

Wednesday evening

I rested my arms on the café table and sipped the rich, red wine Danny had chosen. The popular Mediterranean café had filled quickly tonight and noise from neighboring diners had risen.

I watched Danny read both sheets of paper I'd handed him. Finally, he looked over at me. "And you got these names from Quentin Wilson's notebook? I'm still surprised Sylvia Wilson let you see it."

"Yeah, I was too. But I think it was a case of each of us had information the other didn't have. So it was mutually beneficial. Those last two names on the other paper, Montclair and Kasikov, came from my brother-in-law's notebook. I took that to Loretta as well. I'm hoping she can figure out what Eric was looking for."

I took a sip of the velvet cabernet. Cherries, blackberries, and more. "By the way, I hope the security firm doesn't mind, but I gave Sylvia Wilson their contact name and phone number. I advised her to have her townhouse gone over and locked down tight. Whoever bugged Natasha's phone knows the congresswoman has her husband's notebook."

"Too many notebooks floating around. Too many questions. I'm glad you finally put all of this information on the page in one file. You should do that with Karen's and Celeste's notes. And Wilson's notes too. Put it all together, so you can analyze it better." Danny retrieved his wine glass and leaned forward over the table, dropping the pages beside the candles. "I can tell you're convinced that Natasha's murder wasn't an accident."

"Yes, I am. And the more I learn, the more sure I am there's a connection. We know Karen was murdered, but we'll never know for sure if Jed Molinoff did it to protect his reputation or if there was another reason. He was hanging around with Ryker and Holmberg that night at the Dumbarton Oaks reception. And he was handling the Epsilon Group's contribution to Congressman Jackson's reelection fund. Both Quentin Wilson and Natasha, asking questions about the same topic Karen was. Both dead." I took another sip. "Too many coincidences to suit me."

"And then there's Celeste," Danny said with a frown.

"Then there's Celeste. Who was doing the same research. And she had her apartment broken into. She swore the intruder was messing around her computer and flash drive storage files. I remember your saying the guy was sending her a message because the break-in was so brazen and obvious."

"But who sent the message? That's the key."

"Maybe Larry Fillmore. If so, he was definitely taking orders from someone else. Someone much higher up is behind all this. It's way above Fillmore's pay scale." I stared off into the busy café.

The waiter appeared then and poured the rest of the delectable cabernet into our glasses. Danny looked over at me as we both sipped the wine and smiled.

"I'd hate to think we're going to waste this superb vintage talking about the likes of Larry Fillmore. I had other plans for tonight."

I returned Danny's smile and lifted my glass. "Larry who?"

TEN

Thursday morning

AT THE SOUND OF my name, I paused at the glass doors leading
outside into Senator Russell's manicured gardens. The senator
strode toward me, Peter right behind.

"You'll be at the dinner tonight, won't you, Molly?" Russell said
with his teasing smile. "I've heard that you and your former Marine companion have been seen at several Washington cafés these
last few weeks when we didn't entertain. I believe Luisa refers to
him as 'the Colonel.'"

I grinned at the senator and Peter. "I see that I've fallen into a
nest of gossips. It's not enough that Luisa keeps track of my social
life, now there are spies throughout Washington watching me." I
shook my head dramatically. "You're all conspirators at heart."

Russell chuckled as he turned to accompany Peter down the
hall toward the front door where Albert stood waiting. "We're your
extended family, Molly. So think of it as 'fatherly' interest." Just
then the senator's cell phone rang and he reached into his inner

pocket. "Excuse me for a moment," he said as he walked toward the living room.

"It'll be good to see you and the senator enjoying yourselves at home instead of working for a change," I said.

Peter sighed as he looked out into the gardens. "I'm simply looking forward to getting away from the Hill for an evening." Suddenly he frowned and turned to me. "I just remembered something I wanted to ask you. Back in August you brought me a disc with Karen's notes she'd made of subjects she'd researched. Her notes mentioned the organization Epsilon Group. I recalled that yesterday when the senator received a contribution from them. A significant contribution, I might add. Did Karen ever go into more detail about why she was researching them?"

I chose my words carefully. "No, she didn't. She indicated that she always checked out every new contributor to Congressman Jackson's campaigns. Apparently they're an organization that was established by some wealthy investment banker in New York years ago to educate legislators and others on global financial issues. In fact I went to one of their lectures at Dumbarton Oaks last spring. Former EU foreign minister Ambassador Holmberg was speaking. Lots of facts as I recall, but pretty boring."

"Molly, you amaze me. Even my staffers didn't learn that much background about the group," Peter said.

"Thanks, Peter, but I have to give credit to Samantha Calhoun. Whenever I want to know about something or someone in this town, I ask her first." I winked.

Senator Russell finished his phone conversation and Peter started toward the door again. Feeling playful, I couldn't resist. "I see Eleanor MacKenzie will be in attendance this evening. It'll be good to see her again." I gave the senator a devilish smile. "Eleanor makes a wonderful hostess."

Russell caught my drift and grinned, wagging his finger at me. "Now who's being a conspirator?"

I did my best to look innocent—always difficult for me—and replied, "It's always a pleasure to see the Queen Mother."

Senator Russell threw back his head and let loose a basso roar of laughter that followed him down the hall. Peter simply grinned at me and shook his finger.

I walked through the glass doors and down the steps leading to the gardens below. I enjoyed a few moments of mid-morning quiet before the catering trucks appeared in the driveway and the house sprang to life with caterers and assistants and wait staff. Luisa was in seventh heaven. Noise and hustle and bustle had returned.

I sipped my coffee as I strolled through the gardens, sunshine warming my back. It was a truly gorgeous autumn day, leaves already flaming with red and gold, yellow and orange. The sort of day that appears regularly during autumn in Washington. Mild temperatures still in the sixties and sometimes seventies. Sunny skies. No hint yet of the winter to come.

Senator Russell's gardener had already pruned the hedges and mulched the plants, preparing for winter. There was a bush in my townhouse backyard I needed to tackle. It needed pruning badly, having been neglected for quite a while. I'd found some pruning shears in the garage, so I had no excuse to avoid it except for my horrible track record at pruning. I tended to get carried away with the clipping and didn't know when to stop. I could reduce a healthy full plant to a footstool in a few minutes' time.

My cell phone's music interrupted my stroll; Samantha's name flashed on the screen. "Hey, there, Miss Thing. Have you had a chance to contact that security company?"

"As a matter of fact, they're coming out tomorrow. I'm sure your good word helped speed up the process."

"Not mine, I'll bet. Danny probably called them."

"Well, thank him for me, please. I wanted to give you an update on what has come in so far on your information requests. I have to leave in a few minutes to meet with Sister Bernice and the Walter Reed group for lunch."

"Wow, you're really getting involved with them."

"Well, once I saw what a difference they were making in the lives of our returning wounded from Iraq, I knew I had to join their efforts. I tell you, Molly. My heart went out to them."

I could hear the compassion in my dear friend's voice come over the phone. "I'm sure it did. And I'm not surprised you've become more involved."

"I even met an old acquaintance I'd known at Ole Miss years ago. He'd gone to West Point and had served in Vietnam as well. He's retired now and has been donating his time to these military charities. I told him I'd thought of contributing money toward a small foundation to help these wounded veterans, and he promised he'd help me organize it."

"Oh, that's wonderful, Samantha. You know, Eleanor is someone else who would be most interested in participating. Have you shared this with her?"

"Absolutely. She'll be attending one of their meetings with me next week. In fact, the old girl has even loosened the leash lately, if you can believe." Samantha's amusement was obvious.

"Doesn't surprise me a bit. You've shown her Sensible Samantha was still there. The Merry Widow merely chased her away for a while."

Samantha gave a genteel snort. "Sensible Samantha. *Gawd.* That sounds so dull. I'm not sure I can stand it."

"Sensible, surviving, call it what you want. It's simply your personality, Samantha. You've always been smart and savvy, ever since we were teenagers. That's who you really are. Not the 'let's see how I can shock them today,' Samantha."

She laughed softly. "All right. I'll take smart and savvy. Now, let me tell you what my mice have found out so far. I've heard from several since we talked the other day. The general consensus about Ryker is what we've already heard for a while. He's gotten richer over these last few years. Word is he invests in some pretty high-level hedge funds. The same is true for Senator Dunston. But there're more details. It seems Dunston has invested a lot of money in European banks in addition to American hedge funds. And there was a rumor that his son works for a bank in Germany. Maybe that's where he invests."

"That confirms the notation I saw in Quentin's notebook. He'd written the word 'son' beneath Dunston's name and then Stuttgart. Quentin was right."

"Yes, he was. Bless him. So now, I'll ask my sources specifically about that Dunston family connection to Stuttgart when I talk with them. Meanwhile, the stuff on Holmberg is what we already know. A former EU finance minister, professor at the Sorbonne, he has a list of credentials as long as your arm. Mostly he gives lectures and speeches all over the country about international monetary policy. Stuff like that. He's become a fixture in Washington and even has a house over near Woodley Park. That's all I've got for now. I'm sure the mice will come up with more, but I have to leave for that meeting."

"Nothing on that Spencer name?"

"Nope, not yet. That will take more time. One name is kind of vague. Talk to you later."

"Thanks, Samantha. Enjoy the meeting," I said, listening to her click at the other end of the line.

I drained the last of my coffee and headed back up the steps. My nature escape was over. Spreadsheets were calling.

Thursday evening

Larry Fillmore edged around the International Hotel's ballroom, eyeing the crowd of politicians, donors, lobbyists, staffers, and various camp followers. He spotted Congressman Jackson, immersed in conversation with two other Midwestern congressmen. He'd leisurely stroll over to join them in a few minutes. But first, he needed to find Spencer.

Being tall was an advantage, especially when it came to crowded rooms. He could easily scan over heads to find someone he was looking for. Like now. Spying Spencer Graham standing between two West Coast senators, Larry weaved his way around clusters of people who were talking and drinking, arguing and drinking, cajoling and drinking. Finally, he edged to the outskirts of the threesome. Larry deliberately positioned himself so he could catch Spencer's eye. After a couple of minutes, Spencer glad-handed both senators, guffawed at a joke, then moved away, angling toward Larry. He stood about two feet away.

"What have you found out so far?" Spencer asked, not looking at Larry but smiling out into the room instead.

"Thanks to the photo, I was able to run a search in the Congressional employee database. And I struck paydirt." Larry couldn't help bragging.

"Excellent. Who is she?"

Now came the tricky part. Spencer was not going to like the answer. "Loretta Wade. She's a senior researcher for the Congressional Research Service. A career employee. She's been with them for over twenty years."

Spencer turned to stare right at him. Larry could see a mixture of anger and apprehension in his eyes. Spencer spit out a raspy whisper. "*Dammit to hell!*"

"Yeah, I figured that was not good news. Do you think Malone got this Wade woman to follow up on the same research Quentin Wilson was doing? You said Raymond's guy saw Malone hand her a notebook."

"It looks that way." Spencer leaned back his head and drained his glass.

That huge diamond Spencer wore on the little finger of his left hand caught the lights overhead and sparkled, flashing with its brilliance. *Damn, that was big.* Larry wondered how much that ring had cost Spencer. He'd seen it on Spencer's hand ever since Larry had met him a few years ago.

"I sent you an email right before I came here with all the info from the employee database. Loretta Wade's fifty-six years old, a D.C. native, grew up here and went to American University, degree in history. Then got her master's at George Washington University. Was married, now a widow with three sons. I did a separate search to find out that one is an officer in the Navy, serving on the destroyer USS *Arleigh Burke*. Another is at Cornell, and the youngest is a junior at Gonzaga High School. She lives over on Potomac Avenue. I Googled it, and it's across the street from that Harris Teeter grocery store." Larry felt like thrusting his chest out but restrained himself.

Spencer eyed Larry and a small smile crooked his mouth. "Impressive, Larry. You didn't get all that from the employee database, I'll bet."

Larry couldn't hide a small smirk. "As you know, I have my own sources." He couldn't conceal his self-satisfaction.

"That's why we use you, Larry. You bring value." Spencer looked over his shoulder. Probably searching for the bar, Larry figured. "We can definitely make use of that."

"I figured you could." Larry was feeling so good about himself, he couldn't help adding, "You know, that's one helluva big-ass diamond you've got there." He smiled and pointed to Spencer's ring.

Spencer glanced briefly at his hand. "Yeah, it is. And it never leaves my hand. Couldn't even get it off for surgery." Pointing at the corner, he said, "I'm heading for the bar. You coming?"

"Naw, I'd better rejoin Jackson. I don't want him to think he can get along without me."

Spencer gave a snort. "Amen to that. We'll be in touch. Meanwhile, why don't you keep checking into Loretta Wade. Discreetly of course. Keep track of her. We'll let you know if she meets with Malone again."

"You know where to find me," Larry said as they both turned and went in opposite directions.

Later that evening

I stood in the side hall leading from the kitchen to the main hallway of the Russell mansion, sipping an excellent white wine. Ever since I'd taken over the Russell entertaining accounts, I'd made it a point to oversee the expenses of what Luisa referred to as the "wine cellar." It was more of a temperature-controlled closet, but its contents were outstanding. Thanks to my cousins Nan and Deb, and their advice, I'd been able to save the senator a good deal of money. Since they had their own entertaining business, their counsel on wine suppliers was spot-on. The senator didn't need any advice as to vintages. His taste was excellent.

The caterers were their normal organized, well-oiled machine. Various tempting appetizers appeared on trays as the serving staff from Preferred Professionals worked their way through the distinguished guests mingling in the Russell living room and spilling out into the gardens. Since Daylight Saving Time was in effect until this weekend, there was still enough light to beckon people outside.

Servers Aggie and Ryan smoothly brought appetizers and refilled drinks, moving effortlessly around the rooms. Bud, the bartender, was his usual quiet, efficient, speedy self as he mixed drinks and poured expensive whiskies, Scotch, and other liquor. I'd chatted with all three, Aggie, Ryan, and Bud, as they set up the dining table as a buffet table. The International Trade and Finance Subcommittee had twenty-two members. Add spouses and staff and ex-officio members, and the number swelled. I didn't even want to think about how many would be in attendance if the senator decided to entertain the entire Senate Committee on Banking, Housing, and Urban Affairs.

I noticed experienced server Aggie glance my way, then scurry down the hallway toward me. I met her halfway, not wanting her to take time away from the senator's guests.

"It's good to see you again, Aggie. The senator's hiatus from entertaining gave you folks some evenings off, I imagine."

"Well, we missed you, too, Molly," Aggie said with her warm smile, her gray eyes twinkling. "I hope you enjoyed the time off as well."

I could tell from the twinkle in her eye that she'd been talking to Luisa, so I willingly played along. "As a matter of fact, I have. As I'm sure Luisa has kept you all informed." Wagging my head dramatically, I added, "Such a bunch of busybodies and gossips."

"Washington runs on gossip, Molly," Aggie said with a grin as she headed down the side hallway to the kitchen.

"Well, you'd better get back in there and learn more," I said as she turned the corner. I walked toward the main hallway. Casey strolled over my way, doing his usual security monitoring of attending guests.

"Luisa is certainly happy tonight," he said with a smile. "But I imagine you're counting up the dollars as you watch all this."

"Oh, yes. Accountants can't help it. It's the way we're wired. We're always thinking about the money." I raised my glass. "But Luisa is in hog heaven. She hasn't stopped smiling all day, I swear."

"Oh, yeah. Even Albert looks happier."

"They were both bored. I'm afraid they've gotten addicted to those early months of the senator entertaining everyone in Congress."

Casey's smile vanished and he looked at me. "You still look like you're worrying about something. Maybe it's my imagination, but ever since Natasha Jorgensen was murdered you've been … preoccupied, I guess. Maybe it's my imagination."

Casey had good instincts. "No, it's not your imagination; I have been preoccupied. I've been asking a lot of questions and talking to different people, and I've started to make some connections."

He peered at me. "What kinds of connections? Are you talking about Natasha's murder?"

"Yes. Ever since you told me the cops found a bug on Natasha's phone, I started to get suspicious. If someone had been listening in on her calls, then they would have heard Congresswoman Wilson's call. They would have learned about Quentin Wilson's notebook. Heard the names of a prominent congressman and a senator mentioned. And they would have heard my call with Natasha. Heard me ask her for a copy of any notes she took. And they would have heard us make plans to meet that Thursday morning on the Canal towpath."

I watched Casey's intent gaze deepen on me as I spoke. Clearly he was making the same connections I had.

"Are you saying what I think you are?"

I nodded. "Yes, I am. I believe that Natasha's killer knew where to find her and when. She wasn't the victim of a random rapist lurking beneath the bridge but a planned attack."

Casey's expression turned skeptical. "That's a helluva lot of speculation, Molly."

"Maybe. But Natasha promised to give me a copy of her notes when we met that morning. And police said there was no paper found on her body. I think that's because the killer took it. Someone doesn't want those prominent names spread around."

"Then why kill her? He could have just mugged her. Stole the paper and her phone."

"Maybe she was killed to silence her. To keep her from giving information to anyone else."

Casey didn't answer right away; he just stared at me, clearly skeptical. "I don't know. It sounds like too much speculation to me."

"I realize that. That's why I'm still asking questions."

Albert waved at us from the kitchen hallway. Casey started to move away. "We'll talk some more about this."

I turned back to Senator Russell's reception. I had no doubt Casey and I would have this conversation again.

ELEVEN

Friday

"Hey, I wasn't expecting to see you this morning," Raymond said as Trask walked down the hallway of his office. He couldn't help noticing the familiar takeout bag with the golden arches symbol in Trask's hand, coffee in the other.

"Yeah, the Wade woman is settled in at her office and won't reappear until after five, so I thought I'd come over and check on Malone. I also stopped by to pick up some fast food." Trask gave him a crooked smile.

"You read my mind," Raymond said as he accepted the takeout bag and coffee. He could smell the breakfast sandwich inside, and his stomach growled. "Thanks for this. I didn't have any breakfast."

"I figured." Trask took a drink from his takeout cup and settled into the chair beside Raymond at the long table with the video monitor screen. "Actually, I was hoping to get a better look at Malone's boyfriend. I only got a glimpse of him in August before I left for Europe."

Raymond took a sip of the creamy hot liquid. *Damn, that felt good.* "Well, he has an erratic schedule. Sometimes he's here, other times he's not. When he's here, they go running early, then she heads for her office at Senator Russell's house. The guy comes and goes at different times. Some mornings he's already gone by the time I get in here. Other times, he leaves right after Malone. And when he leaves the house, he never looks toward the camera."

Raymond sank his teeth into the breakfast sandwich. Sausage, egg, and melted cheese on an English muffin. He closed his eyes and savored. He'd forgotten how good these were. Greasy and delicious. You couldn't beat it.

Trask chuckled, watching him. "I would have brought two if I'd known you were that hungry."

Raymond didn't answer because his mouth was full. He devoured the rest of the sandwich, then took a big drink of coffee. "He's here now because his car is in the driveway. The black Jag parked behind Malone's car."

"Well, if we can get a good look at him, we can run a check. So, all we need ... hey, isn't that him?"

Raymond glanced at the large monitor screen and spotted a man closing the front door to Malone's townhouse, then walking toward the driveway. "Well, I'll be damned. That's him, all right. Perfect timing, Trask."

The man pulled a cell phone from inside his jacket and held it to his ear as he approached the car. Trask and Raymond both leaned forward over the table, closer to the video screen.

"That's it, slow down and answer the phone," Raymond coached.

"Now turn around so we can get a good look at you," Trask said as the man stood outside the car, still talking on the phone.

As if heeding their advice, the man turned and leaned against the car as he talked. "Perfect. Now let's take a closer look." Raymond picked up the controls and began zooming in on the man as he stood talking. Every now and then, the man would turn slightly so he faced the cameras. "There you go. Just what we need." Raymond clicked the camera twice.

"Son of a bitch!"

Raymond turned to see Trask sitting bolt upright, his face contorted with a grimace. He'd never seen that expression on Trask's normally icy, composed features before.

"What's the matter?" Raymond asked, surprised. "You know this guy or something?"

"Hell, yes," Trask snarled.

"From the look on your face, I'm guessing you two were not best buddies."

Trask stared at the screen, transfixed. "I was in his squad in the Marines. He's the sonofabitch that got me thrown out! *Motherf—*"

Raymond watched as Trask let loose a stream of profanity aimed at the man on the video screen, who was still calmly talking on his cell phone in Malone's driveway. "What the hell happened?"

"He caught me taking money from another guy's gear and dragged me to the commander. They brought me up on charges. Sons-of-bitches gave me a dishonorable discharge and shipped me back home."

Raymond heard no emotion in his voice, but the rest of Trask fairly radiated with rage. Suppressed rage. "That's ancient history, Trask. We all have people that have screwed us in the past. We move on."

Trask didn't answer, he simply kept staring at the screen, while muscles in his jaw twitched with the obvious effort to hold back whatever response he wanted to give. Raymond watched him carefully, then pulled the open laptop computer toward him and clicked onto several different screens, opening files. Finally, he found the one he wanted.

"Okay, what's that guy's name? Do you remember? Let's see if this is a case of mistaken identity."

"DiMateo. Daniel DiMateo," Trask said in a low voice, still staring at the screen. The man opened the door to his car, got in, and proceeded to back out of the driveway. Within a minute, the car had disappeared from the video surveillance screen.

Raymond read the document file he'd opened on the screen. "Bingo. Looks like that's your old Marine buddy. Daniel DiMateo. 4567 Quinn Street, Arlington, Virginia. Probably one of those high-rent condos overlooking the Potomac near Rosslyn, so I'll bet your boy stayed in full-time, then retired. Probably been consulting since then. That's my guess."

Trask didn't say anything; he simply stared at the screen, even though the object of his fascination was gone. Raymond observed him carefully. He'd never seen Trask lose his cool over anyone or anything. He was the consummate professional, which was exactly what Raymond needed. So, this change in Trask's temperament was disconcerting. And, worrisome.

"Do you have any idea where else this DiMateo served?"

Finally, Trask broke his trancelike stare at the video screen and turned to face Raymond. His expression had just about returned to its normal emotionless mask. Almost.

"I heard he got into Special Forces. That's all I know."

"Interesting. Did you ever hear anything about him or catch a glimpse when you were a mercenary years ago? I always tried to stay clear of those guys whenever I was doing work for hire."

Trask shook his head, then sipped his coffee. "Nope. Never did."

"Okay, let's see what we can find out about this guy. We were only occasionally checking on Malone back in August. We'd gotten the official 'hands off' so I didn't pay much attention. She and her boyfriend were just doing their thing."

"Okay, let me know what you find. Meanwhile, I'm going to check around Loretta Wade's neighborhood. Take a look at Gonzaga. I went there for a basketball game once. I'll see what info I can get on her kid too. All that preliminary info about her is pretty clean. Let's see if there's any dirt hiding." Trask quickly rose from the chair and started for the hallway, then looked back at Raymond. "Why don't you get outside in the sun this weekend? It would do you good."

Curious at Trask's comment, Raymond retorted, "I'm afraid of getting skin cancer," he said with a wry smile.

Trask's lips twisted slightly. "Suit yourself. Email me whatever you find on DiMateo, okay?"

"Sure thing. Listen, Trask. Why don't you take your boat out this weekend? Go for a sail. Relax. You've earned it."

Trask slipped his shades from his jacket pocket. "I'll think about it." Then he was down the hallway and gone.

Raymond stared after him. He had a bad feeling.

———

I tabbed from column to column in Peter Brewster's rental property spreadsheet. Another hour and Danny would pick me up for dinner. Tonight, we'd be heading downtown to a favorite steakhouse and grill. It was hard to go wrong with steak.

My personal cell phone came alive with a mellower sound. "Desperado" played for a minute before I answered. Loretta Wade's name flashed on the screen.

"Hey, Loretta, how's that puzzle solving going?"

"Actually, it's kept my sanity several times these last couple of days. I tell you, supervising people is the most frustrating part of my job. I swear, some of these folks are gonna put me in an early grave."

I laughed softly as I relaxed into my desk chair, coffee mug in hand. "Well, I'm glad taciturn Eric Grayson could rescue you from aggravation."

"Escaping into his notes was a lifeline. The man was so organized and methodical. The subject matter was as dry as you predicted. I wish I could tell you I had some great revelations while going through his notebook, but I didn't. I did, however, get an idea what that word meant that Grayson had indicated so many times in his notes. You know, *geo.* Something about that word buzzed in the back of my head until it finally came to me. It might have been an abbreviation for 'George.' George Trudeau was a senior researcher during the time when Grayson was doing his research. I saw Eric Grayson and George talking together many times during those months. I worked with George when I first moved into this division. He was a role model, of sorts. Super smart, and a brain that was greased lightning. He had so many facts and figures at his command, it was formidable. So, I think George Trudeau must have been the senior researcher helping Eric Grayson; that's why the abbreviation for his name was written down."

I sipped my coffee, considering what Loretta had said. "That kind of makes sense. Geo was an abbreviation. But why would Eric Grayson write that guy's name over and over so many times? It's not like he was going to forget who he was."

"Yeah, I wondered about that too. But I didn't come up with any answers. I guess you could always ask the man himself. I checked and George Trudeau lives over in Arlington, near Ballston. He retired a few years ago. Had a big retirement party too. He didn't have any family as I recall. You could probably call him. See if he remembers working with Grayson. I can email you his phone number. I corroborated his number with the public directory."

"Do you think he'd mind if I called? I mean, I'm a stranger. I didn't work with him or anything."

"He'd probably enjoy it. Old researchers love nothing more than talking about it. So, he might welcome it. Give it a try, Molly. I'd be curious to know too. Tell him I sent you. I think he liked me. At least he never scowled at me or anything." She chuckled.

"Okay, I'll give it a try after this weekend. I think Danny and I are going to finally get away into the Blue Ridge and see some leaves and relax."

"Sounds great. I'll be sitting on gym bleachers. Basketball season is starting in a month and practice has already begun. They'll be doing some preseason games with other schools too."

"You go, Mom. That brings back memories. Those gym bleachers are hard."

"Let me know if you talk with old George, okay? By the way, I took a look at those other names you gave me. I've found some things, but I don't really want to talk about these folks over the phone. You know what I mean?"

That caught my attention. "I know exactly what you mean. Maybe we should meet for a pub dinner. When are you free?"

"Let's meet after the weekend, like Monday night around six thirty, after I get dinner for my son and he starts his homework. There's another Irish pub on the opposite section of Eighth Avenue. Right across from Barracks Row. Let's meet there, okay? I'll email George's phone number later. I've got to hang up now. Two calls are waiting."

"Sounds good, I'll see you then," I said, then clicked off. I'd let Danny know he'd be on his own for dinner that night. Whatever Loretta found must have been important.

TWELVE

Late Sunday afternoon

RAYMOND UNLOCKED HIS OFFICE door and stepped inside. To his surprise, there was a fast-food bag sitting on his front desk along with an extra-large takeout cup of what smelled like coffee. The aroma of a hamburger sandwich inside the bag beckoned him forward.

"Trask?" Raymond called.

"Yeah, I'm back here," Trask's voice came from down the hall.

Raymond dug out the first of two sandwiches from the takeout out bag and tore into it. The coughing had kept him awake most of the night, and this morning he hadn't felt like eating. Until now. Maybe he should just forget about eating regular food and head for the drive-thru instead. He sipped from the creamy hot coffee as he walked down the hallway to the inner room with surveillance monitors on the desk. Other cameras and computers lined the walls, their screens dark, no longer in use.

120

Trask was seated beside the table, staring at the monitor screen showing the front of Malone's townhouse. He leaned back in the chair, hands behind his head.

"Damn, Trask, don't tell me you spent all weekend here?"

Trask gave a little smile. "Most of it. After you sent me all that info on DiMateo, I decided to do some digging of my own."

Raymond wasn't sure, but he thought he spotted the hint of a smile. He sank into the chair beside Trask and took another deep drink of coffee to soothe the pain in his throat, which had started to throb last night. "I sent you his Special Forces duty tours, Trask. I doubt you could find out more than that."

"Let's just say I added some background. Put it in context, so to speak. I thought Malone might find it interesting."

Raymond peered at him. "What in hell are you up to?"

Trask gestured to a file folder on the table. "Take a look."

Reaching for the folder, Raymond opened it to find several 8 x 10 photos. DiMateo standing beside several uniformed men, gold braid covering their shoulders, along with other men in business suits. Was that Ryker in the group? Another photo showed DiMateo standing in a group of other military men in fatigues, jungle foliage in the background. Rifles in hand, each man held what looked like a severed head. A third photo showed another jungle background and DiMateo squatting with other uniformed men around naked bodies piled in a heap. Some looked to be children. *What the hell?* There were enlarged newspaper articles with headlines. Nicaragua. Columbia. Raymond scanned a couple. Finally, a single page had words typed in all caps: "DO YOU KNOW WHO YOU'RE SLEEPING WITH?"

Raymond glanced at Trask, who was watching the monitor. It showed Malone's empty front yard. He had only one question. "Why, Trask?"

Trask merely smiled, just a little, as he continued to watch the monitor. "Just thought I'd let a few snakes loose into their garden."

"Not smart, Trask. This guy's gonna get pissed and try to find out who sent the photos."

Trask's smile turned smug as he continued to lean back in the chair. "There's nothing to find. Some old newspaper articles. Old photos. A little Photoshop. Anybody can do that on a laptop. There's nothing to trace."

"Don't be so sure—"

"Well, well, they're back. They left yesterday morning. Small suitcases, so they didn't go far."

Raymond took a deep drink of the coffee as he watched Malone and DiMateo get out of his car. "You've delivered this package, I take it?"

Trask nodded. "Early this afternoon. I used the express delivery uniform and truck. Package is sitting beside the front door. Okay, the show's about to start."

Raymond didn't say anything else. He pulled out the second sandwich while he watched the monitor screen.

———

"I'll bring the suitcases in right after I return this call," Danny said as he flipped open his cell phone. His car trunk popped open.

"Want some coffee?" I asked as I approached the front door.

"Sure, then we can head uptown for dinner." He leaned against the side of his car.

A courier mail package sat beside the entry door. I scooped it up. I wasn't expecting anything. Could it be intended for Senator Russell? I saw it was addressed to me, so I pulled the strip on the back and reached inside. I pulled out a file folder with no markings. Inside I saw pictures: 8 x 10 blowups of black-and-white photos. Photos of Danny in some junglelike surroundings with a group of soldiers. Guns were everywhere. On their backs, in their hands, on the ground. And each of these men was holding something in front of them. What was it? It looked … was that a *head*?

I turned to another photo. Several men in suits, standing together. Some were naval officers in white uniforms. Danny in a suit, talking to a guy beside him. I stared at the photo. Wait a minute … was that Ryker? *Good God!*

A chill settled over me as I turned to the last photo.

It showed Danny in another jungle setting crouching down with a bunch of other soldiers. Naked, dead bodies lay in a pile on the ground in front of them, blood smeared all over their faces. Smaller bodies, like children, lay beside the others. The men were crouched around the entire gruesome scene along with Danny. Like hunters, surrounding a trophy elk. *Did the men kill all those people and children?*

My stomach lurched as I turned to the newspaper articles and started reading. News stories reporting guerilla armies fighting in Central American countries. Government troops attacking. Old memories of decades ago and the wars that ravaged South and Central America. I remembered the news stories as I recalled the wars in those chaotic years. Africa. The Middle East. So much fighting. So much war. So much killing.

I turned the pages until I found the last one and read the question typed there. "DO YOU KNOW WHO YOU'RE SLEEPING WITH?" An icy cold shot through me.

"Here, I'll open the door," Danny said as he approached, carrying both bags under his arm. "What's in the envelope?"

I looked up at Danny and stared at him. No words came.

Danny peered at me. "Molly, what's wrong? What's in that package?" He dropped the suitcases and reached out.

"The past," was all I could say.

He grabbed the folder and started going through it. I watched his face darken in anger. "What the hell! What sick sonofabitch would send you this?" He glanced up at me, and I saw Danny's expression change as he stared at me.

I just stared back at him, as every doubt I'd ever had slithered from the underbrush in the back of my mind. Hissing, whispering.

Lies. All of it, lies. Everything he's ever told you. You can't trust him. Lies. Lies. That's why he doesn't tell you where he goes and what he does. He's still killing people. Cannot trust him. Lies. All lies.

"Molly, these photos are fake. Doctored. I've never spoken to Edward Ryker in my life. And you knew I was in Nicaragua and South America, because I told you myself. But all these are fakes, I swear they are. Whoever the sonofabitch is that sent you this crap, I'm gonna—"

"Danny, *stop!*" I blurted, holding up both hands.

"Molly, listen—"

"*No!* I can't listen. Just go. I don't want you here right now."

"But, Molly—"

"Stay away. I ... I need to think," I said, backing toward the front door, hands still up, ready to push him away if he approached.

But he didn't. Danny stood watching me, his face reflecting some of the same emotions that wrenched through me now. Pain. Confusion. Then he grabbed his valise from the stoop and backed away, still holding the folder with the incriminating past.

"I'm gonna find the sonofabitch who did this, Molly. I swear I will. He's after me, but he's going through you to get to me. I'm going to call Prestige and have protection on you starting tonight." Then he turned and strode to his car, backing out of my driveway with a squeal of brakes.

I stared after him, then grabbed my small carry-on and headed for my own car. I couldn't be alone tonight. Not after this. I needed to think. I dug out my keys and jumped into the car, revving the engine loudly.

Drive. Get away. Right now. I backed down the driveway and headed for Wisconsin Avenue. Meanwhile, my fingers sought out the music player. I punched in my playlist and flipped it on a loop as I headed toward Key Bridge and up the parkway to the mountains.

Those familiar and ominous guitar chords shuddered through the speakers. *Gimme Shelter.* But there was none.

———

Raymond watched Malone back her car out of the driveway and head down the street and off the monitor screen. He glanced over at Trask, who was still leaning back in the chair beside him, the smug smile still in place.

"Satisfied now?" Raymond barbed.

"Oh, yeah."

Raymond dug the last of the fries from the paper bag. "Well, you've released the snakes, but you've also succeeded in pissing off this guy. Not smart."

Trask just laughed, then stood and stretched. Like a cat who'd been crouched in the grass, waiting for a bird to appear.

"You've also broken the cardinal rule, Trask. Never make it personal. Do that, and you become vulnerable."

"Don't worry about it, Raymond. I'm not. DiMateo will never find me."

Raymond sipped the creamy coffee. "Trask, you've been in this business long enough to know we never say never."

Only then did Trask's smile fade.

Later that evening

I curled my legs up beneath me on Samantha's library sofa and clasped the ceramic mug of coffee with both hands. The warmer autumn temperatures were fading away. Tonight was chilly. So much so that Samantha had started a fire in the fireplace across from us. The flames licked up the last of the kindling as it snapped and popped.

Soon Daylight Saving Time would officially end, and the sudden appearance of dark night skies an hour earlier would be jolting. Suddenly bright light shone outside the library windows looking out on Samantha's front yard. Now that her home had the security totally upgraded, bright spotlights shone outside along the entire perimeter of her house whenever the motion detector sensed movement.

"I'm waiting for my neighbors to complain about the lights coming on in the middle of the night," Samantha said as she sat in the stuffed armchair next to the sofa.

We both faced the fire, which had grown. More heat radiated toward us, and it felt good. Even though I wore a sweater, I was still cold. "I'm sure they understand your need for security." I sipped my coffee. "I'm just glad your house is totally locked down like mine. No one will get in without you or your housekeeper allowing them."

Samantha swirled the bourbon in her glass. "I'd like to thank Danny for calling Prestige Systems and recommending me."

I pressed the warm mug to my chest, absorbing its heat, as I stared into the flames, licking higher now. "It's okay. I'll write down his email for you."

Samantha sipped her bourbon. "Molly, I can understand how shocked you must have been, seeing those photos, especially the awful ones, but everything you know about Danny tells you he's a good man. He'd have no reason to lie to you about meeting Ryker. Why would he? And if he says those photos are fake, phony, then I'm inclined to believe him. Why won't you?"

I let out a tired sigh. "I want to believe him, but those pictures were so ... so horrible. Dead children lying in a pile." I closed my eyes and shuddered. "I don't know if I can get them out of my head."

"I understand, Molly, believe me, I do. Just ... just promise me you'll listen to him when he tries to talk to you. I know he will. You told me he said he was going to find out who sent the photos, and I don't doubt he will. Frankly, I think you should be worrying more about who sent that package. Clearly, someone has been watching your house or something. How else would they know Danny was staying there with you?"

Samantha made sense, I knew that. The anxiety about someone watching me hadn't had a chance to penetrate yet. Those sickening photos still claimed my attention. Whenever I closed my eyes, there they were—haunting me. Children with bloody faces lying dead in a pile. Danny and comrades in arms kneeling behind them. My stomach lurched again.

There was a light knock on the library door, and Samantha called, "Yes, Anna?"

Gray-haired, matronly Anna stepped inside the room. "Excuse me, Mrs. Calhoun, but you have a phone call. The gentleman said he had an important message for you. A mister DiMateo."

I stared first at Anna, then Samantha. "Why is he calling?" I said, suddenly anxious.

Samantha rose from the armchair's embrace. "Probably because he knows you're over here. Thank you, Anna. I'll take the call here." She walked over to her cherrywood desk and picked up the phone. "Good instincts, Double D. That is your nickname, right? Molly's here with me, and she's staying the night."

I watched Samantha hold the phone, obviously listening to Danny's response.

"I see," Samantha said after a couple of minutes. "I'll tell her then. Do you have my address here in McLean?"

That caught me by surprise. Was he coming here?

"That's very interesting. I'll be sure to tell her. Oh, and Danny, thank you for referring me to Prestige Systems. I appreciate it. And … good luck." She clicked off the portable phone.

I sat up so quickly I nearly spilled my coffee. "I can't see Danny now. Not yet."

"Relax, he's not coming here. He's abiding by your demand that he stay away. He even said that right now." Samantha paused by the liquor cabinet and poured more bourbon into her glass.

"Then why did you give him your address?"

"Because he told me he's already arranged for Prestige Systems personal security service for your protection," she said as she returned to the stuffed armchair. "One of their escorts will pick you up tomorrow morning and take you home so you can get ready for the office. He'll be here at 6:30 a.m."

I stared at her. "That's ridiculous. I don't need a security escort."

"Well, after hearing what Danny has learned so far, I think you do. He said Prestige did a perimeter check around your property, looking for cameras of any kind. And they found one on the utility pole directly in front of your house. From that angle, Danny said they could see anyone arriving and the entire front of the property and driveway." Samantha eyed me over her glass as she sipped.

That got my attention. Good God! Somebody really *was* watching me. *Why?*

"Danny also said he's going to find out who's doing this, Molly. And from the sound of that man's voice, I do not doubt it." She swirled the bourbon. "He also told me those photos were phony. Probably Photoshopped, or whatever they call it. And I believe him."

I stared at Samantha, but didn't have anything to say. Too much was running through my head right now. *Why would someone be watching me? And why would they send me doctored photos of Danny?* It didn't make any sense.

"I … I don't understand. Why would someone do that? Why would they be watching me?"

"Danny also said it wasn't about you, Molly. It's about him. Someone from his past is behind this."

The past. Come back to haunt Danny. The sins of our past. None of us can escape them. No matter how far away we run. Not even Danny.

THIRTEEN

Monday morning

I STARED AT THE fresh-faced young man standing on Samantha's front step, clearly waiting for me to join him. A jet-black Lexus was parked in her circular driveway. No lettering on the side. "I really don't need an escort," I protested. "I've been walking safely to Senator Russell's house every day for months."

"I understand, ma'am. But my superiors said the situation has changed. Someone is watching you, following you. So you need protection. By the way, I'm Jeremy." With his blond, buzzed-cut hair and square jaw, I guessed he was probably right out of the military. He still had the starched look of a salute about him as he stood waiting by the open passenger door.

"All right, all right. It's too early in the morning to argue with superior powers." I gave an exaggerated sigh and walked to the car. "What about my car?"

"Don't worry, ma'am. We'll bring it over to your house for you."

"Molly, why don't you give me the keys and I'll follow behind you two. Then this nice young man can bring me back home. Would that pass muster with your superiors, Jeremy?"

"Yes, ma'am. That would be very convenient. Thank you."

"Are you sure you want to be driving in this awful rush hour traffic?" I asked Samantha as I dug the keys from my purse and handed them over. "This is a little early for you, isn't it? I'm amazed to see you dressed." I couldn't resist.

Samantha flashed one of her brilliant smiles as she took the keys. "A little fresh air in the morning will do me good," she replied, then slipped on a jacket and headed to the side driveway where my car was parked.

Jeremy closed the door after me and scurried around to climb into the driver's seat. He quickly started the car, then glanced at me and paused. "Seat belt, ma'am."

I dutifully complied and held my tongue. Getting bossed around "for my own good" was hard enough. But I didn't think I could take the "ma'am" for very long.

———

Albert approached me as I stood in the doorway of my office. "Molly, Luisa and I are going out on some errands. Is there anything you need while we're out?"

"Thanks, Albert. I'm good. A fresh pot of Luisa's coffee is in the kitchen. That's all I need." I saluted him with my mug and watched as he headed for the hallway leading to the back entrance. I also noticed Casey walking my way. From the look on his face, I had a feeling he'd already been updated on the change in my "security situation," as escort Jeremy referred to it.

"You have a minute, Molly?" Casey asked as he approached.

"Sure. I can tell you've either talked with my new escort Jeremy, or you've had a call from his superiors at Prestige Systems."

"Yes, Jeremy and I did have a talk after you arrived this morning. But I also had a call from Danny." He looked at me, clearly concerned.

I glanced away and walked back to my desk chair. "Well, then, you know about the unknown watcher."

"He won't stay unknown for long. Danny told me he's arranged for Prestige to shadow you for the next few days. He thinks this guy is obviously watching you and may be following you as well. If so, Danny thinks the security guys can take photos and they'll start matching them against files. Identify this guy."

I sank into my chair and stared up at Casey. "What files? This guy could be anybody."

"Danny thinks he's former military. Probably served with Danny. Something must have happened for this guy to hold a grudge so long. When you've been a career Marine, you've pulled a lot of tours all over. You're bound to make some enemies. Hopefully not a lot." He gave me a half smile.

"Okay. That makes sense. But why now? And if Danny is this guy's target, why go through me?"

"Well, we haven't figured that out yet."

"*We?* Have you been snared into this drama as well?"

Casey gave a good-natured shrug. "I'm anxious to help any way I can. Above all, we want to keep you safe."

I leaned back in my desk chair and took a sip of coffee. "So, let me get this straight. I'm now going to be 'shadowed' or followed everywhere I go by a security team from Prestige, right?"

"Correct. But you'll never notice them. Their job is to stay unobserved and photograph everyone in your vicinity."

"Well, tonight will be a good test, then. I'm going to meet Loretta Wade at an Irish pub in Eastern Market. So that ought to be fun. These security guys are going to be busy watching all the pubgoers."

He furrowed his brow. "Who's Loretta Wade? I don't recall you telling me about her."

I smiled. "I don't tell you about everyone I know, Casey. Loretta is a senior researcher at the Congressional Research Services. Natasha Jorgensen told me she was the researcher who helped Quentin Wilson, so naturally I called her up to find out what he was looking for back in July. And it turns out Loretta knew Karen and was close to Celeste Allard. So she's helped me a lot whenever I've had questions."

Casey nodded. "Which is most of the time. You must have even more questions if you two are meeting for dinner." His cell phone started to ring then. "Don't worry. These guys are professionals, so they'll handle the pub crowd," Casey said as he reached for his ringing cell phone and backed out of my office.

I turned my attention to the computer screen and all the new emails waiting for me. *Professionals, huh?* Then why did I feel like bait? They were definitely using me as bait. Trying to draw this guy out of the shadows. *Who was this guy anyway?*

Monday evening

"I'm going to cut through some other streets, ma'am. Get out of this Pennsylvania Avenue traffic. We'll cut back over once we get closer to Eastern Market."

I caught Jeremy's glance in his rearview mirror as I pulled out my cell phone. Might as well make some calls while we drove. "Do whatever you have to, Jeremy. Rush hour is wretched all over the city. It's hard to escape. But if you've got shortcuts, go for it."

"Yes, ma'am."

I just sighed, giving in to the respectful "ma'am." Clearly, Jeremy had been doing it for so long in the military, it was a permanent part of his vocabulary. Meanwhile, I figured if I was going to be driven around in a black limo, I might as well enjoy it. And make use of the time spent in the car.

Unfolding a piece of paper I'd stuffed in my purse, I punched in the phone number that Loretta had given me for George Trudeau. I watched Jeremy weave through some of the numbered streets away from the main thoroughfares while I listened to Trudeau's phone ring. He picked up after six rings. His voice was a quiet baritone as he answered.

"Mister Trudeau? My name is Molly Malone, and our mutual acquaintance at the Congressional Research Services, Loretta Wade, gave me your name and number. She suggested I give you a call because I've got some research questions." I deliberately left it at that.

"Oh, yes, Loretta Wade. I remember her. She's a charming woman. Smart too. One of the smarter researchers working there. And I should know. I worked there for thirty years—my entire career."

I decided a little flattery never hurt. "Thirty years? Well, now I know why Loretta suggested I call you. You see, my questions concern some research that former Congressman Eric Grayson did years ago. Loretta said you were a senior researcher then, so you might recall him."

There was a long pause on the other end of the line. "Ah, yes. I remember Congressman Grayson well. Yes, I do recall his coming to the Library of Congress many times. As you said, it was years ago."

"Yes, well—"

"Who did you say you were again? And why exactly are you inquiring about Congressman Grayson's research?"

His tone had changed somewhat, a little sharper, I noticed. "I'm Molly Malone, and I was Senator Robert Malone's daughter. Eric Grayson became my brother-in-law when I married his younger brother, David. You may recall that David served six years in the House of Representatives too. Of course, that was several years ago."

His voice returned to the friendlier tone immediately. "Oh, my, yes... I do remember your young husband, Ms. Malone. And, of course I remember your father. He was quite a man. An exceptional senator." He paused. "I'm afraid we may not see his like again."

I was touched by his comment. "I couldn't agree with you more, Mr. Trudeau. It was another day, I'm afraid. But, I'm presently working for a newly elected senator who has some of my father's strengths. Integrity and passion, for starters."

"Let me guess. Would that be Senator John Russell by any chance?" I could hear the smile in his voice.

"Spot on, Mr. Trudeau. I see Loretta didn't exaggerate when she said you were the smartest one she'd ever met over at Research Services."

"Please call me George. And send your friend my thanks for her compliment. What area of research are you interested in? May I call you Molly?"

"Please do. My niece Karen continued her father's research into international banking and monetary issues and expanded it to cover any financial legislation that's been passed recently. After Karen's death, I decided to continue her research as a tribute to her. She was a very special young woman." I didn't say any more.

George Trudeau was silent for a moment. "I do remember Congressman Grayson speaking about her years ago. And I even met her when she first joined the House staff of Congressman Jackson. She was an impressive young lady." He paused again. "I'll be glad to help you with any questions you have, Molly."

"As you know, I've retired from the federal government, but I am working part-time for the Arlington County Library system. After thirty years of commuting, I really hate to traipse into the District unless forced. Would you mind too terribly if we met over here at the library in Arlington? It's right in Ballston. You could easily take the Metro."

"That's not a problem at all, George. Maybe Tuesday or Wednesday night? I might be able to leave my office here in Georgetown a little early and meet you there. Would either of those evenings work?"

"Tuesday night would be better. I don't have to work late. We're always busy, but there are plenty of quiet corners where we can talk."

"That sounds perfect. I'll see you there tomorrow night at five." I clicked off. Prestige Security's team would certainly get a workout. An Irish pub tonight and a busy library tomorrow. I glanced out the car window and was surprised to see us turning off Pennsylvania Avenue and onto Eighth Street.

"We'll be there in just a moment Ms. Malone," Jeremy announced as he slowed to accommodate pedestrians and jaywalkers.

They were probably going to one of the cafés and coffee shops along that historic section of Barracks Row on Eighth Street in Southeast D.C. The stately brick buildings housing the Marine Corps Barracks rose behind the brick walls surrounding them. This area was once the oldest commercial area in the District of Columbia, because it was so close to the busy Washington Navy Yard. Established in the early 1800s to house U.S. Marines, Barracks Row was now home to the Marine Corps Band.

Jeremy pulled the Lexus to a stop, double-parking along the side of the street. "Don't bother trying to open my door, Jeremy," I said as I reached for the handle. "I'll hop out here. You'll just infuriate the other drivers even more. Shall I text you before I leave or are you coming inside too?"

"I'll be parked in the alley around the corner, ma'am. The security team will let me know when to bring the car around." He glanced over his shoulder.

Sure enough, car horns started to blow, so I exited the Lexus as quickly as possible. Scooting between two parked cars, I stepped onto the curb and looked up at the bright sign illuminated above the pub's front door. My name in lights. Loretta did that on purpose I thought with a smile as I yanked the door open.

————

"Where are you now?" Raymond asked as he steered his car through the traffic morass of I-66 heading into Virginia. What had he told Trask the other day? He actually preferred the congested interstate to the speedy Metro.

"In front of an Irish pub over on Barracks Row. Named *Molly Malone's* if you can believe it," Trask snickered.

"She still being driven around by the security guy?"

"Yep. Looks like he's fresh out of the service. He just dropped her off at the front door and he's headed around the corner. Parking somewhere, probably."

"You got the cycle, right?"

"Yeah. I'll park it and put on the shaggy professor look, then see who Malone's meeting."

"Okay, Professor. Let me know what you find out." Raymond clicked off and sped up enough to cut off another driver from slipping in front of him, just as another round of coughing started.

———

Loretta leaned over the plate of corned beef and sliced brown bread. "I checked all of those names you gave me." She lowered her voice, so I leaned forward to hear in the crowded pub. "The ones in Wilson's notebook—Ryker, Dunston, and Holmberg. And the names Eric Grayson mentioned in his notes—Montclair and Kasikov."

We were seated at a small table along the wall, directly across from the bar in the cozy pub. The owners had done a great job of re-creating that Irish pub atmosphere, and the place was packed.

"Is Dunston's son definitely working for a Stuttgart bank?" I asked, then took a drink of the delicious Guinness. My plate of aged cheddar and pear slices was barely touched. Loretta and I said we'd share, but we'd done more talking than eating.

"Yes, he is. It took a little searching, but I found the foreign employees list." She took a sip of her lighter brew. "What fascinated me the most was digging into these other guys. We already know Ryker and Dunston are politicians. And Holmberg's an economist, former EU Minister, professor, all that. But it took some searching to find the others."

She sampled a sliced pear. "I started off with Montclair. It took a little digging to find someone with that name and an international economic or banking connection. Turns out my money is on Anthony Montclair, who served in two British prime ministers' cabinets at an auxiliary level, not appointed. But his career was mostly in the London banks. Investment banks in particular. He also no longer works for them on a full-time basis. Apparently he consults around Europe and Southeast Asia."

I took a bite of the rich cheddar and savored while Loretta was talking. "Who's this Kasikov?"

Loretta nibbled some of her corned beef. "Now, Kasikov was easier. His name jumped out immediately. I figure it's got to be Dimitry Kasikov, who served as a kind of behind-the-scenes economic adviser to Russian leaders. He made his fortune in oil, then sold off his company several years ago. Meanwhile, he showed up on that Epsilon Group's list of international members as a policy advisor."

"No more until you eat something. Meanwhile, I'll talk. I called George Trudeau today."

"Really?" Loretta said, corned beef hovering at her mouth.

"Keep eating. You're so skinny I'm envious," I joked. "Yes, he and I are meeting tomorrow after work at the Arlington Library. Apparently he couldn't stay away from libraries after he retired. He's working part-time."

"Sounds like George." She took another bite of the delicious-looking corned beef.

"He came across as a very nice man on the phone. Very gentlemanly in his tone. Hey, I'll trade you a slice of cheddar for a slice of that beef."

"Help yourself." Loretta took a deep drink of her beer. "But getting back to these guys, I started checking what kind of connection there might be with those three cities: Geneva, Milan, and Stuttgart. First off, they're financial centers, so I checked the banks with all five names you gave me. I didn't find much. Montclair was working in Geneva for a period of time, and Holmberg gave a talk at a bank in Stuttgart. I didn't get any hits on Kasikov and the banks. Ryker and Dunston show up only as members of visiting delegations from the U.S. I made a copy of my notes for you." She reached into her purse and handed me some folded sheets of paper.

"Thanks, Loretta. I'm impressed. I think you really found out a lot." I raised my glass of Guinness to her, then enjoyed the rich, dark Stout.

"I told you I love puzzles. And I had that window of time to devote because my staffers were training some new hires, and all I had to do was provide advice. So my workload was greatly reduced for two days." She bit into the cheese and closed her eyes. "Oh, Lord. My cholesterol is climbing already."

"One slice won't hurt you," I tempted.

"You are evil, Molly. And a bad influence." She laughed, then devoured the rest of the cheese.

"I can't help it. It's too hard to be good."

"I'll drink to that."

We both laughed out loud as we raised our glasses in a toast to being bad.

Later that evening

Raymond leaned the side of his face against the cold glass of the car window. He'd had to pull onto the side of the interstate highway, the coughing fit had been so severe. His cell phone started ringing. Raymond swiped his mouth with the bloody handkerchief, smearing phlegm and blood.

If he could just make it home. The bottle of molten gold relief could help him get through it. Dark outside already. He always hated that abrupt change and early nights that autumn brought. The cell phone kept ringing until he snatched it.

Trask's voice sounded. "You'll never guess who Malone is conferring with. Intense conversation."

"I'm too tired to play games, Trask. Who the hell is it?"

"Loretta Wade. She brought Malone some papers too."

"*Shit,*" was all Raymond could say as he eased his car back onto the interstate.

FOURTEEN

Tuesday morning

I WATCHED THE STREAM of coffee pour from the coffeemaker spout into my mug. There were a ton of emails waiting for me, so I would need sustenance and caffeine to slog through them. Mostly caffeine. "So, how'd the surveillance go last night?" I asked Casey when Luisa left the kitchen.

Casey stood beside me, mug in hand. We were like thirsty jungle creatures at the watering hole.

"Pretty well. Danny said the team was able to scan the entire pub between them." He took his turn at the coffeemaker.

"That would take some doing. It was pretty crowded. How do they manage that, anyway?"

"He had a camera in a book on the table aiming one direction, and she had a camera in her purse aimed the opposite direction."

That surprised me. "A woman? Wow. I thought it would be two guys."

Casey filled his mug, then turned with a smile. "Nope. A couple is a helluva lot less noticeable. More normal to see a couple having dinner together. We don't want to set off this guy's antennae. He's obviously skillful or you would have spotted him hanging around you before."

I leaned against the counter and sipped my hot, hot coffee. Meanwhile, some stray memories sprang forward from the back of my mind. "You know, when Loretta and I met for lunch in that little park off Constitution, she made a comment about some guy sitting on a bench across from us. She caught him looking at us. Twice she said. We figured we looked like we were conspiring about something and laughed it off."

Casey's expression changed. He looked at me intently. "Exactly when was this?"

"It was last week. I had called her and asked if we could meet. I wanted to give her Eric Grayson's research notebook so she could get a clue about what he was looking for years ago. And I also gave Loretta a piece of paper with some names I'd seen in Quentin Wilson's notebook."

"You said you met Congresswoman Wilson at the Willard, didn't you? Did you notice anyone particular around you two? Or sitting too close?"

I shook my head. "No, no one was seated close to us. Frankly, most of the people in that lobby looked like relaxing visitors or guests, and some obvious tourists with fanny packs and maps. I didn't see anyone suspicious lurking around."

"Well, ordinary is the best disguise of all. We don't pay attention. Tell me, what do you remember about that guy sitting across from you in the park? Anything at all?"

I closed my eyes and reached for that brief glimpse. "I think he had dark hair ... and a mustache. Yeah. A dark mustache. That's it. He was having lunch and talking on his cell phone."

"Okay, that's something. I'll tell Danny."

I eyed him. "Why not tell Prestige? They're the ones doing the surveillance."

Casey smiled. "Yeah, but Danny is directing them. He's got people going over those Irish pub photos already. They're studying faces, getting a file going. So the next time you go out, they'll have something to compare. Facial recognition software."

"Interesting." I was impressed but didn't want to show it. Why, I wasn't sure. Just my contrary nature, I suppose.

"Do you remember any other time you were meeting with Loretta or Natasha Jorgensen and noticed someone? Anyone at all?"

"Oh, boy. Natasha and I often met to run along the Canal before work. I would just be starting my run, and she would be finishing hers. We passed a lot of people. And I never really paid attention to any of them."

"And you two met regularly to run there?"

"Yes, usually when Danny was out of town, and I already know what you're thinking. The killer was probably running there, too, and learned both her schedule and mine." I stared off into the kitchen.

"There's no way you could have known that. We're dealing with a professional. That much is clear. Never leaves a trace. No fingerprints. Nothing. Probably wears a different disguise every time. Smart."

I changed the subject, before those memories of Natasha's body being carried out from under Key Bridge returned to haunt me. "So, will that couple be there tonight? I'll be meeting George Trudeau, Loretta's former boss at the Congressional Research Service. Five o'clock at the Arlington County Library in Ballston. He retired a few years ago and is working part-time at the library. Peter already said it's okay for me to leave early. Jeremy and I still have to fight our way across Key Bridge in rush hour traffic. Then up Wilson Boulevard. Stop and go."

"Yeah, that couple will be there. Disguised, this time, of course. Target won't even recognize them. They'll be a gray-haired elderly couple." He gave me a wink.

"Two can play the surveillance game," I said and raised my mug to him in salute.

Tuesday afternoon

Larry Fillmore picked up his pace as he walked down Independence Avenue, cell phone to his ear. "I lucked out this morning. Jackson was meeting with some of his biggest donors, and they wanted a little private time with him. I was able to slip away to the Congressional Research Services and run a search." He glanced over his shoulder for oncoming traffic as he crossed over South Capitol Street, heading toward the Rayburn House Office Building. "I had to be careful, though. I didn't want Loretta Wade to spot me in her fiefdom. So I used some of the computers on the upper level."

"Good, what did you find out?" Spencer prodded. "Raymond said Wade handed Malone some papers, so she must have been researching something."

"I'll say. She was looking at people and banks. European banks. One was in Stuttgart, another in Milan, another in Geneva. As far as people, her most recent searches showed she was looking at

Ryker, Dunston, Holmberg, then some others. Anthony Montclair and Dimitry Kasikov."

There was a long silence on the other end of the line. Finally, Larry prompted, "You still there?"

Spencer's voice came, sounding a little different than he'd heard before. Tighter. Something changed in the tone. "Yeah. I'm here. Good job, Larry. I'll … I'll be in touch." He clicked off.

Larry pocketed his phone and sped up the steps of the Rayburn Building. With luck, he'd get back to the office before the congressman.

Tuesday evening

"Could you tell me where to find one of your staffers, George Trudeau?" I asked the older woman seated behind the Information Desk at the Arlington Library.

"Yes, I saw him over in the reference section. Ah, here he comes now." She pointed to the tall, distinguished-looking older gentleman who strode toward me. Silver-haired, he could have been a retired senator or judge.

"Molly?" he asked, extending his hand. "I'm George."

I gave his hand a firm shake. "George, it's nice to meet you. Thank you so much for taking your own time to speak with me."

"I'm happy to. Follow me, and we'll find a cozy corner where we can talk," he said as he turned toward the reference section and headed down an aisle.

I followed behind, scanning the various shelves filled with books on different time periods in history. George led me to a corner where there were two small armchairs angled close together. No one else was seated nearby.

"Here's a good spot. Have a seat." He gestured toward an armchair.

I settled into a chair. I had brought a takeout coffee with me, which was the only thing between me and hunger pangs. "This is good. Quiet and no one is about."

I wondered how on earth the Prestige team would arrange a way to scan all the library patrons. So many were standing or sitting in the aisles, spread out everywhere. Lounging on some of the sofas near the center or entrance to the library. Studying at the tables lining the walls.

"Yes, it is. That's why I suggested this place. Because some of what I'm about to tell you is rather sensitive information. So I wouldn't want anyone overhearing our conversation."

Needless to say, that got my interest and I leaned on the arm of the chair, getting a little closer to George. "Let's start at the beginning. What did Eric Grayson tell you he was researching? And did he ever tell you why?"

George shifted in his chair and leaned a little closer as well. "At first, he simply asked me to search for the organization called the Epsilon Group. He wanted to find out what it was and who were the members and if any politicians were involved with the group. He knew they focused on international monetary issues and wrote papers, but he wanted to know if I could find any connections that group had to European banks or other financial institutions."

"Was Edward Ryker a member of the group?"

"Yes, along with Senator Dunston. They were both adjunct members, whatever that means. We were never able to find any information on the organizational structure of the group."

"What about connections to European banks? Did you find any?"

George nodded. "Indeed I did, after a lot of searching. Years ago the Epsilon Group offered grants and economic aid to developing countries, helping them build infrastructure. Wealthy donors and charitable organizations contributed to the fund. The fund was managed by a Russian, Boris Breloff, who had connections to the group through one of its members, Dimitry Kasikov. A couple of years into the funds operation, however, it was uncovered that Breloff had engaged in money laundering for the Russian mafia." George's voice dropped lower when he said that.

"Uh, oh. Not good. Was the Epsilon Group ever involved in any wrongdoing? Any complicity?"

"Not directly. There was never any connection established between the group's members and Breloff's misuse of the fund's capital. Breloff was supposedly going to be charged with misuse of funds or embezzlement, but the case was dismissed a year later on insufficient grounds. Then Breloff simply disappeared from the scene. It was as if he disappeared into thin air. Needless to say, the Epsilon Group discontinued its developmental fund completely."

I stared at my coffee mug for a minute. "And this is what Eric Grayson was researching for all those months?"

George nodded. "Yes. It took us quite a while to comb through all the research materials. This sort of information requires a great amount of digging. It's a lot of minutiae."

"And none of it proves any wrongdoing by any of the people involved. Except that Russian guy, Breloff. But it looks like he never went to jail either. So I still don't understand why Eric was so determined to take time from his own committee work to dig into something like the Epsilon Group. They still come off looking squeaky clean."

"Not quite. You see, Eric was also digging into the investment activities of one of Congress's most powerful politicians, Edward Ryker. And he found not only a connection between Ryker and the Epsilon Group's development fund, but he also learned that Ryker had taken money from a huge agricultural conglomerate and a mining company. Ostensibly the money was intended as contributions to Epsilon Group's development fund. But we found a letter from an employee who was convinced Ryker was skimming off a healthy percentage of the donation for himself. There's a letter in the files. Unfortunately, the man never formally accused Ryker or brought charges, and he left the company within months."

I stared at George as long-ago memories crossed my mind of my young husband Dave's desperate attempt to expose Ryker's underhanded dealings with a large mining company. But Ryker let loose his hounds of destruction that smeared Dave's reputation and ruined his career. Ryker had once again successfully kept all charges of his corruption out of the public eye. No one dared speak of it, only whispers around the outskirts lest the hounds be set on them. Everyone had seen what had happened to David Grayson.

Those memories must have shown on my face, because George looked at me solicitously. "I can't help but remember your husband David and his fight against Edward Ryker. David was never able to bring any of the rumored bribery witnesses to give statements against Ryker. It was tragic how it ended."

"Yes, it was," I said with a sigh. "And it looks like Ryker's corruption and greed increased over the years. And his tactics have become more sophisticated."

"You're right, Molly. And that's the second level of Eric Grayson's research." George reached inside his suit jacket and withdrew a CD in a plastic case and handed it to me. "Eric never put anything he found involving Ryker in his notebooks where someone could see it. He was very careful that way. He put all of his Ryker research on this CD. And he always gave it to me to keep whenever he left the Library of Congress." George gave a rueful smile. "Poor Eric. He was so careful. And then he died in such a tragic accident." He shook his head. "I've been keeping this CD for all these years. I would have given it to his daughter Karen except I remember Eric saying one of the reasons he was being so careful was he didn't want anything to hurt Karen's blossoming career. Knowing what was on this disc, I decided to just put it away and hoped there would be an opportunity to tell Karen about her father's research, but that time never came." He glanced away.

I sensed George wouldn't have brought the disc with him tonight if he hadn't intended to give it to me. "It sounds like you want me to have it, George. Am I right?"

He smiled. "Yes. It's obvious you're serious about uncovering wrongdoing. So, I think Eric Grayson would approve of my handing over his research to you. I sense you'll make good use of it."

I accepted the plastic case, my curiosity growing. "Thank you, George. I promise I will definitely make sure this information comes to light. Somehow."

"It won't be easy. There was never a case of anyone putting their accusations against Ryker on paper. But there are layers and layers of allegations, from the mining company to the agricultural conglomerate. We also found instances when Ryker steered legislation that benefited the mining company years ago. Rumors of bribes. Eric

151

tried to get something concrete. He even spoke with two different men in Montana who claimed they knew of Ryker's bribes. They'd seen the money. But then, both those men dropped out of sight. Eric never could find them. They may have panicked at the thought of going public with the charges and changed their minds. Or, they may have simply fled the country. Who knows?"

Who knows, indeed, I thought. They may have had their minds changed for them ... permanently.

"So you can understand Eric's caution," George continued. "To be honest I'm relieved to finally be rid of it. I always felt slightly guilty, holding on to it and not doing anything. I feel better now." He gave a small smile.

"I promise you this, George, I will do my best to make sure this information gets out to the public. I don't know how yet. But I'll figure it out."

"I do not doubt that at all, Molly."

———

I leaned my chin on my hand as I stared at the screen of my old desktop computer. My brother-in-law's concise paragraphs detailed every accusation of corruption as well as every instance of Edward Ryker's meetings with the mining and agricultural companies years ago. Ryker's voting history, public comments, even rumors of bribes heard around the Hill. There was more information concerning the huge agricultural conglomerate and their contributions to the Epsilon Group's development fund. Checking my watch, I saw it was nearly midnight. I doubted I could sleep, so I moved Eric's file and opened a document file of my own. I stared at the blinking cursor. Innuendo and rumors, very little in writing, no one willing to talk.

Eric had never been able to prove any wrongdoing. Possible accusers suddenly changed their minds or disappeared. What made me think I could ever put that information to its best use? I had no idea, but somehow I knew I'd find a way.

FIFTEEN

Wednesday morning

I RACED FROM THE limo to the back door of the Russell mansion and shook my umbrella free of raindrops. A surprise morning shower.

"Morning, Molly," Albert said, taking the umbrella as I stepped inside.

"Thanks, Albert. It's chilly out there."

"Coffee's waiting."

"Ah, music to my ears. Have you seen Casey this morning?"

"About an hour ago. He should be back from dropping the senator and Peter any minute now."

"Good Lord, they leave earlier and earlier every morning," I said as we walked down the back hallway.

"Hi, Molly," Luisa said as soon as I entered the kitchen. "We've got a surprise reception this evening. Apparently some Colorado manufacturing group is in town to meet with the senator and government officials. And you know how hospitable the senator is." She laughed as she wiped off invisible fingerprints from the kitchen cabinets.

"I do, indeed, and I also know that where senators and government officials are, lobbyists are right behind. Looks like the senator's entertaining account will go in the red for the month." Coffee poured into my mug. I was going to need it, what with the rain and overdrawn accounts.

"Oh, you'll find a way to balance it." Luisa pooh-poohed my concerns with a dismissive wave of her hand.

I figured that's how most people thought of accountants. We were magicians who magically made numbers behave and budgets balance. All with a wave of our hand … or a click of a computer mouse.

"I hope you're right, Luisa," I said, leaving her to bustle about her kitchen as only she could. Happiness was having caterers to boss around. Meanwhile, I headed to my office, determined not to let the dark-gray skies outside get to me.

———

Raymond poured three fingers' worth of the premier Scotch into the crystal glass on his desk. That, plus four of the over-the-counter pain killers, had kept the pain in his throat manageable. He took a deep drink of the liquid gold and let it slide down his throat, bringing a blessed numbness. Then he pressed Spencer's number on his phone directory.

Spencer picked up after the fourth ring. "Have you heard anything from Trask?"

"Yeah. Just this morning. He wanted to get more information on that librarian guy Malone was meeting." Raymond felt the cough start to rise and stopped it with a big sip from the glass.

"Who's this guy, again?"

"His name's George Trudeau. He was a senior researcher at the Congressional Research Services when Eric Grayson was digging around. That's why it got my attention. We were never able to find any files or notes on Grayson's home computer or in his desk years ago. Grayson must have kept them at his Capitol Hill office. That's why my buzzer went off when Trask said this Trudeau guy handed Malone a CD. They were sitting in a corner of the library, huddled together, talking. So it doesn't sound like they were discussing the weather."

"*Crap*," Spencer said softly. "How'd this happen?"

"I figure the only way Malone could have heard about this Trudeau guy is through the Loretta Wade woman. She's been at the Research Services for years. So she undoubtedly knew this Trudeau before he retired a few years ago."

"*Dammit!* Every time we've got one leak shut down, another one pops up."

Raymond leaned back in his desk chair and sipped the Scotch. No sunlight streamed into his office this morning. It was gray and depressing outside. He let the Scotch soothe his throat. "Yeah, I know. Malone had stopped poking around until she met with Sylvia Wilson."

"Don't remind me," Spencer growled.

"Too bad we can't get into the congresswoman's house. Trask was going to take a look, but he saw that Prestige Systems company installing security."

"*Jesus!* Didn't Trask have that place bugged?"

"Yeah, and they probably found it," Raymond said with a sigh.

Spencer cursed softly for a minute, then exhaled an exasperated sigh. "Now I'm wondering how much Loretta Wade knows. She may have helped this Trudeau when he was digging up stuff."

"Yeah, I had the same thought. Trask has already checked out Wade's neighborhood. She's in a house on Potomac Avenue, across from that Harris Teeter store. Lots of neighbors around those houses, so he'll have to go in as a repairman or something."

"Okay. Get it done. Let's see if she's got a copy of that CD. Or any other files."

"I'll get him on it and let you know what we find. He may be able to get in there today or tomorrow. Wade is gone all day and so's the kid. Basketball practice over at Gonzaga."

"Keep me posted by text. Tonight I'm attending a manufacturers' reception. Would you believe it's over at Senator Russell's house?" He gave a disgusted snort. "Dunston says Russell's turning really inquisitive ever since he took Karpinsky's seat on that committee. The last thing I need tonight is to listen to another politician sound sanctimonious."

Raymond chuckled. "Malone's got her office there, so if you see her tonight, say 'hello' for me."

"Like hell."

Raymond laughed out loud at the irritation in Spencer's voice, even though he knew it would spur the cough. Some things were worth enjoying.

———

Casey stepped inside my office, coffee mug in hand. "Albert said you wanted to see me."

I paused the mouse over the spreadsheet columns of Senator Russell's soon-to-be-overdrawn Entertainment Account. "Yes, I wanted ask you to please contact Prestige Systems and Danny and tell them I obtained some interesting information last night from librarian George Trudeau. I wanted to share it with them."

Casey approached my desk and looked down at me with what I'd come to recognize as his Big Brother expression. Never having had a brother, big or small, I wasn't sure if that was an accurate description, but Casey's expression was a mixture of concern with a touch of scolding. "Wouldn't it be easier if you called Danny yourself?"

Crazy Ass spoke up quietly. "Don't you think it's time?" I hadn't been able to hear that voice through the dense emotion-charged cloud that had been hanging over me. Crazy Ass preaching forgiveness. That was new. Sober and Righteous, however, responded truer to form with a scowling "No." Stubborn as ever, Sober refused to let it go. Despite the conflicting advice, I could feel that dense cloud start to lift.

I concentrated on the spreadsheet again. "Well, I'd like to have Prestige's input, since they're a security company."

"Uh, huh. Okay, Molly. I'll call Danny. *This time.*"

I glanced back at him and watched him shake his head at me before he walked out of the office. Instead of returning to the spreadsheet immediately, I reached for my personal cell phone and clicked on Loretta Wade's number. She picked up quickly.

"Hey, Molly, what's up? Have you met with George yet?"

"Just last night, and you won't believe what he told me. He gave me a CD with all sorts of research he and Eric uncovered years ago. Eric never put any of this stuff in his notebook. He put it on the CD and gave it to George to keep."

"You're kidding? What in the world is on that CD? Did he tell you?"

"Yes, he did. But I went home and looked at all of it. It focuses on one particular politician and goes into detail. I want to tell you what's on it, but not on the phone. Is there any way we could meet tonight? Even for a few minutes after work?"

"Tonight is hard. I'm going straight over to Gonzaga because Bobby is playing in some preseason games. You could come over to the gym if you want. Believe me, we can find privacy there. We'll just move down the bleachers away from everyone. They'll be screaming their lungs out anyway."

"I remember those games. Sounds like as good a place as any. I'll meet you over there. At six or six thirty?"

"Six thirty would be better. Halfway up the bleachers."

"I'll find you. Talk to you then." And I clicked off. Prestige Systems' security couple would have fun tonight with a crowded gym to cover. They might have to bring some backup.

———

I glanced up from the computer screen at the knock on my open office door. There stood Danny, Prestige Systems' Bennett alongside, and Casey behind him. I ignored the feeling inside me when I saw Danny and beckoned them into my office.

"Please come in, gentlemen."

Casey closed the door, and all three approached my desk. I didn't bother to offer them chairs because this really wasn't a social visit.

"Did your security team get some good photos last night?" I asked Bennett. "It was kind of close surroundings in the library. George and I were over in a corner."

"Matter of fact, that worked to our advantage. It's actually easier to conceal surveillance in a library. Almost everyone is sitting or standing around, bent over a book. And it was an entirely different population. That will help us match faces."

Deciding I really couldn't ignore Danny's presence any longer, I glanced up at him. He was watching me with those dark eyes. "How's that facial-recognition software working? Casey told me you were using it."

"We're making progress. With last night's selections sorted, we've made some matchups. We're also looking at military photos of men who've served in the same locations I did. We'll run that database once we've narrowed down the field." He looked at me intently. "Casey said you learned something from that researcher George Trudeau last night? Can you share that with us?"

"I'll do better than that." I opened a file folder on the side of my desk and took out three sets of printed pages. "I made you all a copy of some of the information on that CD. George told me that Eric never put this information in his notebook where someone could find it. He placed it only on the CD and gave the CD to George for safekeeping. I sat up last night and put all of that information in chronological order. Listed everything. Everything he'd learned about the Epsilon Group and possible corruption here in the U.S. and abroad. Money laundering and the people involved years ago. Rumors of bribes, past and present." I handed one to Danny, one to Bennett, and another to Casey.

Danny scanned the first page quickly, then glanced back at me. "Did he say why he gave this to you, Molly?"

"He wants me to follow through on Eric Grayson's wishes and make this information public. Somehow. You'll notice some high-powered politicians are mentioned, as well as lots of rumors. I'm thinking of releasing it to several news agencies—simultaneously—and perhaps some politicians. Together they'll have the resources to investigate thoroughly. It's time to throw the spotlight on Ryker's corruption. Did he take bribes? Was he involved in money laundering? Let the press find out."

Danny scanned the second page, then caught my gaze. "Pretty sensitive stuff. You did good."

"I didn't do anything. George and Eric did all the work."

Danny smiled that crooked smile I was really fond of. "Yeah, you did. You got George to trust you."

"Do you plan to go out this evening, Ms. Malone?" Bennett asked. "I'd like to advise my team. It would be good if you were someplace different. Someplace that would intrigue this guy to follow you."

"As a matter of fact, I'll be at Gonzaga High School for a basketball game tonight at Loretta's invitation. Her son is playing. So if the intrigued watcher is there, your guys are going to have their work cut out for them. High school gyms are big and filled with yelling people who are jumping up and down." I smiled. "Better bring backup."

Bennett and Danny exchanged glances and Bennett said, "We'll be ready." With that, he and Danny started for the door, which Casey had already opened.

Startled at their abrupt departure, part of me wished they would stay longer. Then Danny paused in the doorway and glanced back at me. "Don't worry, Molly. We're gonna find this sonofabitch. I swear." He was gone before I could reply.

Wednesday afternoon

I noticed the message light flashing on my cell phone as I returned to my desk chair. I checked the screen and pressed to listen. Samantha's drawl sounded.

"Molly, I've heard from my mice concerning the name Quentin mentioned in his notebook. They think it's Spencer Graham. He was Ryker's chief of staff years ago during those early days as Ryker started to move up in Congress. After a few years, Spencer Graham became a lobbyist and has some very influential clients. He's quite wealthy now. Also, he may have a connection to that Epsilon Group, because he's often seen with Ambassador Holmberg when he's giving speeches. I hope this helps. Take care."

Her line clicked off, and I leaned back in my chair and sorted through deep memory. I had only faint images of the people surrounding Edward Ryker all those years ago when my husband Dave was fighting for his political life. No images of Ryker's staff came into view. So I turned to my computer and brought the screen to life. Now that I had a first and last name, it was time to consult the online encyclopedia at my fingertips.

I entered Spencer Graham's name into the Google search box and watched as the screen filled with several websites to choose from. I chose Graham's official site and examined the photo that accompanied his consulting firm's website promo. Silver hair, in his sixties, and a salesman's smile. It brought back no memories. He looked like half of the older politicians, hangers-on, and hacks that filled Washington's streets every day.

Wednesday evening

I quickly refilled my coffee mug and escaped from the kitchen. The noise was deafening. Since this was a spur-of-the-moment entertaining event, the senator's Hill staff was unable to schedule our normal caterers, the wonderful team of Marian and Rosemary— organized geniuses in the kitchen, and quiet. Instead, a flamboyant Argentine tyrant showed up with his army of lackeys, bowing and scraping. The maestro—*El Jefe*—ruled supreme. He even banished Luisa from her own kitchen. I'd never seen Luisa mad before, but she stormed upstairs after a fiery exchange *en Español*. Albert had whispered that she was pacing around in their suite on the third floor, talking to a relative in Veracruz. I planned to leave the Russell abode before guests arrived. Albert could fill me in tomorrow.

Casey stood in the doorway of my office when I returned, a package in his hand. "Danny gave me this when he arrived and asked that I give this to you. He says it's the original version of the photos this guy sent you."

I took the package, reluctantly. "I really don't want to see these again, Casey. It's been hard to get those images out of my mind."

"I think you owe it to Danny. After all, the photos you saw weren't the real ones. They were faked, deliberately to shock you and arouse that reaction. Danny found the originals, he said. With the date stamp on them."

"Okay, okay. But can you stay here? That way you can throw them in the fireplace afterwards."

"I'll be glad to."

I opened the clasp on the envelope and slid out the file folder inside. Hesitating for a moment, I opened the folder and saw an 8 x 10 photo of Danny standing with a group of men. But this time the group showed several men in military uniforms. Navy whites. One was an admiral with a lot of braid on his shoulders. On the bottom of this photo was a time stamp. Edward Ryker was nowhere to be seen.

Beneath this photo I found the one showing Ryker standing beside Danny. On this photo, however, someone had used a marker to show exactly where the photo had been doctored. There was no date stamp on the bottom of this photo.

"You can see how it's done, Molly. That guy is good. Good enough to fool most people. But the photo lab guys can spot a fake."

I felt a muscle deep in my chest let go. Something that had been held tight relaxed at last.

"You'll see that's exactly what he did with the rest of those photos," Casey said.

With that encouragement, I turned to the next photo, the awful one with the piles of dead bodies. This time, the photo showed Danny and the other soldiers kneeling behind a pile of rifles, pistols, and various other weapons. I deliberately did not even glance at the fake photo, but slipped it behind the original and turned to the last one. Danny stood holding a string of fish rather than a severed head. So did the rest of the men. I saw the date stamped below, and it coincided with what Danny had told me of his tours of duty. He'd never gone into detail about the missions, and for that, I was glad.

I closed the folder. "You're right. I can see that they were faked. All of them." I paused for a second. "Tell Danny 'thank you.'"

"It would be better coming from you, don't you think?"

I handed him the folder. "I know. Would you burn this, please? I don't want to see it again."

"It'll be my pleasure. But think about what I said, Molly." He looked at me with that brotherly expression again as he left the office.

I did think about it as I settled into my desk chair. Danny deserved to hear it from me. I picked up my personal phone and scrolled through the directory for Danny's number. My finger hovered for a moment, then I pressed the text message. One of the perpetual feuding voices in my head, Crazy Ass, made clucking chicken noises while the other, Sober and Righteous, urged caution. I keyed in a text message. "Thank you for sending the original photos, Danny. It really helps."

My finger hovered over the keys again, but I couldn't think of the right words, so I pressed "Send." Even though it was a cowardly text instead of a phone call, I still felt better. I took a sip of cold coffee and was tempted to get some more, but I really needed to return to these spreadsheets, so clicked on the mouse, bringing them to life on my screen again.

I was just about to enter new expenses when I heard the phone buzz with a text message. It had to be Danny.

I clicked on the phone and read: "I'm glad. I don't want you hurt. Enjoy the game. The Prestige team will be there in force. By the way, Bennett told me they found the same type of listening device in Congresswoman Wilson's townhouse when they were installing security. She told them a 'friend' advised her to check. I'm betting that was you."

I stared at the text. My instincts had been right. Quentin Wilson was being monitored. And whoever was doing it knew his whereabouts. That means they knew Quentin had gone to Samantha's home that night. The night he died.

A myriad of thoughts started bouncing around my head then. *Who were these people or person?* Clearly they were able to gain access to Wilson's townhouse while he was on the Hill. Memories danced in my head—walking into my own home and finding that an intruder had entered and gone through my computer documents and desk drawers. My home was bugged, Quentin Wilson's home was bugged, and Natasha Wilson's phone was bugged. *Who were these people?*

I had no answers, simply more questions bombarding me. Work was waiting. I clicked on the computer mouse and returned to Senator Russell's expense spreadsheets. Only numbers could chase away nagging thoughts. A heavy dose of numbers.

SIXTEEN

Wednesday evening

"Here, help me eat this popcorn," Loretta said as I climbed into the bleacher section where she was seated, halfway up the Gonzaga side of their gym.

"Thanks, I only grabbed a banana, so I'm starving now," I said as I sat. I'd dashed to my home and changed into a sweater and jeans before leaving to meet Loretta.

"Good, because popcorn is one of my weaknesses. Here, take it and save me from myself."

She handed over the half-filled box, and I greedily dug into the crispy popped kernels. "Which one is your son Bobby?"

"Dark blue shirt. Number thirty-three." She pointed toward the group of tall, lanky boys racing down the basketball court. Their white-shirted opponents had the ball and were closing in on Gonzaga's basket fast.

I checked the scoreboard. Gonzaga was not in the lead. Arms and elbows clashed beneath the basket as shots went up and missed, then tried again and were blocked. A Gonzaga guy stole the ball and dribbled like mad down the court toward the opposition basket. The pack was right on his heels, the sound of sneakers squeaking on a polished wood court. Fast stops. I'd forgotten that sound. That's what I loved about basketball. It was nonstop action until a whistle blew, like right now. Foul against Gonzaga. One of the opponents got a free throw. I watched the player go through his own personal routine of preparation for the shot. Bouncing the ball, again and again, then letting it fly. *Swish.*

"*Damn!* That kid is way too good. He's killing us with free throws," Loretta complained, then sipped her cola.

"Hey, Father, say a prayer for us, okay?" a balding man on the bleachers ahead of us called loudly.

I looked over and saw a man in clerical collar and Gonzaga jacket climb the bleachers, carrying a popcorn bag and a cola. "Don't worry, I will," the sandy-haired, bespeckled man replied with a smile as he went past us, climbing higher into the nosebleed seats.

"We could use some prayers," Loretta said, shaking her head.

Another whistle blew and the official called time-out for Gonzaga. I decided this was as good a time as any to update Loretta. Plus, it would get her mind off the game. The other team was ahead by a lot.

"Listen, Loretta, I wanted to tell you what I learned from George the other day." I glanced over both shoulders. "Should we move down a little, just to be careful?"

We both scooted down the bleacher row a few feet, so there was no one close by. I'd noticed that the gym was only half full; obviously preseason games didn't have the same draw for attendance.

"What did George tell you?"

"Basically, the CD has all of my brother-in-law's research into Ryker's corruption. All meticulously detailed by Eric. The disc also has those other names you saw earlier, Dunston, Holmberg, Montclair, and Kasikov. Eric goes on to list allegations of money laundering that even touched the Epsilon Group. Years ago the group had a developing nations investment fund in Europe. It was run by a Russian who had ties to Kasikov. This guy, Breloff, was implicated in a money laundering scandal in Europe. Ryker, Dunston, and Holmberg withdrew their investments in the fund. Breloff was supposed to be indicted, but charges were suddenly dropped. No links to Montclair or Kasikov were ever established, but the Epsilon Group closed its developing nations fund soon afterwards. Montclair and Kasikov were on the governing board. Breloff disappeared from the scene."

Loretta stared at me, her dark eyes wide. "Good Lord, Molly. Do you think that Epsilon Group is actually involved in money laundering?"

"I don't know. There's no proof Montclair or Kasikov knew what was going on. But it raises a lot of suspicions. But the disc also contained all the allegations made against Ryker starting back with that mining company years ago. Eric and George gathered a lot of detailed information. Listing different people who'd talked 'off the record' about their personal knowledge of Ryker taking bribes. They even found a copy of a letter that someone with the mining company wrote years ago, alleging the same."

Loretta looked at me. "What are you going to do, Molly? I can tell you're chewing over something."

"George said he was giving me the disc because I would follow through on Eric Grayson's wishes. I would find a way to make it public knowledge. But I haven't decided exactly how yet. Last night I made a file and copied all the allegations and charges and listed them in chronological order. So it will be easier for people to investigate. My first instinct is to give the information to the press. Distribute it to multiple media outlets anonymously. But Ryker, with all of his cronies and his accumulated wealth, might be able to trace the source of the information back to George and me. And who are we to accuse the most powerful member of the U.S. House of Representatives? Chairman of the House Financial Services committee."

Loretta shook her head. "Molly, I've heard enough stories about that man. You need to be careful."

"That's why I think I may need to give the information to some politicians at the same time. They could find allies in Congress to confront Ryker. He's made many more enemies in all those years since he set out to destroy my husband Dave."

Suddenly a loud buzzer sounded, signaling the end of the game. "Good Lord, the game's over." Loretta looked up, shocked.

A skinny teenaged boy in a Gonzaga uniform came bounding up the bleachers, long legs sprinting over seats. "Hey, Mom, Brian's having the team over at his house for pizza after the varsity plays. Joe said he'd drop me back at home. Okay? Homework's already finished." He flashed her a winning smile as only teenaged sons can when they're trying to wheedle concessions from their moms.

Loretta nodded. "Yes, you can, but you'd better be back before ten thirty. And where are your manners, young man? Say hello to my friend Molly Malone. Molly, this is my youngest, Bobby."

"Hey, Bobby. You guys put up a good fight. But the other guys had some beasts under the basket."

Bobby grinned and gave me a schoolboy nod. "Nice to meet you, Mrs. Malone." He started to turn away, then paused. "Oh, yeah, Mom … Coach cut practice short because of the game, so I went home to grab some new sweats. And this guy was coming out of our house. Some computer guy. Truck said 'Geeks, Inc.' Told me you had problem with the computer and he came to check on it. What's up with that?"

Loretta's eyes popped wide. "What the—? He was coming out of our *house!*"

"Hey, Bobby! Get down here!" A guy in a Gonzaga jacket waved his arm, beckoning Bobby back on the court.

"That's Coach. See you later, Mom." Bobby leaped over the bleachers like a gazelle, heading for the court.

"Who in the hell would be in my house?" Loretta demanded, clearly outraged.

A cold feeling settled in the pit of my stomach. *Oh, my God! This guy was checking Loretta now!*

"Loretta, you're going to have to get a security system installed at your house right away! I never told you this, but someone got into my house last summer and went through my computer files. I could tell because he left the back door partly ajar. Who knows how he got in. I had security put in that very afternoon."

Loretta turned to me, dark eyes wide. "What was he looking for on your computer?"

"I had files on flash drives of Karen's research, and Celeste's too. And someone broke into Celeste's apartment last spring. But he deliberately left signs that he'd been there. He moved things on her desk, opened closets, stuff like that."

"Someone went into Celeste's place?!?" Loretta looked truly shocked.

"That's what really drove her out of D.C. and her job. She told everyone else the office politics were driving her out, but she confided to me the break-in spooked her so she didn't feel safe anymore. She gave me flash drives with her research on them. Now I'm worried that's the same person who broke into your house today."

Loretta stared at me. "Now you're scaring me, Molly."

"That's exactly how I felt when I came back from Senator Russell's one morning and found my computer running, the chair pushed back, and the desk drawers open." I looked into Loretta's eyes. "And I think someone's been following me. If that's true, he's seen the two of us together. He's seen us pass papers to each other. Maybe that's why he broke into your house. He wanted to look at your files."

She looked skeptical. "Just because someone got into your house doesn't mean he'd be following you, Molly. You've been watching too many movies."

"This guy has sent me a package with photos of people. People I know. That told me he was watching. That's when the security company started monitoring me. They were at the Irish pub the other night, and they were at the library when I met with George." I glanced out into the gym, only a third filled with fans. "And they're here now. They're sorting through faces, looking for people who would show up at all three locations."

Loretta stared out into the gym. "Good Lord ... you think someone followed you here?"

"The security firm says they've made some matches already, so they're hoping to narrow it down after tonight. After all, how many people who went to the Irish pub also went to Arlington Library and Gonzaga gym tonight?"

"What are they going to do when they find a match?"

"Danny says they'll catch him. He's convinced."

"Danny's this guy you've been seeing, right? The former Marine?"

"Yeah. And I believe him." I realized I meant it. Now, I had to let Danny know. "Anyway, I feel responsible, Loretta, that this guy has started checking you too. So I want to make sure you've got the same kind of security I've got. This firm will make sure no one gets into your house again who isn't supposed to."

Loretta frowned. "I don't know, Molly. Maybe Bobby was mistaken. Maybe this guy was just trying the doorknob or knocking on the door. Maybe he wasn't really inside."

"Whatever. I'll feel better if someone comes with us to check your house. And I know exactly who." I slipped my phone from my purse and found Casey's number in the directory. "Casey Moore is the security guard for Senator Russell. Former military with lots of experience. Plus he knows what happened at my house. He can take a walk through your house with us, just to be safe."

"*What!*" Loretta screwed up her face. "I don't want some strange man going through my house!"

"He's not going through your house, he'll just be there to make sure that ..." I wasn't sure how to put it.

"What's he going to do? Check to make sure there's no one hiding under the bed?" Loretta looked aghast. "Molly, I have to tell you, I think your imagination has totally gotten hold of your good sense."

I admitted it did sound outrageous. Casey's voice came over the phone then. "Hey, Molly, what's up? How's the basketball game?"

"Gonzaga's not doing so well. Listen, Casey, can you get away from Senator Russell's for about an hour? I'd like you to meet Loretta Wade and me at her house. Her son saw a guy coming out of the house this afternoon when he came home from school. The guy told him Loretta called with computer problems. Of course, Loretta says—"

"No such thing! I didn't tell anybody to go to my house!" Loretta enunciated close to the phone.

"Is that her?" Casey asked.

"Yes. So, given what happened at my house, you can understand why I'm concerned. My antennae are going off, Casey, and you know what that means."

"Yeah, Molly. I've learned to pay attention to your antennae. Let me check with Peter. Everybody's still drinking and talking with the senator and will be for hours it looks like. I probably could slip away for a little while. I gather she'd like me to go through the house with her."

"Yeah, I think Loretta needs someone to check out the house, and—"

"Loretta does *not!*" she said sharply.

"Okaaaaay. Sounds like she's not really buying that, but I agree with you. It wouldn't hurt to have a look around."

"Good. I'm also trying to convince her she needs security installed."

"Good idea. What's her address?"

"Loretta, what's your address?" I asked her.

Loretta frowned, obviously debating whether she wanted to reveal that information or not. Finally she recited it and I repeated the Potomac Avenue location to Casey.

"Okay, I'll leave in a few minutes if it's okay with Peter. See you there."

"We'll wait outside. Is that okay, Loretta?"

She rolled her eyes. "Tell him to park at the Harris Teeter across the street. We'll meet him inside the store."

"I heard that. See you soon." I recognized the amused sound in Casey's voice.

———

I took another sip from the Styrofoam cup of coffee as Loretta and I hung out in the café-like area near the front of Harris Teeter grocery store. I was perched on a chair stool at one of the tall, round tables. Loretta, on the other hand, was pacing back and forth in front of the windows looking out onto Potomac Avenue. At nine thirty at night, there weren't any others seated around us. Only the cashiers looked at us strangely. And the uniformed security guard, who was stationed near the front door. He glanced at us from time to time. He'd recognized Loretta when we first entered, so she told him we were waiting for someone. We'd been waiting for five minutes and Loretta had paced the entire time.

"Senator Russell is entertaining at home tonight so I'm sure that's why Casey is delayed," I said, glancing toward the door again.

"Hmmmph!" was Loretta's reply. She'd "hmmmphed" several times already.

Just then, I saw Casey push open one of the glass doors and hold it open for an elderly woman to enter ahead of him. "There he is," I said, trying not to sound relieved as Casey glanced our way.

"That's him?" Loretta asked looking toward the door. "Hmmmph."

She stood, hands on hips, as Casey walked our way. I stood up, too, just in case. I could sense from the tilt of Loretta's chin and her tone of voice that she was going to make sure Casey knew she was none too pleased with the situation.

"Hey, Molly," Casey greeted me with a smile, then looked at Loretta. "You're Molly's friend, Loretta Wade, I take it? I'm Casey Moore, security for Senator John Russell." He extended his hand.

Loretta glanced at his hand, then back to Casey's face. She'd already given him the once-over as he'd approached. Loretta pursed her mouth for a second, then gave Casey's hand a quick shake. "I'm not going to say I'm pleased to meet you, Mr. Moore, because I'm not. I'm not the slightest bit happy with the idea of having two strange men traipse through my house today."

"I totally understand, Ms. Wade. I'm sure—"

"Don't *Ms* me. I don't like it. It's Mrs. Wade or it's Loretta." Chin even higher.

"As you wish, Mrs. Wade, I'm sure you felt that your privacy was invaded—"

"You're damn right!" she flashed. "Who is this cretin anyway? Prowling around respectable people's houses."

"Molly's security firm, Prestige Systems, is working on uncovering this man's identity. And I agree with Molly that you need to have your house secured—"

"I do not want to have a whole team of men prowling around my house, attaching wires or what-have-you everywhere!"

I let Casey try to explain the procedure to the highly annoyed Loretta while I simply stood and watched this tennis match in progress. I must have looked like those spectators at Wimbledon, nothing moving except their eyes, as the ball flew from one side of the net to the other.

"I understand, ma'am—"

"Don't you *ma'am* me!" Loretta snapped, clearly indignant. "You're the same age I am."

To Casey's credit, he never flinched; he simply listened to Loretta's indignant replies, recalibrated, and ventured forth again with another point in the security argument.

I decided I wasn't watching a tennis game at all. Hell, this was a fencing match. Thrust, parry. Point. *Fascinating.*

"I promise to respect your privacy, Mrs. Wade. Molly and I simply want to make sure your home is safe. Is your house nearby?"

"It's right across the street. How long will this take?" she challenged. "My son will be home from having pizza with the team by ten thirty and I don't want him to see you here. I don't want him worried."

Casey held up both hands. "Twenty minutes, no more."

"Well, then, let's get it over and done with," she ordered as she grabbed her purse and headed for the front doors.

Casey and I followed dutifully behind. I kept my mouth shut and deliberately did not try to catch Casey's gaze. However, the older security guard—who'd been watching this exchange with great interest—spoke up as we approached the door.

"Good to see you, Casey," he said with a bright smile.

Casey glanced his way and broke into a grin. "Hey, Sam, I didn't see you there. How's it going?" He grabbed Sam's hand for a hearty shake.

"Just fine. Thanks again for that reference."

"Glad to do it."

"You helping out Miz Wade?" Sam nodded toward Loretta, who was standing in the open doorway watching this exchange.

"Trying to, Sam. Take it easy now."

I followed Loretta through the open door, Casey right behind.

"How do you know Sam?" Loretta interrogated while she quickly walked across the wide Harris Teeter sidewalk.

"He and I served together in the Marines. Sam was in one of my platoons in Desert Storm."

Loretta paused on the curb as a truck passed by on Potomac Avenue. "My husband Gabe was in the Marines. He died in Somalia."

"I'm sorry."

Loretta sped across Potomac Avenue toward the row of townhouses that lined the other side of the street. Several houses were still alight since it was not yet ten o'clock at night. However, Loretta headed for the gate of one that was completely dark.

Casey stepped up and opened the chain-link gate to the front yard and walkway. "Do you always leave all the lights out when you leave?" Casey asked.

"No, I don't. But then I usually arrive before dark," Loretta said as she pulled keys from her purse and sped up the steps, quick as a rabbit. Casey and I hopped up the steps in her wake.

The front porch was wide and had a wrought iron and cushioned-chair set and table. The two-story brick was the same vintage as the other townhouses along that stretch of the street—1920s or 1930s. Maybe older. Prime properties in the eyes of real estate developers and investors.

Loretta unlocked the glass-paneled front door, reached inside, and snapped on the lights. A polished walnut hallway stretched beside the staircase leading upstairs. High ceilings all around. Loretta tossed her purse onto a nearby foyer table and hurried into the living room. A desktop computer sat atop an old-fashioned mahogany desk in a corner.

Casey and I both walked into the living room. Casey glanced all around while I admired the obviously original house molding in the cornices and surrounding the fireplace. Probably early 1900s, I guessed. Highly sought after.

"Loretta, how have you and your neighbors kept these houses? Real estate investors must be knocking on your doors."

"It hasn't been easy. One landlord owns most of these houses. I own mine." She bent over the computer and moved the mouse. The desktop monitor brightened immediately, revealing a screen half-filled with icons. "*Damnation!*" She jerked her hand away from the mouse as if it were hot. "He's been in my *computer!* I never leave the monitor on!"

"Do you think your son might have left it on?" Casey asked as he approached the desk.

"Bobby never uses the desktop. He only uses his laptop. And he uses it down here where I can keep an eye on what he's doing." She made a face. "That cretin *was* in my house!"

"Would you like me to check the rest of your house, Mrs. Wade? Just to make sure nothing else is disturbed."

"Yes! Who knows where that … that freak prowled around! *Disgusting!*"

I pulled my phone from my purse. "You two go on and check the house. I'm going to call Danny and ask him to contact Prestige Systems right now. Maybe they can come out tomorrow and get your house secured."

"Good idea, Molly. Lead the way, Mrs. Wade." Casey gestured toward the hallway.

"It's Loretta. We'll start in the kitchen." She stalked away, Casey in her wake.

I pressed Danny's name on the phone directory. He answered on the third ring. "What's up? Prestige escort said he let you and Loretta Wade out at the Harris Teeter grocery store. Then Casey showed up and all three of you went across the street into Mrs. Wade's home. Casey already updated me on the intruder situation. Did he actually enter her house?"

"Looks like it. Loretta checked her computer and it's still running. I'll bet the bastard did that on purpose just to let her know someone was there. Loretta did not take it well. Casey's walking through the house with her now to make sure nothing else was disturbed. Do you think Prestige Systems could come out tomorrow to install security here? Loretta's really freaked out."

"I'll check with them right away. Considering who we're dealing with, they'll probably move Loretta to the top of their list."

"Are you guys getting any closer to identifying this cretin, as Loretta calls him?"

"Yeah, as a matter of fact. After the basketball game tonight, they were able to separate out some faces that showed similarities to ones who showed at the pub and the library. Appearances are all different, though. Clothes, hair color, stuff like that. This guy obviously uses disguises. But it's harder to conceal facial shape. Beards can disguise to a point, but not completely."

"It sounds like you're really making progress. What happens when you finally find out who he is?"

"Then it'll be a cat-and-mouse game. We'll have to draw him out into the open somehow."

Loretta and Casey came down the stairs. "I'm going to get those antiseptic wipes and clean every inch of that computer. In fact, I'm going to wipe down everything in here," Loretta said before heading for the kitchen.

"Casey's here, did you want to talk to him?"

"Yeah. Listen, Molly, once we narrow these faces down to three or four, I'd like to show them to you. See if you recognize anyone. Would you mind if I came by tomorrow night after you're home? It won't take more than a few minutes."

"Sure. No problem. Here's Casey." I'd wanted to say more but didn't know what exactly. I couldn't think fast enough. As Casey approached, I handed over the phone. "It's Danny," I said and stepped back while Casey and Danny discussed plans on what to do next.

I already knew what I had to do. I had to stop the cretin and his associates. And there was only one way to do it. As soon as I got home, I was going to copy the files I'd compiled of Eric and George's information onto multiple discs, and tomorrow I'd get it out to people who would throw the white-hot glare of publicity onto every past activity Edward Ryker and his cohorts engaged in. Expose every nook and cranny where they thought they could hide their secrets. No more.

"Is that security guard still in there with them?" Raymond asked as he stretched out on his living room sofa. The television was turned low, the local weatherman was running through the weekly forecast. Sunshine for several days.

"Yeah, the lights went on upstairs so I figured the security guard took a walk-through with Wade," Trask said. "Checking if anything's out of place."

"Is it?"

"Nope. I was only at her computer. Nothing's there. Her son came home early, but I'd already checked all her files. No research files, just family records. And no storage drives in the desk drawers. Kid must have told his mom I was there, because I watched Wade get agitated while she and Malone were sitting at the game. That's when Malone got on her phone."

Raymond took a sip from the crystal glass he held close to his chest. The Scotch had finally soothed tonight's coughing spasm. "What do you want to bet Prestige Systems shows up at Wade's house tomorrow?"

"Oh, yeah. I don't doubt it."

"Considering how much business Prestige has gotten because of us, we ought to get a commission."

Trask laughed low in his throat. "Don't count on it."

"Well, you can leave the Wade woman alone from now on. Whatever she knew, she must have written it up at her office and passed it to Malone. We'll never get it."

"I agree. But that Trudeau guy knows a lot. I can tell. He gave Malone a disc filled with information, and we need to see what's on it."

Raymond hesitated. He had a bad feeling about another hit so close to Natasha Jorgensen's. "I don't know, Trask."

"It would be easy. He works late twice a week. I could wait for him in the parking lot. It's pretty dark out there."

"Yeah, and it's in Ballston. Lots of singles living in those condos, and they go out at night, walking around. And that library isn't far away from the main streets. Luck hasn't been with us the last few times, Trask. Look at today. Wade's son just happened to come home and see you coming out of his house. You were lucky to talk your way out of that."

"Yeah ... but Trudeau is one of those loose ends that you always talk about. Dangling out there."

Raymond snorted and felt the cough start to tickle. *Damn.* "He's just gonna have to dangle. We've got several out there. Nothing we can do about it now."

Trask didn't answer, so Raymond took a deep drink of golden heat. That could soothe the cough, but it couldn't chase away the bad feeling in the pit of his stomach.

SEVENTEEN

Thursday morning

Escort Jeremy held the car door open as I exited the limo. I looked at him and smiled. "I'm not sure how long I'll be, but I imagine you'll be waiting when I come out."

"You're right, ma'am." He glanced at the three-story white brick townhouse where we'd parked in front. On R Street, near Reservoir Road, it was only a few blocks from my house and Senator Russell's home. "Are you sure Congresswoman Wilson is at home?"

"Yes, indeed. I talked to her only moments ago," I said as I turned toward the brick steps leading to the walkway above.

Since it was only ten minutes after seven o'clock in the morning, the gray skies and lower temperatures brought a hint of autumn's chill to come. Now that it was November and no longer Daylight Saving Time, the days would shorten even faster as the season hastened toward Thanksgiving. Winter was hovering out there, waiting to strike when we least expected.

I hurried up the steps to the front stoop and rang the doorbell. A matronly woman answered the door so quickly, I figured she'd been watching for my arrival.

"Molly Malone, here to see Congresswoman Wilson. She's expecting me," I said as I stepped inside the foyer. The rich tones of maple woods warmed the entryway.

"Yes, she's waiting for you in the parlor." The woman gestured toward the room on the right off the hallway.

The parlor reminded me of Eleanor MacKenzie's in décor and tasteful furnishings. Mahogany and luscious red velvet upholstery. Sylvia rose from behind an antique secretary desk and walked over to greet me. Once again I envied her wardrobe budget.

"It's good to see you again, Molly. No matter the time," she said with a wry smile. "I must confess I was surprised by your early call this morning."

"I'm sorry to come so early, but I thought it was the best time for us to be uninterrupted."

"Well, it certainly sounds interesting." She gestured to the nearby sofa. "We'd better make ourselves comfortable. Would you like coffee?"

"No, thanks, I've already had two cups." I settled on the luxurious sofa and opened the portfolio on my lap. Sylvia settled at the other end of the sofa. Her gorgeous and expensive Italian heels caught my eye. Too rich for my salary.

"I wanted to thank you again, Molly, for your recommendation of Prestige Systems security company. I was most impressed with their work. And I'm very grateful you suggested it. When they discovered that listening device, I confess … my blood ran cold." She caught my eye.

"I felt exactly the same way, Congresswoman."

"Sylvia, please."

I smiled and pulled out a slender folder from the portfolio. "Well, Sylvia, I believe I've finally found the way for us to even the score with the people who invaded our privacy. I believe I know who is behind it. He's extremely powerful and has many resources at his command, many people to do his bidding, so the only way to combat him is by exposing his past history of shady dealings to the glare of publicity. Lots of publicity." I held up the folder. "My brother-in-law, former Congressman Eric Grayson, dug into this man's past and found one instance of corruption after another. Unfortunately, Eric died in a car accident before he could make the information public years ago. But he left the information on a computer disc, which I recently discovered. And I have written up all the information so that news media outlets and anyone else who's interested can delve into this congressman's sordid past. Expose him to the glare of daylight at last."

Sylvia Wilson sat wide-eyed during my entire dramatic recitation. "Is this congressman still in the House?"

"Indeed, he is. And he's probably the most powerful member. Congressman Edward Ryker."

I watched Sylvia's response as her eyes widened even more and her cheek paled slightly. "Molly, what on earth have you found?"

"I'll let you judge for yourself." I handed over the file folder. "After I leave here, I'll arrange special deliveries of the exact same file to five of the largest global news media outlets. Maximum exposure so there will be no place to hide."

Sylvia Wilson took the folder and held it gingerly. "And what do you expect me to do with it? I'm a first-time congresswoman, filling in the remainder of my husband's term. Appointed by the governor, not even elected." She looked at me expectantly.

I caught her anxious gaze. "I believe you'll find a way, Sylvia. Once the news media start asking questions and raising issues from the past, others will come forward. Ryker has made even more enemies in Congress since he set out to destroy my husband years ago. They'll sense vulnerability now and move in. But I thought it fitting that you should strike an early blow. I believe Edward Ryker is responsible for your husband's death."

Shock flashed through Sylvia Wilson's eyes then. "Wh-what? But how? *Why?*"

I chose my words carefully, knowing I was walking a very fine line. "I've learned that Congressman Wilson overheard Ryker talking to EU Ambassador Holmberg about a bill in his committee controlling transfers of funds to European banks. That's why your husband Quentin was researching those international banking issues. Unfortunately Ryker must have learned of your husband's eavesdropping. Thus, the listening device found in your wall. I believe your husband's accidental suicide was deliberate murder. Made to look like suicide."

Sylvia's shocked gaze narrowed. "Molly, do you realize what you're saying?"

"Yes, I do. And I realize it's pure speculation. There's absolutely no proof. But my instinct says Quentin Wilson was eliminated just like my niece Karen, her staffer friend Celeste, and Natasha Jorgensen. All of them had been investigating Edward Ryker and the Epsilon Group, all within the last seven months while this banking bill was moving through committee."

Sylvia glanced down at the folder in her lap. "I have to admit, I've been thinking about all those deaths ever since you mentioned them last month."

"Too many coincidences."

"Still ... there's no proof."

"In the file you'll find other instances of Ryker's past corruption. Allegations of bribery from several different sources. None were ever brought forward successfully then. But now, I sense there will be more people willing to dig deeper into those past incidents. And if the press gets their teeth into it, they'll definitely bring all that dirt to light." I gave her a crooked smile. "You know how to deal with the press, Congresswoman. I've seen you on TV. Use whatever you find in that file you can without putting yourself at risk. Then, let the hounds of the press go to work. They have very sharp teeth, and they'll make a meal of Edward Ryker. And they'll love every minute of it."

A slow smile teased across Sylvia's face. "You are a woman after my own heart, Molly. I just have one question. How did you learn that Quentin overheard Ryker talking with Ambassador Holmberg?"

I deliberately glanced out into the beautifully decorated parlor. "I learned it from a highly reliable but confidential source. So, I'm not at liberty to say." I looked back at Sylvia Wilson and saw the light of recognition spark in her eyes.

"I understand. Well, Molly, I can promise you that I'll do my best. Not being on those subcommittees or committee does make it harder to approach. But I promise I will try."

"I have no doubt of that, Sylvia. And if I may suggest, Congresswoman Sally Chertoff is on that committee. I have met her several times and she has spoken of doubts about that legislation. So you could find a valuable and experienced ally in her."

"Thank you, Molly. I appreciate that suggestion."

"You're smart and tenacious, Sylvia. Those are qualities that will help you succeed in Washington. As the widow of a congressman who was trying to expose corruption, you have more reason than most to speak out." I gave her a wicked grin. "Besides, bringing down the powerful is an old, established tradition in Washington. The press will love you for it."

Sylvia Wilson simply laughed.

A little later

"You ready for another surprise?" Trask's voice came over the phone.

Raymond closed his eyes and leaned his head back on the desk chair. "God, no. But tell me anyway."

"The security guy didn't drive Malone to Senator Russell's first thing this morning as usual. Instead she went over to Sylvia Wilson's house a little after seven. Wilson was there, and Malone was inside with her for over half an hour."

"*Aw, crap,*" Raymond said softly.

"Yeah, I didn't expect that. What do you think she's up to?"

"Probably sharing whatever is on that disc."

"Too bad we didn't find out about Trudeau sooner."

"No way we could. Looks like Loretta Wade is the only one who knew about him. By the time you saw Malone meet him, it was already too late. The moment Trudeau gave that disc to Malone, there was nothing we could do. If she starts leaking what's on there, Spencer will have to deal with it. It's out of our hands." Raymond took a sip of hot coffee. Soothing. "I wonder why she'd spend so much time with Sylvia Wilson. She's low woman on the totem pole on the Hill. No power."

"Well, Malone's full of surprises. She also didn't go right to Russell's house after she left Wilson. Driver stopped at an express delivery service on Wisconsin Avenue. She went inside with a briefcase."

Raymond felt his gut clench this time. "*Damn, damn, damn...*" he muttered.

"Yeah, I know. I figure she's sending out that info."

"Not good. No telling where she's sending that stuff. Those guys are not gonna be happy."

"I'll stay on Malone."

"Hell, yes. No telling what she'll do next. By the way, they killed the video feed," Raymond said, taking another soothing sip. "Prestige driver aimed at it this morning and zapped it. When I came in, there was only static. I ran back the video and saw him do it."

"I'm surprised they didn't find it before."

"What makes you think they didn't?" Raymond challenged. "I'd better call Spencer. Be careful surveilling her, Trask."

"I'm always careful. Hell, I even used a bike this morning. Backpack and Redskins jacket. Just another commuter."

"Well, take my advice and stay low. I'll let you know what Spencer says."

"Roger that."

Later morning

I stepped from my office into the hallway. "Peter, do you have a minute?"

Clearly lost in thought as he hurried down the hallway toward the front door, Peter quickly glanced my way and broke into a smile. "I've got a few. Casey's waiting for me outside to take me back to the Hill. What's up?"

I beckoned him inside my office and picked up two separate portfolio folders from my desk. "I know how pressed you and the senator are for time, but I wanted to give you these folders. Same information. One for each of you. The information inside is extremely sensitive and explosive."

Peter took both packages and peered at me. "What sort of information is this, Molly? Where did you get this?"

"It's my brother-in-law's research on Congressman Edward Ryker as well as others in powerful positions. Eric found multiple instances of Ryker's corruption and raised many questions about other peoples' involvement. I discovered his CD days ago and learned he planned to make the information public, but his early death prevented it. I'm simply carrying out his wishes."

Looking at the packages in his hands, Peter frowned slightly. "Edward Ryker, huh? Well, I've been on the Hill long enough to hear the rumors. Eric actually found proof? I always heard Ryker was able to silence any potential accusers. No one ever would go on the record."

"Eric actually obtained statements from two different mining company owners saying Ryker had demanded bribes in order to obtain government contracts. When they refused, their companies were each eliminated from consideration."

Peter shook his head. "That was a long time ago, Molly. And it's still only their word against Ryker's. If they're even willing to confront him now. I understand your feelings about Ryker, especially after your husband's death, but ..."

"I know what you're saying, Peter. It's all accusations. Allegations. But Eric has listed scores of them. He's even found information about Ryker's connections to international financial institutions. There are suspicious ties to money laundering and foreign banks. Senator Dunston is mentioned, as is former EU Minister Ambassador Holmberg, as well as other highly placed individuals in international finance, even the Epsilon Group."

That caught Peter's attention immediately, as I knew it would. "Are you serious?"

"Quite serious. You and the senator will see when you go over the file. Definitely keep it private. I wanted Senator Russell to have this before it's made public."

Peter stared at me. "Good Lord, Molly, are you planning to go to the press with this?"

"Special packages are being delivered today to five major international news outlets. Once the media sees all those allegations piled on top of each other, rumors and speculations, the press won't be able to resist. They'll dive in with investigators and start digging. They'll bring out the dirt for all to see." I gave him a crooked smile. "Ryker's made a lot of enemies over the years. Once they smell blood in the water, they'll come out with a vengeance."

Peter gave me a knowing smile. "Take no prisoners, right, Molly?"

"Never. All I've ever wanted for Ryker is exposure. For the public to see who and what he really is. Corrupt, venal, and dishonorable. He doesn't deserve to be in public office."

"I'll make sure the senator and I take time to go over all this to-night. There're no functions planned and no meetings." He looked at me with concern. "You're aware the media will descend on you once they receive the packages. I'd better alert Casey to prepare for reporters on the doorstep."

"Don't worry, my name isn't on it. The sender is a mythical Washington Media Corp. The address is real. But it's an Episcopal church on G Street. Almost across from the Washington Press Club. I figured any reporters who showed up there could use some prayer-ful reflection."

Peter's eyes lit up as he laughed. "You're even more diabolical than I imagined. The senator will get a laugh out of that. We won't squeal on you. Have you shared this information with anyone else?"

"Only the researchers who helped prepare it. And believe me, they treasure their privacy. I did give Sylvia Wilson a copy. Her hus-band Quentin was investigating Ryker on his own before his unfor-tunate death last summer. I figured if anyone in Congress could start asking questions about Ryker's past, who better than the widow of an idealistic congressman fighting corruption."

Peter looked at me, clearly surprised. "You amaze me, Molly. However do you find out so much of what's happening in Con-gress without setting foot on the Hill?"

I had to laugh. "Sometimes you need to get away from the fog to see clearly. And I have very good sources."

"I'm impressed." He wagged his head with a wry smile. "The Widow Wilson. Who would have thought?"

"We've seen her in action already. I think she can handle it. She'll have plenty of help from the press."

"I promise the senator and I will give this our full attention tonight." He turned toward the doorway to leave.

"By the way, Peter. Were you aware that Senator Dunston has a son who works for a bank in Stuttgart?"

Peter spun around. "*What?* Where'd you hear that?"

I pointed to the folders. "It's in there. If I'm not mistaken, there was recent legislation in the senator's subcommittee that dealt with transfers of U.S. funds to European banks."

Peter nodded. "Thanks for the heads up. I think I'd better start reading this in the car."

"Happy to help, Peter," I said as he hurried from my office. Meanwhile, I settled in my desk chair, took a deep drink of coffee, and returned to the daily email onslaught.

Late morning

"*Jesus, Mary, and Joseph . . .*" Spencer's voice came over the phone. Soft enough to sound like an actual prayer.

"Yeah, I'd say we'd better start praying to all three," Raymond joked. "No telling where that information is going to turn up."

Spencer was quiet for a long moment. "This is not going to be received well."

"I figured that. How did Montclair react when you told him about Loretta Wade? You know, all those searches Fillmore discovered she was doing."

Another long pause. "I didn't tell him."

Uh, oh. Raymond heard the hesitation in Spencer's voice. Not a good sign.

"I . . . I let the committee think we stopped Malone's snooping with Jorgensen's death. They calmed down after that."

"Okay…" Raymond could tell Spencer was afraid of telling Montclair. He could hear it in his voice. Normally loquacious, Spencer was now quiet. "Are you going to tell them about Malone? Or just wait and see what happens?"

"God knows…"

Raymond picked up on the hint of panic behind the fear in Spencer's voice. He felt a warning jab inside. *His instinct.* Not having anything else to give Spencer, he said, "Who knows? Maybe we'll get lucky and whoever gets that information will just sit on it."

Spencer gave a disbelieving snort but said nothing.

Raymond didn't believe it either. But he didn't have anything else. Their luck had clearly run out.

Thursday evening

The doorbell rang, and I hastened to my front door, opening it to see Danny standing there, illuminated in the bright security lights. "Hi, Molly. I wanted to bring these photos over so you could take a look at them."

Seeing him standing in the doorway now, smiling, reminded me how much I'd missed him. Seeing him. Being with him. The feeling had never left, actually. I'd just been able to push it away. I realized I no longer wanted to push it away. Or him.

"Sure. Come on in."

"I promise it'll only take a few moments. I've heard how busy you've been lately." He looked at me with that familiar amused expression as he walked inside. "Jeremy said you took several packages for special delivery."

"Prestige is doing a good job of keeping track of me, I see." I gestured toward the living room sofa.

"I'm guessing you sent out that research on Ryker and others." Danny sat on the edge of the sofa, as if he expected to jump up and leave any second.

"Good guess," I smiled at him. "First, I took out all references to Karen's or Celeste's notes and wrote up only Eric Grayson's research, focusing on the scores of allegations against Ryker and others. Bribery, connections to money launderers. Then, I printed it out and sent copies to five global news outlets. Let them dig up the dirt on Ryker. That way the press can bring him down."

He caught my eye. "Good job, Molly. Let's hope it works."

"It better. Ryker and his cohorts are behind all of this. That guy breaking into houses, following me around, spying on Loretta. It's got to stop."

"We're going to stop it. I promise. Ryker's only part of it, though. Those connections go farther than you think."

I eyed Danny carefully. "You and Prestige have figured that out?"

He grinned. "Not all by ourselves. I've shared the information you gave me with some of my military associates. I figured you wanted me to. That's why you gave me the file."

"You figured right. I want to shine as much light on them as we can. Drive the rats out of the corners."

"Oh, yeah. We'll also drive out the rat who's spying on you."

Danny opened the file folder he'd brought with him. Inside I saw several photos. He spread different photos on the coffee table. Three different men. Or, it looked like three different men. One had shaggy blond, longish hair, mustache, and wore a brown sweater. The next was an older man with fuzzy gray hair and black-rimmed glasses, he looked kind of old, judging from the lines on his face. The third had touseled black hair and a mustache. I stared at the photos.

"Do any of these men look familiar, even slightly?"

I examined the shaggy professor, the old man, and then stared at the dark, mustached guy. "I think this one looks like the guy who was on a park bench across from Loretta and me about two weeks ago. We met for lunch so I could give her Eric's notebook and the notes I got from Sylvia Wilson. Loretta said she caught him looking at us twice. I only noticed him checking his phone."

Danny pointed to the shaggy-haired man. "This guy was at the Irish pub. And this guy was at the library." He pointed to the gray-haired man. "Jeremy also spotted a cycle or a bike several cars behind him every day. The guy was usually wearing a helmet and had different clothes. But he was able to spot him remove the helmet once. And this is the guy." He pointed to the dark-haired man.

I stared at the three photos. "I wish I could bring back more memories. But I didn't even pay attention to the people at the pub. Loretta and I had so much to talk about. Same thing when I was at the library with George. Darnit. I wish I'd looked around more."

"How about at the Gonzaga game," Danny said and placed another photo on the table. This one showed a man with blond hair, wide face, and spectacles—and wearing a black clerical collar. As well as a Gonzaga jacket.

I stared at the photo. "The priest! Yes! I remember seeing him at the game. He walked right past Loretta and me, going up the bleachers. Some guy shouted out to say a prayer and he said he would." I looked at Danny, incredulous. "A priest? That can't be right."

Danny gave a wry smile. "It's a damn good disguise. Most people don't even notice the face. The clerical collar stops them. It's like staring at a nun in full habit. You don't want to stare, so you glance away."

"So you're saying all four of these photos are the same man?"

He nodded. "Facial recognition software shows the same facial structure and features; even with a mustache, the program can tell. The priest's face is the most exposed. I have a feeling this guy doesn't think anyone is checking on him. Yet."

"You think you'll be able to identify this guy?"

"Oh, yeah. We're getting really close. In fact, he resembles someone I knew. Just a hunch." He slipped the photos back into the folder and stood up suddenly. "Thanks, Molly. You've confirmed what we've found. Now, keep an eye out for those faces you've seen so far." With that, Danny walked toward the door.

I was surprised by his abrupt move and followed him to the door. Now that he was here, I realized I didn't want him to leave. "What … what will you do when you find out who he is? Confront him or something?"

Danny turned toward me and smiled. "Oh, yeah. I definitely plan to confront the son of a bitch. Depend on it."

"Good. I want to be there when you do."

"I'll see what I can arrange," he grinned. Then he looked away. "I'd better go."

I reached out and grabbed his jacket. "Not so fast," I said, looking into his eyes as I yanked him toward me. Danny tossed the folder aside and reached for me.

We grabbed each other. Our mouths hungry. Clothes disappeared, tossed, torn, dropped—in the living room, up the stairs. We reached the bedroom just barely. And there we stayed. Skin against skin, devouring each other, satiating ourselves until morning.

EIGHTEEN

Friday morning

I WALKED INTO MY upstairs bedroom and saw Danny, still damp from the shower, towel draped around his hips, standing at the window and staring into the breaking dawn. "C'mon out, you little shit, so I can get a good look at you."

"You think he's outside already?" I handed one full coffee mug to Danny as I sipped from the other.

"You left early yesterday, so he may assume you'll do it again today. We killed the video feed, so the only way for him to keep track of where you're going is to show up." Danny took a drink. "Thanks. This may be breakfast. I can let Prestige know I'm taking you to Russell's. Do you want to stop at a café on the way?"

"No, I want to get there early. I have a feeling Peter and the senator will want to talk to me this morning before they leave for the Hill. I gave Peter a folder with all the information on Ryker, Dunston, Holmberg, and the Epsilon Group. The money laundering connection with that Russian guy years ago. Ryker's bribery charges, everything. The senator's subcommittee handled the international banking legislation recently, so it really got Peter's attention." I pulled off my tee shirt and began dressing.

"Hey, hold on. I've missed this," Danny said with a grin. He leaned back against the bed pillows and watched as he sipped his coffee.

"Are you going to try to leave before he appears? After all, he thinks he broke us up." I caught the last bra hook, then slipped on the lacy panties from Samantha's favorite lingerie shop.

"Naw. I want him to see my car and figure I was here overnight. Then he can watch us leave together. If this guy is who I remember, that will piss him off. And that's what I want." He took another sip while I pulled on pantyhose.

"Is that what you're doing? Trying to goad him into showing himself?" I walked over to the closet.

"Yeah, if I can. But he may not bite. I've been thinking, once we get his face isolated, we may need you to go someplace where there are less people around. Someplace where he'll stick out more if he shows up."

I zipped up my skirt and slipped on a short-sleeved sweater. "Well, I'm game. Whatever it takes to catch this guy. Put him away ... or whatever."

"It'll be more *whatever*, if I get my way." Danny's smile disappeared.

I slipped on my heels, then picked up the coffee, taking a sip as I walked closer to the bed. "Oh, by the way, I was wondering," I said with a wicked grin. "Did the makeup sex live up to your expectations?"

Danny laughed so hard, he spilled coffee all over the bed and himself.

———

"My, you're early this morning, Molly," Luisa said as I stepped inside the Russell mansion foyer. "You must have a sixth sense. Peter said he and the senator wanted to chat with you in the library as soon as you arrived."

"You're right—that sixth sense has kept me out of trouble over the years. Let me drop my purse and briefcase and I'll—"

"I'll do it. Coffee is already in the library. Now, you go in and see the senator and Peter." She made a shooing motion with one hand as she relieved me of my things with the other.

"Yes, ma'am," I said and hastened down the hallway, pausing to knock on the half-open library door.

"Come in, Molly," Senator Russell's basso voice rang out. It always sounded deeper in the mornings.

"Good morning, Senator, Peter," I smiled at both men as I entered. "I thought you two might want to chat this morning. So I came early."

"Perceptive as ever, Molly," Senator Russell said with a smile as he leaned back in one of the armchairs near the desk. "Make yourself comfortable."

I hastened to the tray with the white porcelain coffeepot and saucers. "Ah, Luisa's nectar. Oooooo, and are those cinnamon rolls?" My mouth started to water. "Heavenly."

Peter sat behind his desk, cinnamon roll in hand. "Take one of these—Luisa baked them fresh this morning."

"If you insist." I snitched a smaller roll from the plate on the corner of his desk, then settled into a matching armchair near the senator. He wore one of the dark-gray suits that set off his silver hair perfectly.

"If it weren't for the cinnamon rolls, I'd say this would be a perfect photo to send to the Colorado constituents. Hard-working senator and staff—not quite nose to the grindstone, more like stuffing our faces." I took another bite.

"Molly, I wanted to thank you for sharing your brother-in-law's research with Peter and me," the senator said, leaning forward, both hands clasped between his knees. "Your assessment of the information as potentially explosive and sensitive is indeed astute."

"I started going over the folder in the car and Albert had to force me out when we reached the Hill." Peter's intense blue gaze focused on me. "You were right when you said 'allegations.' But the money laundering connections between the Epsilon Group members and those European financiers are really troubling to say the least."

I took a deep drink of the dark brew. "I thought so too. That's why I wanted you to know of it, Senator. Even though there was never anything that showed the Epsilon Group members were involved in that Russian guy's money laundering schemes, simply shining the light of public scrutiny on those past activities should stop any potential threat now. If there was any group out there who hoped to divert U.S. funds transfers for illegal purposes, they'll abandon those plans. Once the press starts digging, they're bound to uncover these past activities, and all of this should come out. At least I hope it will."

"It's already started, Molly," Senator Russell said. "Phone calls started late last night. One of the networks had a breaking news story on the ten o'clock news. I'm surprised you didn't see it."

Danny and I were already in bed by ten o'clock and not watching television. I tried to hold back the smile as I remembered last night. I honestly answered, "Oh, I was already in bed. I missed it."

"Well, you'll have plenty of time to catch up today." Peter gave a small smile. "The other networks are starting to run with it. The *Post* had a story on the inside pages, but I'll bet it will be splashed all over the front page tomorrow."

"Good. I have to admit I will enjoy watching Ryker squirm. Ambassador Holmberg will probably leave the country. And the rest of those financiers will go to ground, quickly." I sipped Luisa's rich coffee. "Nothing like the bright light of publicity to drive rats out of dark places."

Senator Russell laughed softly. "I never knew you were a muckraker at heart."

I shrugged. "I suppose we've all got a little of it inside. Corrupt politicians have always roused my ire. I guess I inherited that from my father." I took another bite of the sweet, cinnamon pastry. Buttery goodness.

"Well, I promise I shall keep this information confidential, but the press has already started asking questions. Some of the more senior members of the Senate committee have gotten calls."

"You'll be called too," I reminded him with a smile. "But I'm not worried about you, Senator. You're not involved."

Peter glanced at his watch. "We'd better be leaving, Senator. This is going to be a long day. Molly's right. The press is bound to start asking questions about Dunston now that the rumors are bouncing everywhere."

I finished the rest of my coffee and stood as the senator and Peter gathered briefcases and papers. "Well, Senator, I promise I will be glued to the television tonight and see what the press has brought forward. Frankly, they've moved on this even faster than I thought." I walked toward the library door.

"That's because it's potentially such a juicy scandal," Peter joked as he and the senator followed. "I'd leave the television on. You don't want to miss anything."

Senator Russell paused in the hallway and put his hand on my shoulder. "That was good work, Molly. Bringing all this to light. Your brother-in-law would be proud. As well as your father."

That made me feel really good, which surprised me. "Well, it isn't my work, Senator. It's Eric Grayson's. He deserves the credit."

"Ah, but you put it together, my dear. And you knew what to do with it. Not everyone is smart enough to do that. Don't be modest."

"You're very kind, Senator. Now, I leave that information in your capable hands because you have the instincts to know when and how to use it. If at all." I gave him a sly smile.

Senator Russell laughed and wagged his head. Peter gave me a wink as he followed Russell out the front door.

Friday mid-morning

I had just gotten a coffee refill and barely sat down in the desk chair when my personal cell phone burst into life. Springsteen's "Dancing in the Dark." I had to scramble to find my purse, then dig out the phone, so Bruce and the E Street Band had a full minute of my attention. A beat so strong, you could follow it home.

Samantha's Southern drawl broke through the beat. "Molly? Have you seen the news? Cameramen and reporters have been chasing Ryker through the halls of the Capitol. They've cornered him several times already. He's sweating buckets. *My Lord!* If his face gets any redder he's going to have a heart attack right on camera!"

"Oh, my," was all I said, then sipped my coffee.

Samantha's contralto laugh sounded. "Molly, this has your fingerprints all over it. You have got to tell me what you've been up to. I know you gathered all that information, girl. Now, you owe me the details. I'm canceling lunch plans, and I will bring a gourmet lunch over to the Russell ranch. We have to talk. I want *intel!*"

Now, it was my turn to laugh so hard, I spilled my coffee. "Okay, okay. I'll see you at lunch. We'll go sit in the garden and I promise I'll give you all the details. For your ears only. It will be the biggest mouse dropping you've ever seen."

Samantha was still laughing as she clicked off her phone.

———

"Now we know what she did with the info," Trask said as he leaned back into a café chair. It was sunny outside, but November's morning chill chased the outdoor brunch crowd inside the cozy French café. The sound of traffic along M Street was muted.

"Oh, yeah," Raymond's voice came over the phone. "Gotta hand it to her. She hit them where it would hurt the most. Nothing gets their attention like publicity. Lots of it."

Trask tasted the fresh-squeezed orange juice the waitress set before him. Along with a plate of fresh croissants. "All major news outlets at once. Those guys are probably frothing at the mouth. What did Spencer say?"

"I haven't talked to him. It's still early in today's news cycle. The press has probably camped out around Ryker's home. This melodrama is just starting. We're gonna watch it play out. Now you know why they had you eliminate Eric Grayson years ago. They had to keep that information under wraps."

"Well, they bought themselves more than ten years. No one else has raised questions since."

"By the way, what's Malone been up to? Any early morning visits?"

"Nope. She already had a visitor. DiMateo must have wormed his way back into her good graces. His car was already in the driveway when I got there, and he drove her to Russell's. No escort."

Raymond chuckled. "My condolences, Trask. That must have been a disappointment. But, you know... women are fickle."

"Yeah, yeah. I'll keep an eye on her. Who knows what other surprises she's got planned. More politicians. More press."

"Keep track of her. Let me know if she contacts anyone else. Meanwhile, stay low."

"Don't worry. I always do."

Friday noon

I smeared a spoonful of duck pâté on a super-thin cracker and savored. Luscious and deadly. I didn't even want to know the fat calories. Off the scale, no doubt. Ducks were fat, anyway. I remembered watching the caterers spooning off rendered duck fat from their roasted creations.

"Oh, this is divine," I said to Samantha before I took another sinfully rich bite.

"Isn't it, though." Samantha polished off her last bite of pâté and chased it with a fat green olive. "I thought we deserved to celebrate. Thanks to you, Molly, one of the biggest bastards in Congress is finally going to be exposed. *Hallelujah!*"

I grinned. "Amen, to that. But it's Eric Grayson's doing, not mine. And I know I can trust you to keep my role in this totally private."

"No one will ever hear it from my lips, girl." Samantha leaned back against the bench in the shaded gazebo at the edge of the Russell gardens.

All the fall plantings had been mulched and pruned and were ready for winter. Boxwood hedges were neatly trimmed and had fresh pine bark layered around. So did the other perennials. I wasn't ready. I was never ready for winter or cold weather. Colorado's low humidity made winter much easier, especially with all the sunshine. But I was back east now, the damp, humid east, where the cold penetrated and winter lingered. *Brrrrrr.*

"Let's hope the press doesn't let up on him. Ryker has always been able to slip away from scandal before." I held up crossed fingers.

"Don't worry. The press is more vicious now. They've drawn blood already. People have started to talk. All those skeletons will come out of the closet." She poured more of the sauvignon blanc into the wineglasses she'd brought along.

"A gourmet picnic basket. I love it." I lifted my glass. "To us. And to fighting the good fight."

Samantha raised hers as well. "May we keep it up. Bloodied but unbowed." She sipped, then gave me a smile. "I still can't believe you gave that info to Sylvia Wilson."

"I thought it only fair, considering it was Quentin's notes that provided clues to help Loretta unravel the puzzle." I took another fruity sip. "Without Loretta's digging into Eric's and Quentin's information, we wouldn't have discovered anything. And Loretta led me to the retired researcher Eric used years ago. He'd been keeping Eric's detailed research information on a disc all these years. That was a gold mine."

"What do you think Sylvia Wilson will do? Will she jump into all of this?"

"I'm hoping she will. She's a pit bull. We've seen that already. And she's hungry enough to want to make a name for herself."

"True enough."

"I told her as the widow of an idealistic young congressman who wanted to expose corruption, she had more reason than most to raise questions about abuses of power. So, let's see what she does."

Samantha stared into her wineglass. "Talk about politics making strange bedfellows. I trust my name never came up."

"No. I promised you that. She did ask how I knew that Quentin had overheard Ryker and Holmberg talking."

Samantha closed her eyes. "I knew it."

"I told her my source was completely reliable but confidential, and I wasn't at liberty to reveal it. Sylvia smiled just a little and said she understood."

"You're kidding!" Samantha looked shocked.

"No, I'm serious. I think it's over. The Widow Wilson has seen what happens when she's on the bad side of the press, and I don't think she's going there again. Besides, I gave her the chance to curry favor with the press. Far better to help bring down the powerful." I grinned.

Suddenly I heard Luisa's voice calling my name. I leaned out of the gazebo. "Hey, Luisa! Is there a call for me?"

"No, no. It's that congresswoman on TV." She beckoned from the garden steps. "You're going to want to see this!"

Samantha and I looked at each other. *Congresswoman.* We bolted from the gazebo and into the mansion. Luisa beckoned to us from the kitchen as we sped down the hallway, laughing as we ran.

"She's talking now. See!" Luisa pointed toward the television screen located on the kitchen counter.

Sure enough, there was newly appointed Congresswoman Sylvia Wilson, in a drop-dead gorgeous crimson-red suit, hair and makeup perfect, looking straight into the camera.

"Naturally, I was curious what my late husband's notes meant when I found them. I could not understand why he would research topics like international banking regulations. His committee assignments had nothing to do with financial matters. But after watching recent news broadcasts, I realized I had to speak out. You see, my husband Quentin had also written the names of Congressman Ryker and Senator Dunston in his notebook."

She held up Quentin Wilson's spiral notebook, and the press erupted in a raucous chorus of shouted questions and demands. Cameras pushed forward, zeroing in on the now-notorious notebook.

"You go, girl," I said, laughing softly.

Samantha wagged her head slowly as she smiled. "I'll be damned. Quentin must be laughing his ass off, wherever he is."

Shouts of "Congresswoman!" "What did he know?" "Did he tell you?" clogged the air.

"Quentin never mentioned this subject to me before he died. But I have the feeling my husband overheard a conversation or accidentally learned something that was not intended for him. And these notes were his attempt to reveal it. Quentin was an honorable man and spent his entire career as a district attorney fighting corruption. Unfortunately, he died before he could bring this information to light."

This time the press shouts were deafening. Shouts of "Was his death an accident? *Congresswoman!* Did someone kill your husband to shut him up!"

I stared at the chaotic televised eruption. "Whoa . . ."

"Good God," Samantha breathed.

Luisa stared at the television, clearly shocked. Then crossed herself.

A young man stepped in front of the congresswoman and waved his arms. "No more, please! Congresswoman Wilson has a meeting. She has nothing else to say at this time."

He took Sylvia Wilson by the arm while others I figured were staffers surrounded her as he escorted her out of camera range and away from the baying hounds.

Samantha and I simply looked at each other solemnly for a minute. Finally, my dearest friend spoke. "It looks like she took your advice, Molly. Talk about bringing down the powerful."

"Brilliant. Simply brilliant," I said, letting admiration fill my voice. It was even better than I'd hoped.

Friday afternoon

My cell phone flashed beside my elbow and I clicked on before the music started. Danny's name. "Hey, there. Thanks to Samantha, I've been catching up on the news coverage. Watching Ryker try to fight his way through those gangs of reporters everywhere he goes just makes my day. Of course, Sylvia Wilson's performance was the *pièce de résistance*. Masterful."

Danny laughed. "I figured you'd enjoy all of it. Ryker's trying to stonewall reporters now, but that won't work. Listen, we've finally made a definitive match with the software. And it *is* the guy I remember from years ago. He hated my guts because I got him thrown out of the Corps. I caught him stealing money from another Marine's gear, and I brought him up on charges. He was out. Dishonorable discharge. He hated me, that's for sure. And he's the kind that would try to get even."

"Really? After all this time?"

"Some guys never let go of a grudge. We traced him through every system, and he got hired on as a mercenary for some guerrilla outlaw group in South America not long after his discharge. He even worked for gun runners in Africa. So he's gotten his hands dirty in different places. Plus, he's made enemies along the way. Some real bad guys. Then, he dropped off the radar screen entirely. We figure that's when he started working for whatever group Ryker's connected to. Believe me, Trask is not the brains behind something like this. He's a hired gun, that's all. There're others who are calling the shots. We've just got to find out who."

"Is that his name, Trask?"

"Yeah. We were thinking we might try to flush him out and get a really good look at him tonight, if you're comfortable with going someplace this evening alone."

"As long as it's not a dark alley. This guy sounds dangerous. Before I just thought he was a sleazy stalker."

"No dark alleys. We thought the National Gallery around seven thirty tonight. You'd let Jeremy take you home, then after he leaves you can slip out the front door and walk toward Wisconsin. Let it look like you're trying to give Prestige the slip. You'll take a cab to the gallery. We'll already be in position, staking out all the entrances and exits. You won't be alone, for sure, but there will be less tourists this time of year on a late weeknight. Gallery closes at nine."

"What do I do there, wander around?"

"You'll go straight to the café downstairs, get some coffee, sit at a table, then wait. Bring a magazine to read. Keep looking around like you're expecting someone. Check your watch every few minutes. Wait till they're announcing the gallery is closing, then go upstairs and leave. There will be practically no one there by then. So when you leave, we can hopefully catch him leaving afterwards. He'll be convinced you were waiting for someone who didn't show."

I felt a slight feeling of unease in the pit of my stomach, but I ignored it. We needed to catch this guy. "Okay. I'm in. The National Gallery, it is."

NINETEEN

Friday evening

THE TAXI DRIVER PULLED to the curb on Constitution Avenue, right in front of the National Gallery. I glanced out the window at the impressive marble façade above. Dark now at seven thirty, but the building was beautifully lit, shining in the night.

"Keep the change," I said, handing the driver a twenty dollar bill as I opened the door.

"Thank you," he called out in accented English as I slammed the taxi door and resisted the urge to look around for my constant shadow. Instead, I hurried up the long flight of steps leading to the brass doors above.

I had visited the gallery twice since I'd returned last spring. Once with family and another time with Samantha for a concert. Danny and I had been in the Sculpture Garden and all the surrounding areas and neighboring walkways during the spring and summer. But I'd been too busy to indulge in a leisurely browse like I loved to do.

Now we had ourselves and our belongings scanned upon entry. Sign of the changed times. I took the information booklet from a kindly museum docent who reminded me that the gallery closed at nine tonight. I was counting on it.

I'd said I would go directly downstairs and pretend to wait, but I couldn't resist visiting one of my favorite spots. I skipped up the greenish marble steps that curved around the landing leading to the upper floor, which held my favorite exhibits, and headed straight for the fountain in the center beneath the gorgeous domed ceiling. I stood for a moment watching Mercury, still balanced gracefully, water splashing down, and remembered. Remembered all the field trips, all the family trips, all the trips with my daughters young, and daughters older—all stopping for a moment at this pleasant restful spot.

I checked my watch and did a speedy walk-through of the gallery wing, which held my favorite paintings and peeked at some of the old masters. Old friends. Clearly I would have to return when I had more time. Right now, I was on assignment. Assignment: sit and wait. I headed for the marble staircase again and returned to the first floor, then went to the staircase that led to the lower level. If my shadow was following, at least he'd get a workout.

Following the winding hallway toward the bookstore, gift shop, and café, I deliberately paused at the bookstore and browsed. I made a point to look up and glance around, then check my watch. Nearly eight o'clock. I'd noticed the gift shop and bookstore had a fair amount of people in them still. I chose one of the Gallery's beautiful booklets on French Impressionists. Hoping that peaceful scenes of Paris and ballerinas and cafés would be calming, I felt my heart racing already and I was only browsing. I must not be cut out for this work.

As I paid for the booklet, I checked my watch again and glanced around. I saw students, older people, younger ones, business suits, casual gear, but no dark-mustached guy. I also didn't see any shaggy blonds, no older gray-haired men, and no priests.

I used the coffee machines in the only open area of the café and sat down at a table along the edge. People walked by on the way to the entrance to the Hirshhorn Museum. The artistic wall of water was directly across from me, providing a soothing sound of water falling and splashing on rocks. Artistic rocks, of course. I glanced around again, over both shoulders, checked my watch, 8:15. I opened the booklet and proceeded to wait; I stared at the beautiful paintings on the pages. Paintings that should have given me pleasure. This time, I barely saw them. I concentrated on studying every line, then reading every word of the description.

I checked my watch, 8:30, then glanced around. There were definitely fewer people here now. A tall man in an overcoat with graying red hair and a thin face. Couldn't be the same man. Elderly woman with a National Gallery shopping bag. A young woman with a briefcase. Two tourists with Asian features who were holding maps and guidebooks. A guy with a leather jacket and "Hells Angels" emblazoned on the back.

Puzzled, I returned to the booklet and memorized a Degas. Then a Toulouse Lautrec. I checked my watch: 8:43. I glanced around. The two students were still there. So was the Hells Angel guy, talking to the girl behind the cash register. The elderly woman had a pile of books in her arm, still browsing. The tall man had left.

Just then a voice sounded overhead, announcing the gallery would be closing in fifteen minutes. "Please finish up all purchases and leave. Tomorrow's opening hours are ..."

I glanced around again and saw the Hells Angel guy finishing up his purchase, the elderly woman right behind him. The two students were hurrying down the hallway.

Assignment completed. My orders were to leave now, and I was more than ready. I grabbed my purse, tossed the empty paper cup into a nearby trash can, returned the book to the shelves, then headed for the hallway and the stairs. Hells Angels guy was checking out more books and Granny was at the register.

I resisted the urge to race down the hallway and made myself walk at a leisurely pace, listening to the sound of my high heels echoing in the empty hall. The sound bounced back from the marble at me as I walked alone. I rounded a corner and headed for the lower staircase leading to the first floor above, my footsteps echoing after me.

The sound of a person's whistle floated farther behind me as I started up the long flight of stairs. A tuneful whistle, quite good, actually. Whistling a familiar tune. I continued to climb as the whistling followed me. What was that melody?

Suddenly I recognized the tune, and the words came to my mind. "In Dublin's fair city, where the girls are so pretty, there lived a fair maid named Molly Malone ..."

I froze there on the steps. I couldn't move. I couldn't breathe. All I could do was listen to the whistle as it sounded behind me. Coming closer. The familiar words were the only thing in my head.

"She wheels her wheelbarrow through streets broad and narrow, singing 'Cockles and mussels ...'"

Run!

The command came from deep inside me. I raced up the stairs as fast as I could. The whistle still echoing behind me. Reaching the landing, I sped for the front door, ignoring the docent's "Come again." I shoved open the first brass door I came to and raced outside. I gulped in a huge breath of chilly, damp air and flew down the long flight of steps leading to the sidewalk below, praying I wouldn't trip and break my neck.

I hesitated briefly at the edge of the sidewalk, then sprinted into Constitution Avenue, arm outstretched, frantically waving down a taxi. Blessedly, one pulled up in front of me. I jumped inside. *Anywhere. Anywhere but here.*

———

Trask pushed open the brass door and peered at the traffic-filled street below. Malone was frantically waving down a taxi. He smiled, just a little. *Run, little rabbit. Run.*

Then he stepped behind one of the massive columns, slipped off a curly gray wig and woman's raincoat, and stuffed them inside the Redskins jacket he was wearing beneath. Leaving the National Gallery shopping bag behind the pillar, he walked down the long flight of steps to Constitution Avenue.

———

I fumbled at my cell phone, trying to bring up the directory. Then the phone rang in my hand. Danny.

"Molly? What's the matter? You ran out of there like you were shot out of a cannon. Was he there? Did he approach you?"

"He was there. But I didn't see him. I … I heard him."

"*What?*"

"I kept looking around, but I didn't see anybody that looked like those guys. Then it was time to go, and I started walking up the steps. The gallery was almost empty. And then I heard him ... somewhere behind me ... whistling. He was following me ... whistling 'Molly Malone.'"

"Son of a bitch," Danny muttered.

I closed my eyes, feeling the fear of those moments return. "I've never been so scared in all my life, Danny. I just panicked, and I ran out of there as fast as I could."

"You did exactly right, Molly. You got the hell out of there and away from that sick sonofabitch. But we got a photo of him. It's Trask, all right. We were watching everybody who left the gallery and spotted an older woman come out carrying a shopping bag. But instead of walking down the steps, she went behind one of the columns outside. A few seconds later, Trask stepped from behind the column and walked down the steps. And we got a clear shot of his face."

I stared out the window of the cab, watching traffic flow past on Constitution Avenue. "The old woman! That was *him*?"

"He's clever, I'll give him that. But we've nailed him. Now we just have to flush him out. Listen, where are you now? Where's the cab?"

"Uhhhhh, looks like we're on Constitution just passing Sixteenth Street."

"Have the cabbie drop you at the Willard. I don't want you going home alone without me. I'll meet you there as soon as I can get my car. Stay in the lobby around a lot of people. Or go to the bar. I'll be right there."

"Hurry up."

"I'm already gone."

Later that evening

Raymond stood beside the expanse of window in Spencer's office and stared into the darkened streets below. Nighttime traffic flowed along Pennsylvania Avenue, lights illuminating buildings on either side. Traffic lights—red, yellow, and green—headlights, and flashing orange signal lights brightened the night like early holiday decorations. Blinking, twinkling, all along the avenue to the very brilliantly lit white ornament at the top of the tree—the U.S. Capitol. Shining alabaster white.

He took a deep sip from the crystal glass. Spencer's Premium Scotch. Once more, the golden heat coated his throat. It was the only thing that could. "Funny. I never get tired of this view," he said to Spencer, who stood beside him.

"Yeah, I know what you mean." Spencer swirled the Scotch in his glass.

"You've had this office for, let's see ... nearly twenty years, right? When I came, you were in another smaller place on Sixteenth. Damn, that's been twenty-five years."

"Yeah. Long time ago. Ryker was just starting his third term in Congress." He took a deep drink.

Raymond couldn't miss the edge in Spencer's voice. Those old memories weren't so fond anymore. He turned to face his friend and colleague. "How's Ryker taking it? Being forced out, I mean."

"Not good. But he's got no choice, and he knows it. He has to resign the chair of the House Financial Services Committee if he wants Montclair and the group's protection, get help in fighting any bribery or other charges that come up."

"It's gonna be hard for him to give up that power. What if he refuses and tries to hang on?"

Spencer turned away from the view, and a hint of anger flashed across his face. "Then he'll do it alone. He'll get nothing and neither will his family. The press will tear him to pieces, no matter what. He's finished in Congress, anyway. There's nothing left for him to hang onto. He just doesn't know it yet."

Raymond watched another emotion flash across his old colleague's face. *Fear.* He'd heard it in Spencer's voice on the phone. Now he saw it on his face. "What are you going to do now? Take a vacation?"

Spencer stared into his glass. "Yeah, Montclair thinks I need to get out of D.C. for a while. He's inviting me to his place in the Bahamas. Take it easy for a few months, lie in the sun, relax. Then he'll try to find a spot for me in one of his consulting firms in London." He glanced back at Raymond.

Raymond could see the panic banked in Spencer's eyes, and felt his own warning bell go off inside. He could read the writing on the wall. "Well, it sounds like he didn't go ballistic. That's good. I was afraid he would when he found out Malone was the one behind the leaks."

"Yeah. I was surprised too." He abruptly turned and walked over to the liquor cabinet across the room. "Let me refill that for you. Listen, Raymond, I'll call you once I get settled in there. And make sure you call me if you need anything."

Raymond glanced around the office, the luxurious furnishings, so familiar after all these years. "Will do. And thanks again for the Scotch. It's the only thing that eases the cough."

Spencer reached over and poured until Raymond's glass was half full. Then he looked at Raymond, genuine concern in his eyes. "You need to get that cough taken care of. We won't be needing those higher-level services for a while. So this would be a good time for you to go to one of those medical resorts or something. See a doctor. Hell, get a massage or something."

Raymond laughed softly, then took a deep drink of the best medicine he knew. "Yeah, I've been thinking I might do that," he lied. "Relax, sit in the sun, like you said. Winter's coming here. It'll be rain and snow and gray for months."

Spencer settled into the leather sofa and glanced around his office. "You're right. Winter's coming. It'll be good for us both to get away. I'll let you know once I settle into a place in the Bahamas. You might want to come out and bask in the Caribbean sun." He caught Raymond's eye. "You're going to clear out your office, right? Computers, files, everything."

Sinking into the loveseat across from him, Raymond felt his insides sigh as he relaxed into the leather. "Don't worry. It'll be swept clean. I'll let you know when it's done. I'll call Trask on the way back to Virginia. We'll start tomorrow."

Spencer glanced at his watch. "Damn, it's past ten o'clock. I'm sorry to call you here so late. Why don't you stay at the Willard tonight. I keep a suite there for visiting clients."

Surprised and a little touched by his colleague's considerate gesture, Raymond smiled. "That's nice of you, Spencer. I appreciate it."

"It's nothing. I'll call them and authorize everything. They'll bring you anything you need. If you want a steak tonight, just ask for it."

Raymond started to laugh, until that cough began to rise in his throat. "I'll think about it. As long as there's some of this Scotch, I'll be fine."

Spencer grinned, one of his old familiar grins. "There's a whole case of it there, Raymond. My private cache. Oh, and if you want any adult company, I can arrange for that too."

This time, Raymond started laughing and didn't even try to stop. *Damn the cough.* A few years ago, he'd have taken Spencer up on his offer. Right now, however, an evening's entertainment might kill him.

———

"Keep the change," Raymond said as he handed the cabbie a large bill, then climbed out of the taxi.

"Good evening, sir," the Willard bell captain greeted as he sped down the steps to meet him. "Will you be staying with us tonight?"

"Yes, I will. No luggage," Raymond said as he slowly walked up the carpeted steps to the Willard's old-fashioned grand entrance.

The bell captain quickly sped around him and was up the steps and already holding open the polished brass door. *Might as well enjoy all this,* Raymond thought. It would be easier to get an early start on clearing out his office tomorrow.

Remembering that he hadn't yet called Trask, Raymond reached inside his suit jacket for his cell phone as he walked through the door into the Willard's large foyer, which opened in several directions. He stopped and was about to scroll through his cell phone's directory for Trask's number when he glimpsed not one, but two familiar faces. Very familiar faces.

Molly Malone and Daniel DiMateo. They were walking out of the Willard bar and heading toward the front doors. Raymond couldn't help but stare.

Well, I'll be damned. What are they doing here? Wonder if Trask's around?

Raymond poised his finger over the cell phone again, pretending to be busy, while he watched Malone and DiMateo from the corner of this eye. They actually stopped not that far from him. Malone smiled up at DiMateo, and he gave her a quick kiss before they walked outside.

Raymond watched them through the glass as they stood at the bottom of the steps. *They made a nice couple.* An attendant brought DiMateo's car around and Raymond watched them drive off.

He pushed Trask's number and listened to it ring a couple of times before he answered. For all he knew, Trask was outside somewhere.

"Hey, I called earlier, but it went to voice mail."

"Yeah, I was with Spencer. Listen, we're gonna have to break down the office tomorrow. Spencer wants it cleared out completely. They're folding their tents. They sure won't be needing our services. So we need to get those computer hard drives out and destroyed. Bring a truck with you tomorrow. We'll need it. I'm going to get there by eight."

"Okay, will do. I kind of figured they'd go to ground, what with old man Ryker getting hammered. Those reporters have dug up stuff from thirty years ago. He's gonna be in court for years. Hope

224

he has a good lawyer. The committee will probably help him with that."

"Yeah, as long as he does what he's told and resigns. That's what Spencer's doing too. He's heading out of Washington, out of the country." *That's what he hopes.* Raymond had a bad feeling. "And we're gonna have to get out of here too. After we clean everything, so there's no trace."

"Copy that."

"Hey, did Malone go anywhere tonight? Did you follow her?"

"Yeah, as a matter of fact. Escort dropped her home, but she left right after that, walked to Wisconsin, then took a cab to the National Gallery. I figured she was going to meet someone. She waited down in the café over an hour, looking all around, but whoever it was didn't show, so she left. She ran off to get a cab before I could follow her. Probably went home."

"Nope. I just saw her leave the Willard bar with DiMateo, so they must have met. Who knows? Maybe he was supposed to meet her at the gallery. Funny you weren't following her. You're usually right on her tail."

"Well, she kind of ran out of there real fast. So I just let her run."

Raymond picked up on the slightly amused sound in Trask's voice. "That's not like you, Trask. What happened? Don't tell me you made contact."

Trask laughed softly. "Not exactly. The gallery was closing, so it was empty, and sound really echoes in those marble halls. I couldn't resist. She was on the stairs just ahead and couldn't see me. So I started whistling that little Irish tune. You know, the one about the lass that wheels her wheelbarrow through Dublin."

"Molly Malone. *Damnit, Trask!* You broke cover just to taunt her? You know better than that!"

"Relax. She never saw me. But she heard me, all right. She started running up those steps fast. By the time I got outside, she was already flagging down a taxi."

"Congratulations, Trask. You just succeeded in scaring an unarmed woman in an empty building at night. What's next, frightening little children in the street?" Raymond didn't bother to hide his sarcasm.

Trask just laughed.

"Well, Malone didn't stay scared for long. In fact she and DiMateo looked pretty happy when I saw them a few minutes ago."

"For now."

Raymond didn't like the sound of that. "Leave 'em alone, Trask. This is over. We've finished this job. Nobody has any reason to look for us. Unless you give them one."

"Don't worry about it, Raymond."

Trask's voice had that smug sound Raymond had been hearing lately. Clearly, Trask wasn't taking advice. "Whatever. Make sure you get a good-sized pickup truck for tomorrow, okay? We'll need it. See you at the office." Raymond clicked off before Trask could reply.

TWENTY

Saturday morning

LARRY FILLMORE PULLED HIS cell phone from his pocket and stared at the name. He quickly stepped away from the sidewalk bordering the National Mall as a group of tourists approached, tour guide in front. November did not bring a slowdown in tourists visiting from all over the world. Washington, D.C. was a twelve-month, 365-days-a-year tourist destination.

"Hey, Spencer. It's good to hear from you. I'd left a few messages. When I didn't hear back ... well, I wondered. What's happening? With Ryker, I mean?"

"You can see it on the news like everyone else. He's fighting a losing battle."

Spencer's voice had a flat tone that Larry hadn't heard before. It chilled him. "Jeeez ... is he really gonna resign?"

Spencer snorted. "He'll have to. The press isn't going to let him go. They've found people from the past who're willing to testify against Ryker now. They'll finish him off. There'll be nothing left but a grease spot on the pavement. If he's as smart as he used to be, he'll retreat to the Montana ranch and huddle with his lawyers. Try to stay out of jail."

How the mighty have fallen, Larry thought to himself, but all he said was, "Damn."

"Yeah, that about sums it up. Listen, Larry, sorry I haven't gotten back to you. I've been pretty busy. I'm putting everything on hold over here at my office for a while. I've sent my other clients to associates, because I'll be taking a leave of absence. Spend a little time in Europe, change of scenery, you know. So ... I won't need your assistance on any more research assignments, if you know what I mean."

Larry stared out onto the nearly empty green expanse of the Mall; the Capitol and the Lincoln Memorial anchored each end. In between, the Washington Monument stood tall and proud like a sentinel. Keeping watch, perhaps.

Larry knew exactly what Spencer meant, and that little chill spread inside. "Uh, yeah. Sure. No problem."

"Oh, and Larry, my advice is to forget about any of those past projects. Erase them from your memory. You just concentrate on taking care of Congressman Jackson and staying in his good graces. And it wouldn't hurt to be nicer to your staffers. You don't need to make any more enemies than you already have. Understand?"

"Yeah ... I understand," Larry said, as that chilly feeling turned cold.

"I thought you would. You're smart, Larry. So, keep your head down and stay out of trouble, okay?"

"Okay," Larry said obediently, but Spencer had already clicked off.

Larry looked around at the tourists parading by. Young and old, they looked happy as they walked across the grassy green, laughing, talking, and taking photos. It was sunny outside, but there was a hint of winter's cold on the breeze that brushed against his face as Larry silently joined the tourists who were heading across the Mall.

Saturday afternoon

Raymond stood in the front room of his office, empty now except for the desk and chair. Bright midday sun shone through the front window. The office building Raymond had been watching as it slowly took shape was now finished. And it did indeed block off part of his view, just as he thought.

Trask's voice came from the hallway behind him. "Okay, those file cabinets are emptied. I've got it all in trash bags, ready to take the last load to the incinerator."

"Did that guy who works there give you any trouble?"

"Naw," Trask shook his head. "I slipped him three hundred bucks this morning when I brought over the first load. Told him I'd give him more this afternoon. He's even staying around to make sure no one else comes along to get in the way."

"Good. Here, give him something extra." Raymond dug out his wallet and removed several bills, then handed them to Trask. "That should ensure his cooperation and a poor memory afterwards. Did you strip the computers and destroy the files?"

Trask stuffed the money in his pocket. "Yep, circuit boards, memory, storage—you name it, all smashed and burned in the incinerator as well. Empty shells, monitors, dumped into trash bins behind a movie complex on Georgia Avenue." He jerked his thumb toward the back room. "Shelves are empty. All that's left is the table and couple of chairs. Oh, and your little fridge."

"Good, good," Raymond said. He walked over to the desk and sat down in his worn desk chair. "Thanks for bringing the sandwiches. I appreciate it." He gestured to the empty fast-food bag.

Trask sat on the edge of the scarred walnut desk. "I figured you wouldn't take time to eat. How's that Scotch holding out?" He pointed to the silver flask Raymond had filled just this morning.

"Okay. I've got enough to last me till I get home tonight." He gave a small smile. "I've got to clear out a small file cabinet at home, but that's all. I'll have a little roast in the fire pit outside tonight."

Trask looked at him with that concerned expression Raymond had spotted from time to time. "You also need to get that cough taken care of. It's a lot worse."

"Yeah, yeah, I know. I'm gonna take care of it. Spencer suggested I go to one of those resort health places. Maybe I will. There're some in Mexico."

"I hope you're serious." Trask looked toward the back room. "Let me load those trash bags. I've got the truck parked in the alley behind the building. I'll be back in a minute."

"Good idea. I'll give Spencer a call and let him know we've finished."

Raymond pulled out his cell as Trask retrieved the black plastic bags and headed out the office entry. Spencer's phone rang and rang. Five times, ten times. No answer. No voice mail even. First time that ever happened in all these years.

Raymond knew immediately. *They'd gotten to Spencer.* They'd be coming for him soon. As soon as they found out who and where he was. Spencer had always tried to keep identities hidden. But nothing stayed hidden in Washington forever. Raymond slipped his cell phone back in his pocket as Trask came through the door.

"All tied down. Anything else you want me to do before I take this over to the incinerator?"

Raymond sank back into his chair and stared at Trask. "Yeah. You need to get out of Washington tonight or tomorrow. I just called Spencer's number and there's no pickup, no voice mail. First time ever. That means they've gotten to him. He's either been wiped already or soon will be. I'm going to get the hell out of here tomorrow. And if you're smart, you'll get the hell out, too, while you still can."

Raymond saw the reluctance in Trask's eyes.

"Stop trying to settle old scores. Give it up and get away from here. Take your boat and sail far away and stay away. You've got enough money to live life large. Enjoy it, Trask. Take a new identity. Give up trying to get even."

Trask's face hardened into a cold mask. "I just need to tie up a few loose ends."

Raymond stared at him. "Don't be a fool, Trask. Get out before DiMateo finds you. You think that Prestige company hasn't been looking for you? You've slipped away from them so far, but after that little game you played last night, you just made it easier for them. I'll bet you could count on one hand the people leaving the gallery at closing time last night. They've nailed you already. Take my advice and get out of town before DiMateo can get his hands on you. If he does, it won't be pretty."

Different emotions played across Trask's face for an instant, then the mask returned. "I'll be okay. Don't worry."

Raymond saw the set of Trask's jaw and knew he was going to do what he damned well pleased, no matter what happened. Raymond shook his head. He'd warned Trask. That's all he could do. "Okay, then. Watch your back and be careful. And get out of here soon."

Trask gave him a wide smile as he walked toward the door. "Roger that. Enjoy the Mexican resort." He threw Raymond a half salute and was out the door.

Raymond pulled himself up and slipped the flask into his pocket. Time to head home, clear out whatever was there. Get ready to get away. He'd done all he could.

Another thought suddenly appeared out of nowhere. A crazy thought. Raymond paused and let it play through his mind. Maybe there *was* something else left to do. Maybe.

Late Saturday afternoon

"I made reservations for six thirty tonight," Danny said as he slammed his car door. "How's that?"

"Sounds good. Let me give a quick call to my mom and check on her," I said, walking toward my front doorstep. Spotting a white, legal-sized envelope leaning against the door, my heart skipped a beat. "Oh, God. There's another envelope." I stopped and pointed.

"Sonofabitch," Danny hurried over and grabbed it. "I'll get it."

"Wait!" I jerked his arm. "Maybe he's got white powder or something awful inside!"

Danny gave me a dark smile. "That's not his style. He wants confrontation. I can feel it." He tore off the end of the envelope, held it over the grass, and shook it. No white powder appeared. Just a sheet of folded, white paper drifted to the ground. Danny retrieved the paper, then opened and scanned it. "It's not Trask." He handed it over.

Only a few typed lines of text, all caps. Succinct.

"CONGRATULATIONS. YOU'VE OUTPLAYED THEM ALL. BUT THERE'S STILL ONE OUT THERE. IF YOU WANT TO KNOW WHAT REALLY HAPPENED TO ERIC GRAYSON, COME TO LAFAYETTE SQUARE PARK, NEAR SIXTEENTH STREET BETWEEN JACKSON PLACE AND MADISON, TO-MORROW AT NOON. ALONE. A PUBLIC PLACE, PLENTY OF PEOPLE, TOURISTS, PIGEONS. YOU'LL BE SAFE."

I felt a slight tingle, ripple, something run through me. Part fear, part excitement. Those old competing voices awoke inside:

"Go! You've got to! Find out at last!" Crazy Ass urged.

"Have you lost your mind? This is a killer!" Sober and Righteous countered.

"Gotta be one of Trask's cohorts," Danny said, peering at me. "I don't know what he's up to. But you can't seriously be thinking about meeting this guy."

"I have to, Danny. I don't know how, but this guy knows things from the past. I *always* felt something wasn't right about Eric's accident. And this guy knows! I've got to find out." I stared into Danny's eyes.

"On one condition," Danny gave in and frowned. "Bennett's guys are going to be all over that park. And I'll be out of sight but listening. We'll bug you and the freaking pigeons if we have to."

Sunday at Noon

"Thanks, Albert. You don't have to wait. I'll take a cab back to the house." I leaned over and called through the passenger open window.

"Okay, Molly. Enjoy your lunch," he said with a smile, then the window whirred closed.

I watched him pull into Jackson Place traffic before I turned and walked into Lafayette Park. At Danny's suggestion, Jeremy dropped me at Senator Russell's that morning as if I was working. Later, Albert and I drove off from the Russell garage in the back so that my shadow wouldn't know I had left the mansion.

The trees were shedding colorful leaves and some branches were bare already, revealing their graceful bone structure to move in the breeze. Today was wonderfully warm, in the low 70s, but it wouldn't last long. Colder winds and rain were scheduled to blow in this weekend.

I walked past several benches filled with couples surrounded by coffee cups, chatting and sharing lunches, enjoying one of the last autumn weekends before winter set in. I passed another section, benches on both sides. Tourists, weekend workers, talking on their cell phones as they ate sandwiches ... pigeons. I passed another section, benches on both sides were filled with tourist families. Children chasing squirrels. Then up ahead, I spotted a man sitting alone on a bench, not eating lunch and not on his cell phone. And he was looking in my direction.

As I approached the bench, the man looked up at me and smiled. "Hello, Molly. I'm glad you decided to come."

He wasn't what I expected. I thought this guy would be dark and swarthy and dangerous-looking. The man seated on the bench looked to be in his early sixties at least, stocky, short brown hair, mostly gray, and totally ordinary looking. The guy next door. He wore a drab brownish-gray suit jacket and dark gray pants with a raincoat overtop.

"You're the one who wrote the note?" I met his gaze. He had blue eyes.

"I am. Have a seat. Don't worry. You're safe. Besides, Prestige has at least six guys here, so if I so much as sneeze wrong, they'll jump me." His smile turned sardonic.

"Turnabout's fair play," I said as I sat, placing my purse with the bug between us. "You've been watching me for months now."

"*Touché.*" He glanced around. "I don't see your boyfriend, but I'm sure he's not far. Where's the bug? In your purse?"

"They wired the pigeons," I said, pointing to the gray and white birds picking morsels off the sidewalk.

He started to laugh, until a deep cough cut it off. He reached into his pocket and withdrew a white handkerchief and wiped his mouth. "I like you, Molly."

"Who the hell are you?"

He took a silver flask from his other coat pocket and took a drink before answering. "You can call me Raymond. And I'm a service provider, Molly. I provide very specialized services to high-level clients. Your boyfriend will have my name soon enough, once Prestige identifies me. They're taking plenty of photos, I'm sure." He shrugged. "No matter. I'll be leaving soon." He took another drink.

Surprised by his relaxed, almost nonchalant manner, I decided to probe as far as he'd let me. "Who do you work for? Edward Ryker?"

He shook his head. "No. I work for Spencer Graham Associates."

That name jumped from the back of my mind. "The lobbyist? He used to work for Ryker, didn't he?"

He smiled again. "Good research, Molly. I gotta hand it to you. You hit them where it hurt the most. Publicity. Ryker's out there twisting slowly in the wind."

I recalled that notorious phrase from the past, and it gave me pause. Arrogance was always our downfall. "Okay, Raymond. Tell me about Eric Grayson. I always had a feeling something wasn't right about that accident. Eric was a fanatic about being careful. And he certainly would never drink and drive."

"You're right. That traffic accident was arranged. His car was forced off the road by an operative, after two large gas cans filled with gasoline had been placed in the trunk. That ensured a quick and fiery explosion once it crashed into the ravine below the turnpike."

The man's matter-of-fact description of my relative's horrible death sent an ice-cold chill over me. I stared at him, aghast, letting disgust fill my voice. "You cold-hearted bastard."

"I simply follow orders from higher-ups."

"Ryker."

He shook his head. "Way higher than that, Molly. You've already uncovered some of those names. But that web stretches even farther. A committee. Those people had gotten wind of Grayson's research and were watching him. He'd made no secret that he believed his brother David had been right to suspect Ryker of corruption. I was told the committee decided to act before Eric Grayson could go public. They wanted to make sure the information never got out."

The guy's cough started again and sounded even deeper this time, causing him to lean forward and hold onto the bench. I stared out into the park, wondering which bench sitters were Prestige operatives. Danny was out there too. And they all were hearing this man's recitation of how Eric had died. He'd been eliminated. Other names pressed forward.

I waited until the man's cough subsided. He took an even longer drink from the silver flask this time. "Others have gotten too close, haven't they? My niece Karen and Celeste Allard. Were they eliminated too?"

He nodded. "We let Molinoff confess because it shut down questions. Then we wrote his suicide note. And the little staffer on the eastern shore. That gas explosion was no accident. There were a couple of others."

I knew immediately who he meant. "Quentin Wilson and Natasha Jorgensen."

He nodded and wiped the handkerchief across his mouth. I spotted red on the white cloth.

"We dumped sedatives and Vicodin in Wilson's beer. He just went to sleep. Jorgensen was messier. She fought back."

I had to ask. Who knew how much longer this guy was going to sit here and talk to me. "The guy who's following me, did he kill them?"

"Yeah. One operative did them all, including Eric Grayson. And that's why I'm here. Ryker's out of the picture. Spencer Graham is gone. And I'll be leaving soon. But this guy is still out there, and I wanted to warn you. He's got a vendetta against your boyfriend DiMateo, and he's using you. I don't know what he's got planned, but it won't be pretty. I told him to give it up and get out of town now. But he's made it personal. That's always a mistake."

I observed Raymond. Clearly, he was a very sick man; that cough had a death rattle to it. "I guess I should thank you, but somehow I can't bring myself to say it."

Raymond started to laugh again, a hearty laugh this time, until another coughing fit began. Even deeper. I watched him grasp hold of the bench and lean his head between his knees, shaking. Deep racking coughs, droplets of blood dripping onto the ground. I sensed he was already dying, and he knew it. The coughing gradually ceased, but Raymond continued to hold himself over the bench, gasping for breath.

"You really should get something for that," I offered quietly. It was all I had.

Raymond sat up a little and wiped his mouth, smearing some of the bloody phlegm across his cheek. "There's a bottle of thirty-year-old Scotch waiting at my office. That's good enough."

He upended the silver flask, draining it, then shoved the uncapped flask into his pocket. He slowly pulled himself up from the bench. I spotted a gun in a holster below his arm as his jacket fell open. So I pointed to it.

"Were you going to use that on me if I started screaming or something?"

Raymond smiled at me with that sardonic smile. "No, I wasn't going to shoot you, Molly." Then he peered at me. "I can tell you're feeling sorry for me despite yourself. Don't. There's something else you should know." He paused. "Your husband David didn't kill himself. I shot him. He was the first job I did for Spencer Graham and the committee. Your husband was asking too many questions and stirring up too much attention. People really liked him, and they started to believe his charges. That was enough for the committee."

I stared at Raymond, as shock was swiftly overtaken by fury. "*You sonofabitch!*" I whispered as I rose from the bench. Rage burned inside me. I took one step toward him.

Raymond stood where he was. "Watch your back, Molly." With that, he turned and slowly walked down the sidewalk, heading out of the park.

My fists clenched and unclenched as the fury inside slowly ebbed. I wanted to follow him, but I knew Prestige already was. They would know where he was. Where to find him.

Suddenly Danny appeared by my side. He placed his hand on my shoulder. "Molly, you okay? I heard it all."

I turned to Danny and stared into his eyes, letting him read all the regret and anger and grief that I felt churning inside. "I need to get away. Go somewhere to think. Alone."

"I'll take you anywhere you want Molly. And I'll leave you alone. But I'm gonna be right there watching. Just in case."

I simply nodded and grabbed my bag. Danny took my arm and escorted me out of the park.

Later Sunday afternoon

I watched the Potomac rush past. Only a few feet below me as I sat on the riverbank above Chain Bridge. Away from tourists, away from people. This close to the water, I could hear it running fast and deep as it rushed toward the sea. The relentless pull of the sea. Out there, pulling at all of us.

It was deep here. People drowned regularly. Fishermen, drinking too much, would slip and fall, then try to scramble up the bank. But the river's current was stronger than they were. Powerful currents would pull them along, then pull them under. The river could mesmerize you. Trick you into thinking you were safe. Come too close, and suddenly it was too late.

I sat there, not moving. Danny stood way above me on the riverbank, giving me space and time alone with my thoughts. And memories. Oh, God, the memories. And the guilt. Overwhelming guilt had replaced the anger.

God help me. If there was forgiveness out there, somewhere, maybe I could find it. I'd have to find a way to explain to my daughters. How, I didn't know yet, but I would find a way.

Pushing off the boulder where I'd sat, I climbed up the bank. Danny met me halfway down and offered his hand. He held his cell phone in the other.

"I just heard from Bennett. Raymond's dead. The team followed him from the park to an office building on H Street nearby. He had a front office on an upper floor, looking out toward the avenue. They trained their cameras on him and watched as he stood at the window and drank, probably that Scotch he spoke of. Suddenly he put a pistol to the side of his head and shot himself, then fell away from the window. Bennett's calling the police, so they'll check his office."

I stared into Danny's dark eyes. "He said he was 'leaving soon,' and he wasn't kidding. Who was he, exactly? Did they find out?"

"Oh, yeah." Danny looked at his phone screen. "Raymond Montague. Sixty-five. Did two army tours in Southeast Asia, then he quit and became a hired gun. Mercenary for South American guerillas. He was also in Africa and back in Southeast Asia. Then he dropped off the radar screen. That probably was the time he started working for Spencer Graham."

Suddenly I felt very, very tired. I slid my arms around Danny. "Let's go back. I want to go where it's warm. Let's make a fire in the fireplace tonight, okay?"

Danny kissed my forehead and wrapped his arm around me as we climbed the rest of the riverbank together.

TWENTY-ONE

Monday morning

"HOW'RE YOU DOING, MOLLY?" Casey asked as I walked into the hallway from my office. Coffee mug in hand, he was also heading for a refill. Even though it was sunny outside and promised to be warm, I still felt chilled inside.

"I'm doing okay, considering," I said, as we turned into the kitchen. Luisa was out running errands with Albert. "I take it Danny updated you on yesterday's adventures."

"Oh, yeah. I'll bet Prestige had that park covered with their people. Every other bench." He gestured to me, so I refilled my mug with a fragrant black stream.

"Apparently. And they were all listening in on the conversation. That didn't bother Raymond Montague at all. He even joked about it, asking if the bug was in my purse, which it was, actually." I took a hot sip.

"Raymond Montague," Casey said in an amused voice as he filled his coffee mug. "The name sounds like an art appraiser or something, not a hired gun."

I closed my eyes and gave a shudder. "At least I have to thank him for the warning."

"Thank God you've got Prestige watching your house. And you." He looked at me with a worried expression.

That reminded me of something. "Hey, would you check on Loretta, just to make sure nobody strange has shown up? Because of all these things happening, I haven't talked to her in a couple of days."

"Don't worry. I already have. I checked over there yesterday evening after I left here. All was quiet. No strangers, no problems. And she's really glad she has the security. Even though she complains about the lights coming on." He grinned.

"Oh, thank you, Casey. That's sweet of you," I said, making sure I didn't betray my delight that Casey had gone to visit Loretta on his own.

"No problem. She was making red beans and rice. They were delicious." He winked.

This time I couldn't hide my smile. "And you didn't bring me any? You dog. You tell Loretta to send me some authentic red beans and rice next time you see her."

"I'll be sure to tell her," he said with a grin as he headed down the hallway.

Red beans and rice, huh? That's how it starts. I smiled all the way to my office.

Mid-morning

I tabbed through the spreadsheet on one of Peter's rental properties, completely immersed in expenses, so I didn't notice Luisa standing in the doorway.

"Molly, while you were on the phone a few minutes ago, I received a call on the residence line for you."

I broke the spreadsheet trance and glanced up. "Oh, really? Who would call me on the residence line?"

"It was the D.C. Animal Welfare Control. The man said your neighbor had called to report a stray cat wandering in her yard and threatening her." Luisa looked puzzled. "I figured it must be the big tabby that hangs around your house. You said he's been there since you moved in last spring."

I sank back in the desk chair. "Yes, that's gotta be Bruce. He's been, uh … courting the neighbor's pedigree, white Persian kitty. So this woman has been complaining about Bruce whenever she sees me."

"Well, that man said she filed an official complaint so he had to go over and bait a trap for your cat. Some sort of special cage that he put inside the garage. He'll be back later this afternoon to pick him up and take him to the shelter."

"*Oh, damn!* I'd better go over there and see if Bruce is caught in the cage. Darnit! I was just getting into those spreadsheets. Nothing got accomplished Friday, so I wanted to make progress on them today."

"You'd better go over there now. I've heard tell those Animal Shelter fees are outrageous," Luisa warned. "I've heard if you go to the shelter yourself, you can save some money on fines."

Annoyed, I pushed away from my chair and slipped on my suit jacket hanging over the back. "He's not even my cat," I protested. "Who knows where Bruce disappears to every night. His owner never shows up. No ID, nothing."

"He's a mystery kitty," Luisa teased as she walked into the hall.

Mystery kitty. Pain in the ass, kitty. I grabbed my purse and phone and headed out of my office. It was still sunny and warm so it would be a fast walk back to my house. No need to call Jeremy.

––––––

I heard Bruce's loud meow as I walked up my driveway. He must have recognized my footsteps. A raucous meow, hoarse-sounding and coming from the garage. There was a yellow paper taped to the garage door. I yanked it off and read. It was an official ticket. From the D.C. Department of Animal Control. *Damn!* Handwritten itemized fines for animal control and entrapment, cage, and service call for a grand total of *$675!* "Dammit, Bruce! You just cost me $675, and you're not even my cat!"

Bruce meowed even louder, protesting the cage, no doubt. I punched in the garage code and watched the door rattle upwards. There in the back of the garage was Bruce, clawing inside a black cage. Meowing even louder.

"Quiet down, Bruce. I've gotta take you to Animal Control," I said as I walked inside the garage. I noticed the door to the backyard was open and an empty can of tuna was inside the cage. "That's how he caught you, Bruce. It was the tuna."

"Curiosity killed the cat, you know," a man's voice sounded suddenly.

I jumped back instinctively. I saw a man emerge from behind boxes I had stacked in the corner of the garage. Even in the dim light, I recognized the priest's wide face, minus the glasses. Even the smile was the same. But there was a difference. This guy had a gun in his hand. *Trask.* I froze, my heart in my throat.

"You ..." was all I could say.

His smile spread wider. "Yeah, it's me. I figured it was time we finally met face-to-face."

"You were the one following me at the gallery."

"And everywhere else. Don't play innocent, Molly. You already knew that. Those security guys have been trying to find me for weeks. That's why I thought it was time to wrap this up." He raised the gun.

I stared at it. "Are ... are you gonna shoot me?"

"Not yet. I want DiMateo to get over here first. That way, he can watch me kill you. Before I kill him." His wide smile disappeared. "Get your cell phone." He pointed to the bag I'd dropped on the garage floor. "We're gonna send him a text."

Bruce started meowing again as I backed up a few steps to retrieve my purse.

"Damn cat is driving me crazy." Trask aimed his gun at the cage.

"*No!*" I yelled. "Don't shoot him! I—I'll let him go! Please!"

Trask gave me a dark smile. "All right, Molly. Last wishes. Let him out."

I quickly bent down and fumbled with the cage latch until it gave way, Bruce screeching all the while. The cage door swung open and Bruce streaked out of the garage like a rocket. I watched him enviously as he raced to safety down the driveway.

"Okay. Get the damn phone now."

I grabbed my purse and fumbled inside for my phone, feeling it beneath my keys. *My car keys.* I grabbed my phone and my keys, slipping my phone into one hand and holding my keys against my purse as I dropped it to the floor. "Here it is," I held up the phone to Trask while concealing the keys in my other hand.

"Okay, find his name in the directory, and give it to me," Trask directed, holding out his gun-free hand.

I scrolled through the directory to Danny's name and pressed the message button. Then I handed over the phone.

Trask took it and started to enter a message. "Come quick. I need you.' That ought to do it."

While his fingers worked the keys, I dropped the car keys into my jacket pocket.

Trask returned the phone. "That ought to bring him running. He's probably not too far away."

I dropped the phone into my other pocket. "Prestige has probably seen you on the cameras already." I pointed outside.

Trask snickered. "They don't know it's me. I showed up in the D.C. Animal Control uniform with the cage and put the notice on the garage door. Then I opened up a can of tuna all on camera and took the cage around back into the garage. That's when both the cameras on this side of the house started skipping, messing up the video. Funny thing about electronics. They're easy to screw up."

My heart was beating so loudly I was sure Trask could hear it. I had to find a way to distract him. Slow him down until Danny could get here. *And, then … and then what? We'd both get shot?* I didn't have an answer. And I didn't know what to do. Except maybe distract Trask. Throw him off, somehow. Maybe I could try making a run for it like Bruce.

That thought made my gut clench even more. I wouldn't get very far. Danny would simply find my dead body, which would make it even easier for Trask to kill him. There was only one thing I could do to distract him. I shoved both hands into my jacket pockets. Fingering my car keys.

Suddenly my phone buzzed. A message from Danny. It had to be. I flipped open the phone and read Danny's message. "I'll be right there. Five minutes, max," I read out loud. Trask grabbed the phone from me and read the message himself, then smiled. "Okay. Five minutes to go."

I debated whether I should wait closer to the five minutes to use my keys or do it now.

"Sorry, Molly. But I can't let you send out any goodbye phone messages. They'd be too hard to explain. I'm going to make it look like a murder-suicide. Lovers' quarrel, whatever. D.C. cops are over-worked anyway," he said sarcastically.

That was it. I couldn't wait another minute. I pressed the alarm button on my car keys, and the horn started blaring on my car parked in the driveway. Lights flashed, horn blared, making a terrible racket.

"*What the hell!*" Trask yelled.

I raised both hands in surrender and backed up. "It's not me! Something happened!"

"Shut that thing off!" he snarled, advancing on me.

Suddenly Danny burst through the garage back door, gun in hand. Trask whirled around, but it wasn't fast enough. Danny cracked Trask across the face with his weapon. Trask reeled sideways and tumbled backwards over the empty cage onto the concrete floor.

Danny jumped over the cage and stomped Trask's wrist twice. *Hard.* Trask yelled in pain as Danny kicked the weapon away. He backhanded Trask again. Then Danny yanked him up off the floor and slammed him against the wall.

Trask moaned, obviously in pain. Blood streamed down his face as Danny searched Trask's jacket, pockets, under his shirt, pants leg, ankles. He tossed a knife and another smaller pistol out onto the garage floor.

"Damn you," Trask snarled, cradling his wrist.

"Shut up, Trask. Your wrist is broken, that's all. The only reason I didn't kill you is I don't want to have to explain your mangy corpse to the D.C. cops. I'll let your friends take care of you." Danny picked up Trask's two pistols and knife and tossed them onto the shelf.

At the first blow, I had scurried to the other side of the garage to watch, shutting off the car alarm first.

"Sonofabitch," Trask glared at him again.

"You're wasting time, Trask. That wrist is gonna have to be set. I'm pretty sure I snapped all the bones. You're gonna have to go to your place, grab some cash, and make a run for it." He checked his watch. "We've had two days to send out the word to all your old buddies in Columbia and the Congo. Remember them, Trask?"

I watched the color drain from Trask's face as he stared at Danny. Hatred, pure and ugly.

"Well, they remember you. And how you got away years ago. And they've had plenty of time to contact their people here. So, I figure you've got a fifty-fifty shot at getting away this time. Forget about the boat. We had it seized and locked up. There's a chain on it now in the marina."

If looks could kill, Danny would surely drop dead that minute. "Motherf—" Trask let out a stream of curses. Danny stood, unfazed.

"Get your ass outta here, Trask, before I break your other wrist. Your friends are probably already at the airport. So you'd better take a bag of new disguises. I sent them photos of all your others."

Trask kept his mouth shut this time, pushed himself away from the wall and headed out of the garage. He turned just once to glare at Danny and me.

"Time's up ..." Danny said, advancing on him. At that, Trask broke into a limping run, down the driveway. He turned left and headed down P Street. It was after four o'clock now, so the sun was getting close to setting.

I turned to stare at Danny. "Where were you? How'd you get around back without us seeing you?"

Danny gave me a crooked smile. "I snuck back to the house after we left this morning. I've been here all day. I had a feeling Trask was gonna make a move soon. So I was able to see him when he came over in the Animal Control uniform." He snorted disdainfully. "Then Prestige saw the video feeds spiked, so they knew he was up to something. Of course I saw him sneaking into the back of the garage."

"Where were you?"

"I was hidden behind the garden shed outside, watching from a crevice I'd made in the back of the garage." Danny pointed to the right rear corner. "I figured he was setting a trap. Then you showed up and I could hear what he planned. I had to wait till he turned around or something distracted him. Otherwise, he'd see me as soon as I came in the door. Then he'd shoot you first. I couldn't risk that. I was about to call on your phone to distract him, then you did." He pulled me into his embrace. "That was you with the car alarm, I knew it. Quick thinking."

I slipped my arms around him and stared into his face. We were still alive. So far. "He's not coming back, is he? I mean ... that was true what you said, right? About his friends coming to get him?"

Danny kissed me lightly on the lips. "We won't be seeing him again. He's made a bunch of really badass enemies. And they will take care of Trask. Either before he leaves the country, or more likely, once he lands abroad somewhere. He won't last forty-eight hours."

"Promise?" I said, realizing how bloodthirsty I sounded. I didn't give a damn.

"Promise," Danny said, then leaned down and gave me a real kiss.

Monday evening

Larry Fillmore walked down the hallway to the office door bearing the nameplate, *Spencer Graham Associates*. He licked his dry lips twice, then tried the door. It was locked. So he knocked lightly, twice.

Within seconds, the door opened and a man he'd never seen before at Spencer's office appeared. An Asian man. He stared impassively at Larry.

"I—I'm Larry Fillmore. I had a text message from Spencer Graham that I was to meet his associate here at six this evening."

"You may come in," the man said, stepping back and opening the door for Larry to enter.

Larry looked around Spencer's office, hoping to see him, but he was nowhere. "Is ... is Spencer here?"

"No, he is not," the man said, walking toward the door to Spencer's inner office. "His associate is expecting you."

Larry obediently followed the man into Spencer's office. That luxurious inner sanctum Larry had only been privileged to visit once. Instead of the savvy, hard-drinking lobbyist and manipulator sitting behind the mahogany desk, a slender Asian man sat there, smoking a cigarette. Gray streaked through this man's jet-black hair. High cheekbones, thin face, and dark eyes. Larry could spot expensive tailoring even behind the desk. Gold cuff links also caught the light from the decorative hanging light above.

"Good evening, Mr. Fillmore," the man said as Larry approached the desk. "Thank you for coming. I am an associate of Spencer Graham and will be handling this transition."

"And you are?" Larry ventured.

The man gave a small, cold smile. "I am one of his associates. Spencer won't be returning, I'm afraid. He suffered a health crisis after he left Washington a few days ago. He's resting abroad."

Larry got a bad feeling, hearing the words "health crisis." "Uh, I'm sorry to hear that. Please ... please convey my sympathies."

The man took a long draw on his cigarette, then blew out a stream of white smoke. "I'll be sure to. The reason my associates and I asked you here, Mr. Fillmore, is to convey the message that we expect you to act with the utmost discretion if asked about Spencer's whereabouts. We request that you relay only the information conveyed to you. A health crisis prevents Spencer's return to the United States, and his company is presently being liquidated. Do you understand, Mr. Fillmore?"

Larry tried to swallow around the large lump of fear that had risen in his throat. It started when the man raised his hand to his mouth with the cigarette. Larry recognized the huge gold ring with an enormous diamond on the man's left hand.

Spencer Graham's ring. An original, custom-design, that Spencer once said: "Never leaves my hand."

Ice formed around the lump in Larry's throat now, so it took a couple of tries to find his voice. "Y-y-yes . . . I understand. His health is bad. Can't return."

The small, cold smile returned. "Excellent. We appreciate your cooperation. You may show Mr. Fillmore out now."

The other man simply walked over to the office door and held it open. Larry bobbed his head once—in obedience, submission, whatever—backed up a couple of steps then turned and walked from the office. It was all Larry could do not to run.

Wednesday afternoon

I felt the warmth of a tropical breeze brush against my bare skin and it felt good. Danny and I were both lying in our swimsuits on a chaise lounge beneath the shade of a palm tree. The gorgeous turquoise blue-green water of Turks and Caicos Islands stretched before us. Practically deserted because it was still officially hurricane season, the island was perfect. Peaceful and quiet, sunny and warm. Exactly what Danny and I needed. Fresh seafood and tropical fruits awaited us. Delicious, fruity libations already brought a welcome drowsiness as we lay in each others' arms.

And, yet . . . my eyelids couldn't stay closed for long. I let the turquoise water lull me and the tropical birds perched above squawked their melodies, and I tried again. Resting my face against Danny's bare chest, I felt his heart beating beneath my hand. *Thank God.*

"You still haven't relaxed. I can feel it beneath your skin," he said quietly.

"I can't help it. I try. But it doesn't work."

"I know." He kissed my forehead. "It'll get easier."

"Promise?"

"Promise. We just have to do this more. Practice."

"Practice. Okay."

I watched a seagull ride the air currents above the ocean, floating on the breeze, before he folded his wings and dove like an arrow into the surf. That gull might have looked like he was relaxing on the breeze, but he wasn't. He was always watching the busy surf below.

"Can we ever really relax, Danny? I mean, like not worry?"

Danny sighed beneath my hand. "That's different. We can learn to relax but still pay attention. Then we don't have to worry … so much." He kissed the top of my head.

That made sense, I supposed. As much sense as we were ever going to have from all of this. It was over. Danny showed me the photo he received of Trask's dead body—shot through the forehead. Then he assured me the rest of the rats had headed for their hideouts. I didn't care where they went, as long as it wasn't around me … or my friends.

"Close your eyes, Molly. We're safe."

Safe. That felt good. So good, I did what he suggested. I closed my eyes and let the warm tropical breeze, the sound of the sea, and the vestiges of the fruit and rum drink bring back the delightful drowsiness. So easy to drift off. Simply drift off. Away. Breathing slowing down, feeling Danny breathe beneath my hand. Drift away ... slip away ... sleep.

And then ... my eyes blinked open again. As if they had a will of their own. So I lay beside Danny and gazed out at the sea. The beautiful, tranquil, turquoise sea.

THE END